C000048436

MURDER
AND
CORRUPTION
IN L.A.

MURDER
AND
CORRUPTION
IN L.A.

Lower Alabama

Greg Powell

LIBRTY HILL PRESS

Liberty Hill Press
2301 Lucien Way #415
Maitland, FL 32751
407.339.4217
www.libertyhillpublishing.com

© 2020 by Greg Powell

All rights reserved solely by the author. The author guarantees all
contents are original and do not infringe upon the legal rights of any
other person or work. No part of this book may be reproduced in any
form without the permission of the author. The views expressed in
this book are not necessarily those of the publisher.

Printed in the United States of America.

Paperback ISBN-13: 978-1-6628-0023-8
Hard Cover ISBN-13: 978-1-6628-0024-5
Ebook ISBN-13: 978-1-6628-0025-2

Chapter 1

THE CRIME SCENE

I t had been a typical day in the Deep South of Alabama. The
weather had been in the fall temperatures. Everybody loved
the feel of the brisk winter breeze blowing against the skin, until
Deputy Sheriff William Boyd had run across, on a desolated road,
the body of a young girl, whose clothes had been ripped away sav-
agely as if done by a wild animal. He had traveled this particular
road due to where the local youth were known to pick mushrooms
from the cow pastures. Immediately, Sheriff Boyd ran to his squad
car to call in the discovery to dispatch. The body of the victim had
been dragged from the road and laid to rest in the thicket to the
side of the road. Boyd, being of the curious nature, had walked
over the crime scene to see if he recognized the body. This being
his first experience, he had been totally unaware of evidence he
had destroyed in this process. He peered down upon the bloody
mass that had once been a very beautiful woman, and immediately got sick and puked on the body. He had completely contaminated the crime scene. He ran back to his car to regain some
sort of composure, which had been way too late. In the distance,
the sound of multiple sirens had become louder and louder. Boyd
had been working furiously to regain composure. He had been a
newly appointed deputy sheriff, and had royally screwed up the
crime scene. As the other police and sheriff vehicles pulled up at a
rapid pace and had screeched on their brakes, it had sent up a dust
cloud as if a bomb had just gone off. The first officer to jump from

his car had been the sheriff and detective, Roland Smith. Roland immediately yelled, "Bill, where the hell are you, you dumb son of a bitch?" Bill sat in his car and had tried to hide unsuccessfully. After the second belt from Roland, Bill reluctantly answered, "I'm over here by my car." Roland heatedly stated, "Well, why in the fuck are you over there, and why haven't you roped off the crime scene, you jackass?" Absently, Bill had admitted to puking on the body. Roland had been fit to be tied. He stood there and changed all shades of red. As other competent officers arrived on the scene, he finally started to get some sort of investigation started. Bill remained in his car with his stomach a little weak. One of the helpful officers, Randy Cobb, noticed a splatter of regurgitated food on the victim's face and started to take pictures. He pointed it out, but Roland stated, "That was Bill's contribution." Roland still upset, checked for footprints and tire prints. Randy immediately did a systematic search for relevant data. Randy had been busy placing police tape around the immediate area involved when two more police cars arrived with lights going and sirens blaring. These were the local police of the nearby town of Hope.

Roland would have none of this intervention. It was a county affair. Roland being fifty-two, and on the force for over thirty years, would not be bothered by local yokels. Everybody knew Roland by his no-nonsense approach to matters and his past four failed marriages. As he walked up to the local police, Roland recognized both of them, Paul Smith, maybe twenty-two, and Barney Williams, the local drunk with a uniform. "Guys, what brings you here?"

Paul stated, "Looks like we got a case to investigate." Roland began to turn red again and said, "The only case you got is of the gone ass. Now if you will notify Willy Barnes, the vet, I need a temporary morgue." "What the hell? A dog hospital for a morgue? Let us handle this," said Paul. Now Roland had enough, "Fuck you, Paul, and do as you're told, and tell that walking distillery with you. We have work to do and also need a hearse to transport the body. *I hope that will not be too difficult for you.*" Paul started to say something to no avail because Roland had already walked away. Paul stated under his breath, "Prick." Roland turned as if

2

he heard what was said and told Paul, "You can manage traffic also, something you're qualified for, and maybe you could pop out some speeding tickets or a DUI, now git."

Bill had still been in his car drinking some Pepto Bismol when Roland walked up to the car. "Sorry, I didn't mean to be rough on you, but shit, Bill, you puked on the body and walked across the crime scene." Bill was quiet for a moment, then said, "I'm ok now, do you want me to help with photographs?" Roland hesitated, then said, "Ok." Roland walked the perimeter of the crime area very slowly, looking for anything that could be a clue. Footprints were all screwed up, and there were too many of them, or were there? He studied the officers' shoes, and all were standard issue. He noticed at the edge of the thicket, where the body laid, a boot heel imprint stuck out at him; not just any boot, but a curved-in heel-riding boot made for spurs. There was no spur imprint, but some marks on the body looked as if spurs could have been dragged across it. "Bill, bring that camera over here and get close-up pictures of the body and the heel imprint. Do you think you can do that without any more additional breakfast added to the scene?" Roland asked. "Also, get a cast of the heel imprint." It had now bugged Roland, in the back of his mind, somebody local did this, and God willing, he would kill the bastard.

Chapter 2
FRED'S PUB AND PACKAGE

They called it the "meeting place" because if you wanted to
know anything that went on in the county or the town of
Hope, everybody there would know something, whether it was
true or not, and if they did not, they would make up a grand story.
The actual name was Fred's Pub and Package. Opening at noon,
the pub would be half-full with regulars. You could cut the smoke
with a knife. It was an old building with hard wood floors, and old
wooden bar and stools held together with duct tape. At the end of
the bar was Molly. That was her spot. In her younger days, it had
been told she was a sex goddess. Her specialty was known, having
two teeth left in her mouth. Next to her was good ole Marcus, a
Vietnam vet and whiskey drinker. Catching him sober had always
been the challenge. The next stool down was Sparky. He was
called Sparky for his quick wit. He had three teeth a little more
to brush. He had retired from the local hospital as a lab tech. He
had a big round belly and a bald head. There were various others
in the bar just to see what had been going on. The bartender was
Amber, and she was a crafty one. One never knew what side of her
face she talked from. She was a God in her own mind. She was
the one to keep the leash on the crazies at the bar.

Molly whispered to Marcus, "I heard she was naked with her
legs spread wide open." Marcus yelled out, "You getting naked?"
Then Sparky said, "Shall we pray not." Molly butted in, "Damn

it, not me, though you know I'm the best, I'm talking about that girl they found this morning."

Amber innocently stated, "What girl?" Then the whole bar exploded. "What girl?" Someone yelled from the back, "Why you should have known she left from here last night." Amber responded, "How would I know? I deal with all you nuts. Who the hell knows what happened?"

Marcus spoke up again, "So when are you taking your clothes off? I'll bet those titties of yours will drop to the floor."

A voice from the back had spoken loudly, "I heard a wild boar was eating on her, that's why they took her to Willy's Vet Hospital." Sparky chimed in, "Well, if it was a wild boar, then I wouldn't mind having a piece of that, heard she was a looker, what was left and all."

"Is it murder? I mean, did someone kill that young girl?" wondered Amber.

"Who said she was young?" stated a new voice from the back. Everyone had turned to see who made the statement; to find out it was Johnny, the town AM radio station owner and DJ. You could hear a pin drop. "It was just a guess," stated Amber. Johnny had looked at her queer-like, and had been studying her body language and not liking what he was seeing.

The door flew open and Doc came in the bar. There were murmurs from the patrons, for they always gossiped about Doc. His name wasn't Doc; it was Richard McClusky. People called him Doc because he used to be an RN nurse. He gave free medical advice to whoever would ask, and tried to be helpful as best he could. Amber especially did not like Doc because he got more attention than she did, and this would piss her off. She would always start gossip about Doc, just to see how far it would go. Doc was of a slim build, weighing around 165 pounds, and had long hair to his shoulders, which he assumed a lot of the older women liked. He walked up to the bar and took a seat. He looked over at Marcus and stated, "Hey Marcus, how the ole legs feeling today?" Marcus looked up at Doc, and through glazed-over eyes and with a thick tongue, said, "Molly's going to take off her clothes, and I got a front-row seat." Doc, looked confused, looked up at Sparky, and he had shaken his head, as were others. Molly turned red and said nothing.

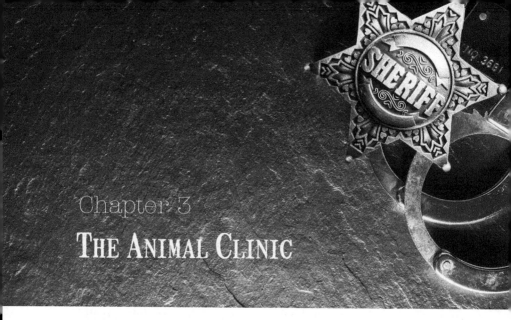

Chapter 3

THE ANIMAL CLINIC

H ope had been established in 1901 and had grown to a popu-
lation of roughly 15,000. Willy's Vet Hospital was located
on the fringe of town. Downtown had a historical train station,
which had been converted to a museum. There were about ten
local police. They usually arrested the youth for sewing their wild
oats. There was one young male, about seventeen, a little intoxi-
cated, who attempted to go through his girlfriend's window when
the Hope police had seen this as a major infraction. This young
man was just about to make it in the window when the officers
had apprehended him. Poor kid, just when he was about to get
in, he had been abruptly pulled out. He had been promptly taken
downtown and charged with breaking and entering with minor
consumption added on. This was a big bust.

Roland would not let anyone get in his way of solving this
recent murder. Besides, in the past ten years, there were only three
murders, counting this one. The other two murders were similar
in circumstance. Roland had not been allowed to help with the
other murders because it was not in his jurisdiction, and he always
had been suspicious as to if the right person was charged in those
crimes. Roland would not allow the same thing to happen now.
It was on his turf, and he would solve this gruesome murder if it
was the last thing he did. That was the reason for the change in
protocol on this case.

All the parties involved in the investigation had gathered at Willy's Vet Hospital before the body was dispatched to Montgomery. Roland was the first one there. Dr. Willy Barnes was next, then the deputies. Roland had invited Dr. Price for his input on the cause of death of the victim. Roland wanted all the information he could gather from people he trusted to ascertain the unadulterated facts of this poor girl's murder. As the hearse pulled up with the body, Roland said to Bill, "Bill, I need you to make the call to the Montgomery coroner and tell them we have a body to pick up. It will be at the animal hospital instead of the regular place, Dixon's Funeral Home. Also, I need you to stay outside and do not let anybody in unless you radio me for approval. Do you understand?"

"Yes, but why all the cloak and dagger, Roland?"

"You just do what you're told. Your contribution has been duly noted. Now guys, let's get the body inside before I have an aneurism." Roland talked to the hearse driver, Dr. Willy, Dr. Price, a well-known surgeon, and Deputy Randy Cobb. Randy and the driver, Joe, wheeled the body into the animal hospital to the sound of multiple dogs barking and cats screeching and hissing. Once past the caged animals, they rolled the body into one of the large animal surgery rooms. The rested the body on a large stainless steel table that could fit a horse. There was plenty of room and good light to gather evidence from the body, and Roland had known this. The other place for accommodating a corpse was the local funeral home, and the lighting was poor, and the tables had been designed for embalming. Now that the body was on the table, Roland walked over, pulled the surgery lights down closer, and turned them on. He then unzipped the body bag and asked Dr. Willy and Dr. Price to come closer.

"What do you think?" said Roland to Dr. Price.

"I think someone got sick, and it looks like the Red Flame sausage biscuits."

"That was Billy trying to be of assistance. What I need to know is what the cause of death is."

"Well, let's take a look. How much can I move the body? I do not want to contaminate the evidence."

"Do what is necessary, please."

"Dr. Willy, come over by me, will you? I need your assistance."

Dr. Willy and Dr. Price were at the head of the table, gently moving the head of the victim to the left, then to the right. All of a sudden, Dr. Price stated emphatically, "We got to get an X-ray of the head now!"

Deputy Cobb rolled over the X-ray machine to Dr. Price and Dr. Willy. They manipulated the head of the body very carefully as if she was alive. They placed the film and took the X-ray. Moving the machine away, Dr. Price continued to study the body without comment. Roland watied anxiously for Dr. Price to tell him anything. Dr. Price remained silent and continued to examine the body. He looked at the torso and the markings on the body. Then he proceeded to the lower extremities and the genitals of the body. The body only had torn panties on it. The rest of the body had been blood-smeared and scratched. Finally, Dr. Price stated to Dr. Willy, "Willy, do you see what I see?"

"I do. But what do you think the chances are?"

"Very remote, but it is plain as day."

"What the hell are y'all talking about?" busted in Roland.

"This woman's skull was bashed in, and then she was sexually assaulted," stated Dr. Price.

"Are you sure?"

"Positive. But we will have to wait on the coroner to confirm our findings."

"Was this anything like the previous murders we had in the area?"

"I was not privileged to those, Roland. But from what I have gathered, I would not rule it out."

"I knew I was right."

"What?"

"Nothing," said Roland. He tried to work it out in his head. Roland directed everybody to step back from the body, and he immediately zipped up the body bag and tagged it with an evidence tag. He then asked everybody to stand outside except Dr. Price and Dr. Willy. He turned to Willy and asked, "Do you agree with Dr. Price?"

"It sure looks like it, Roland."

"You know what we got here, don't you?"

"Maybe, just maybe."

"'Maybe' my ass. I know what we got, and now I have to clean up everybody else's fuckup"

All of a sudden, Bill came over the radio, "Roland, Ed Nixon is out here and demanding to come in. What do you want me to do?"

"Tell him to come in and say nothing else." Roland turned to the two doctors and whispered for them to say nothing as they waited for Ed to enter.

Ed walked into the room, which was very silent. He looked to the doctors, then to Roland. Roland was in his sheriff's uniform with his well-known pistol to the side. It was in a western-style holster with a single loop over the hammer of the 44 Colt. The handle was of pearl, and the four-inch barrel was nickel-plated. Ed took notice of the gun, then looked up to Roland. Roland had been with Ed's ex-wife, and he was no friend of Roland's. He did not like Roland. Roland knew this, but it didn't matter. Ed finally spoke up, "Roland, what do you think you're doing? You use my hearse, and you do not take the body to my funeral home as you are supposed to, and you do not inform me of the situation. What is going on here?"

Roland waited patiently, and noticed Ed's neatly pressed suit and tie. He was always with a suit and tie, that gave him, in his mind, some sort of importance, which Roland could care less. Finally, Roland spoke up, "And what is your point, Ed?'

"What's my point? Why, you ass. You know what my point is."

"I'm afraid I don't."

"You have circumvented the protocol. You know I'm the designated coroner, and all accidents and deaths are to go through me."

"Well, Ed, you are wrong, and this was no accident. It was murder, and I'm leaving nothing to chance. I'm going to catch the murderer and see that he goes to the gas chamber."

Ed was silent for a moment, and then said, "I must see the body." And he started to walk toward the body.

Roland immediately cut him off and said, "The hell you will."

9

"Roland, you are interfering with the process, and I will do my job. Now get out of the way."

Roland slipped his hand down to his Colt and softly stated, "You will not take another step."

Ed stopped with a quickness and his face showed panic mixed with extreme anger. His face was red as he said, "What's the big deal here? Why can't I see the body?"

Roland immediately responded, "The body has been sealed, witnessed, and all legal protocol has been followed to the tee. Now I have a picture if you wish to help identify the body?"

Ed reluctantly agreed to look at the picture, for he knew that Roland was very serious, and besides, there were two witnesses to what had happened. As Roland handed him the picture, his eyes got wide and his mouth dropped. His face again got red, and said in a quivering voice, "Why, that's Sue Parrish. She applied for a job with me just last week. I didn't have an opening. I would have hired her if I had something open; she was a looker. This is horrible."

Roland, thinking this was just the break he needed, said, "Do you still have her application?"

"Yes, it's in my file, and I can make it available to you when you wish."

"I wish now. Leave and go with Deputy Boyd and give it to him. You are dismissed."

"Now see here. You can't talk to me like that. I'm a part of this procedure."

"Listen carefully. I will not repeat myself. You will do as you are told, and you will not interfere in this case or I will arrest you for obstruction. Do you understand?"

"God, Roland, there is no need for all that."

"I'm afraid there is now. I will instruct Boyd to follow you to the funeral home. Bye."

With that said by Roland, Ed begrudging left, and in the background, he could hear Roland talking to Boyd on the radio, telling him to follow him to the funeral home.

Dr. Price, a little awestruck, said to Roland, "Did you have to be so abrupt with Ed?"

Roland responded, "You know I did. He has always hated me for getting with his ex-wife, and he was the coroner for the previous murderers. He has got to be out of the loop. Everybody is a suspect. Do you understand?"

"Well, I guess you make a point. At least he can help with that application, and he has put a name to the victim."

Roland sat back a little bit, and concurred with Dr. Price because he had been right. *Well, now it begins. Who was Sue Parrish? Why was she so brutally murdered? Who could do such a thing to such a beautiful young lady? Where to start next?* He would have to establish where she had been for the past week, more importantly, what places she visited.

It was three-thirty at Fred's Pub and Package, and the air had been thick with gossip and speculation of the day's current events. Drinks had been poured, and minds raced with the most incredible stories ever imagined. Johnny had left to find out what was going on from local police to report on his radio show. In fact, he was the only one that had left. Everybody else had been on their phones, trying to get some hint as to what was going on. Doc and Sparky were sitting at the bar with Molly, Marcus, and somebody else they didn't know. Marcus was well on his way to complete intoxication. Molly was feeling no pain. Doc and Sparky were speculating about the day's events and waiting to see if Johnny was coming back. Doc knew that Johnny would get the basic details. Amber, the bartender, had been constantly texting on her phone. She would not be left out not knowing everything, even if she had to make some of it up. There were three other people in the bar, two of whom had been playing pool. The tension was as thick as the smoke in the bar. Everybody had been quiet when Marcus belched, "Who farted?" Everybody looked at each other with surprise.

Sparky leaned over to Doc and whispered, "He probably shit himself."

Doc responded, "Do you think he even knows what's going on?"

"He's smarter than what you think."

Amber spoke up, "Damn it, Marcus, you better not have done it. You know the ventilation is bad. You take it outside if you have the urge."

Marcus replied through a thicker tongue, "This place was so quiet I thought I would wake it up. Don't get on my ass, Amber. You just jealous Molly got the hots for me."

"Marcus, you ain't right."

Molly jumped in, "He sure ain't. He's been trying to rub my leg all day. It's like fighting off a gnat."

Sparky added, "You saying he's small, Molly?"

Amber interrupted, "I'm interrupting. Just got a text from Paul that they found out that the person they found was Sue Parrish."

"Oh my God," interjected Doc. "She was here not a couple of days ago, Amber. You remember, she was looking for a job. God, she was so beautiful. I would have hired her."

Irritated, Amber responded, "I'm sure you would, however, we had no position for her. Besides, she wasn't that good-looking."

"You are mistaken, she was perfect."

Sparky chimed in, "I was here that day, and I would have hired her just to look at her."

Getting red around the neck, Amber stated, "Well, we had no place for her."

This new information had been tragic to a couple of them, while others had no idea who she was. At that moment, Johnny walked through the door. Doc was the first to encourage him to sit at the bar with him and Sparky. Amber jumped in second, rather pissed as to not having gotten in before Doc. Johnny sat next to Doc and ordered a whiskey. Amber went to make his drink with her ears tuned in like radar. Johnny whispered to Doc, "Well, they are calling it murder, and Roland ain't letting anybody get close. I had to talk to Barney, and he said when he and Paul went to where they found the body, Roland was there and immediately ran them off rather rudely. He didn't even let Ed from the funeral home get involved. Barney said Roland pulled his gun on Ed."

Doc was surprised by what Johnny was saying. "How do you know he pulled his gun?"

"Well, Ed went to Barney after he had to get some papers for Deputy Bill, and told him all about it."

"I wonder why he pulled his gun. I mean, Roland has always seemed a logical guy, and that just doesn't make sense."

Amber brought Johnny's whiskey and contributed, "Roland always had an ego, and you all know how proud he is of that pistol he has."

Doc observed, "That has nothing to do with nothing, Amber. There must be something else going on."

Heatedly, Amber responded to Doc directly, "Doc, you don't know everything, and I know for a fact that Roland thinks a little too highly of himself and how important he is."

"Damn it, Amber. Your opinion stinks. Roland is a good guy, and I would rather have him investigate this than the local police. He is quite a bit smarter."

"Don't you cuss me, Doc!"

"Good God, I'm not cussing you. How crazy are you?"

Both Amber and Doc became red around the gills. It seemed like they never agreed on anything. The bar got quiet to watch the show when all of a sudden, Roland and Deputy Cobb walked through the door.

Chapter 4

THE INVESTIGATION

A s soon as Roland had entered, Marcus staggered out of his seat, and attempted to stand at attention to salute Roland. Roland had been familiar with Marcus because Marcus had spent time in the county jail a couple of times. He proceeded to say to Marcus, "At ease, buddy, and take a seat. I'll get to you later." He then turned to Amber, "Is he drunk again?" But before Amber could respond, Bill came over Roland's radio, "Sheriff, the coroner from Montgomery is here to pick up the body, and he wants to know why it wasn't at the funeral home, and he also wants to talk to you."

Roland realized he was in the bar, but did not care. He responded rather abruptly, "Bill, you tell him if he has any question, I will gladly talk to him tomorrow at my office. Also, you can inform him that all protocol has been followed and that this is a murder case under my charge, and I will do what is deemed necessary. Bill, you sign off on everything that needs to be signed. The change of custody can have no errors. Also, tell him I want a preliminary report faxed to me no later than 2 pm tomorrow. Got it?"

"Roger, Sheriff. Dr. Price said you left before he could give you the results of that X-Ray you requested. You know, it was that German shepherd."

"Good thinking, Bill, about that dog, that is. Tell him to meet me in my office in the morning. I sure did forget about my dog, out." I don't think a soul in the bar missed any part of that conversation, and boy were their minds racing. Roland spoke over to Deputy Cobb, "I've got to notify the next of kin over in Willington, and I need you to stay here to interview anybody who knew Sue or even talked to her or even tried to hit on her. I want a statement from each. No one is to leave till you have it. I will get with that local cop up there to show me the way." Then speaking to everybody in the bar, "I want all of you to know that there has been a gruesome murder under my watch. I pity the fool who thinks he or she will get away with it. You cooperate with my deputy to the fullest and do not let me hear otherwise. And Amber, you will not serve Marcus another drink. Do you understand me?"

Nervously, Amber responded, "He has only had two."

"You want to push me?"

"No."

"Cobb, I want a statement from all who might have even known of Sue. You got me? And nobody leaves till I get back from Willington. I'll get with that local cop up there and have him go with me to the family. I should only be gone an hour. If anyone comes in while I'm gone, determine if they know her as well, and if so, detain him or her till I get back. Got it?

"Yes, Sheriff."

Roland immediately left the bar, got into his squad car, and screeched out to Highway 52 toward Willington. His mind raced on how he would give the information to whatever family that might be there. He recounted everything in his mind that he had encountered that day: the horrid mutilation of the body and the similar circumstances that presented themselves from two previous deaths that occurred in the city limits of Hope and were brushed under the rug. Was this the work of one killer? Was it a sick serial killer? How was he going to be able to link it all together? He sure was not going to get any help from the local police in Hope. He remembered the first murder, and it was similar in that she was young and beautiful. Her head was also bashed in with a blunt instrument. The locals pinned it on a local Black man in the area of the body. He had blood of the victim on his clothing, but that was all. He had been convicted on very weak circumstantial evidence. The other girl had been an attractive Black girl, and she was ruled an accident by the local police, but her death was also the result of blunt trauma to the back of the head. This bothered Roland, and he just knew there had to be a connection and a serious cover-up.

Willington was only four miles away, and he now pulled up to the make-shift police station, fire station, and EMS Ambulance. As Roland got out of his car, one of the only two police officers came out to greet him. Willington was considered a community. It had a county school that covered first grade through high school; a very calm and rural community. Roland introduced himself and the purpose of his trip there to the local police officer. He responded, "This is the worst thing that has ever happened in years if you don't take in the fact when Homer got ran over by his tractor in '92. Fell off it drunk from that damn shine he made. Oh, well I reckon you want me to take you to Ms. Parrish's house? My name is Jacob, in case you might want to know."

"What can you tell me about Mrs. Parrish and her husband and any other children they might have? Are they well off? Do they get involved in community affairs or such? Do they have any people that don't like them and such?"

"Wow! You got a lot of questions. What did Sue go off and do? She was never a bad girl; in fact, I wish I had a child like hers. She was an angel, and her mother ain't married. Reckon she was never was. She had Sue at 17. People around didn't like her for that. So she pretty much kept to herself and raised Sue all alone, and did a damn good job if you ask me. Sue is a looker, and her mama ain't no slouch. So, where is Sue?"

"She was murdered, and it was not nice. I need to see her mom now! Will you take me to their residence?"

"I'm afraid I'll have to ride with you, the squad car is in the shop. Something with the transmission, I guess."

They got in Roland's car and proceeded to Sue Parrish and her mother's residence. The area in which they were riding was not rundown. In fact, all the houses and trailers were well kept. It was at the end of the block when Jacob pointed out Ms. Parrish's single-wide trailer. The yard was well-manicured and had flowers up the walk to the front door. The entire trailer was skirted with no discoloration to the structure. Before they had exited the car, Evelyn Parrish had been standing outside the front door with her hands on her hips and a worried look to her face. As Roland looked at her, he could see how right Jacob had been about her appearance. She was a beautiful woman in her own right, and it gave Roland a sinking gut feeling to have to tell her what had happened. In fact, he wanted to get in his car and drive away. But he had a lousy job to perform at this moment. As he walked up to the door, the more he was impressed with this woman. She was very well kept, hair cleaned and pulled back as to reveal her uncanny facial features; not a blemish on her skin. She was perfect in his eyes. This job had just gotten harder. His voice, not as stern as usual, he asked permission to enter the residence so they might talk in private. She agreed, and being a gracious hostess, asked if they needed anything to drink. Both declined. After the pleasantries, Evelyn started the conversation, "Well, I guess you're here to tell me where my daughter ran off to last night? It's not like her not to call me. She is a very responsible young lady, and if you're here to tell me she done something wrong, well it's a damn lie. I raised a good girl, and she was out looking for work so she could finish her degree at the community college. And I'll have you know she was a straight-A student."

Roland raised his hand and stopped her there, "Ms. Parrish..."

Ms. Parrish interrupted before Roland could say another word, "You can call me Evelyn. I've heard of you. Been through three marriages, haven't you? You'd think you might get it right at least once."

Not wanting to be interrupted again, Roland grabbed Evelyn's hand very delicately, and at almost a whisper, told Evelyn this: "Evelyn, your daughter has been murdered. I assure you I will get to the bottom of this and make it right." Evelyn just sat there on her couch with a pale blank expression on her face. She said nothing, nor did anybody else. One could hear the wind blow outside along with a few birdcalls, but nothing else. It was as if the life force had been taken away from Evelyn. It was silent for five more minutes. It seemed like hours. Finally, tears welled up in Evelyn's eyes, and she remained motionless. Roland was lost as to how to comfort her. He felt helpless. He looked at her with complete sympathy. She was dressed in a flowered blouse and tan dress slacks and had her blond hair pulled back, revealing an emotional strain on her face. He finally offered her a tissue he saw on the kitchen counter. Roland felt a little awkward, and asked Jacob to give him and Evelyn a little alone time. Jacob gave no argument and left through the front door. Once he had left, Roland leaned over to Evelyn and said, "I'm taking this very personal, and it happened in my jurisdiction. I will not rest until I find out what happened."

Evelyn, barely able to put words together, asked, "Where is my daughter now? And when can I see her? She was my only child. What am I to do now? How can I go on?" She then broke down emotionally, and Roland embraced her with the best consoling hug he knew to do. After a few more minutes, Roland broke away; feeling the need to be strong for her, he told her the process and what he would do. "Evelyn, as we speak, Sue is being transported to Montgomery for an autopsy to determine the cause of death. This should take no more than three days, and I will have her transported to a funeral home of your choice, at the county's expense, for a proper burial. I am also going to give you my personal number for any questions you might have. I would like for you to make a list for me of anybody who might not have liked Sue or anybody she might have disagreed with. I also want to know all boyfriends or even the ones who thought they were her boyfriends. I do not expect this now. I will come back to check on you as needed. I want you to know I'm here for you anytime and anyplace you want."

Evelyn didn't know what to say, just nodded, and continued to cry. Roland could not stand the thought of leaving her alone. Roland walked toward the door to ask Jacob to come back in for a moment, to which he did immediately. Roland stepped outside and got on his radio, calling in to his office. "Dispatch, this is Sheriff Smith, and I want female Deputy Ann Wade to come to Willington. She is to stay with the victim mother, Evelyn Parrish, till I can make other arrangements. I do not want anybody hounding her. Copy."

On the other end of the radio, the response was immediate, "Copy that, Sheriff. Ann can be there in 20."

"Make it so. Roger out."

Roland remembered he needed to get back to Fred's and went back through the front door to ask Jacob to stay with Evelyn till his deputy arrived, and he agreed without reservation. Evelyn butted in and said, "I don't need a babysitter. I will be ok. I just need some space."

Roland interjected, "It's not for you; it's for me. I do not want news people or radio people or just busybodies bothering you. You are now under my protection, and I will have no one bugging you." Evelyn just looked up at him with a curious eye, but with different respect than she had before. She only knew of his reputation, and that was mostly gossip of old maids and wannabes. For an older man, he took care of himself. There was no fat, just lean muscle. How old was he anyway? Roland proceeded to his car and looked back at Evelyn and gave a mild wave, "I'll be back to check on you." And with that said, he went back toward Fred's.

Deputy Cobb talked to Johnny, the radio guy, at a table away from the bar. The other two he had talked to were Sparky and Molly. These conversations produced no new revelations. "So Johnny, what did our local police officer, Paul, have to offer in the way of news?"

"You know I can't divulge that."

"One thing I do know is that I can give you three hots and a cot for obstruction with an ongoing investigation. How would you feel about that?"

Johnny got a little nervous and said, "This was just found out this morning, and I don't think anybody has a clue as to what really happened, or do they?"

"I ask the questions here. Now, as I was asking you, what did Paul tell you?"

"Well, not really anything except that the sheriff took immediate control and pretty much ran him and Barney off. He did say he saw where the body was found and did not know who it was until Ed told him."

"Ed? When did he talk to Ed?"

"It was when he was leaving the vet hospital to get an application for the sheriff, followed by his deputy. He trailed them to the funeral home."

Deputy Cobb found this information curious, and made a note of it in his book. Johnny had been keenly watching his every move. Johnny reached down deep and asked, "Deputy, what can I report on the radio? I mean, people need to know there is a killer out there, and I need to report the facts. The press has the right to inform the public."

Cobb tried to keep his composure and thought before he spoke, "The sheriff will give you a statement. And then and only then are you to report anything. Do you understand me?"

"Yes, however, I have one question as to why the sheriff pulled his gun on Ed."

Deputy Cobb was beside himself. He stood up drastically and spoke in a loud tone, "Where did you hear that shit? If Roland ever pulled his gun, the person on the other end would be dead. Whoever said that had better recant his statement. I don't want to know who because I know what Roland would do. You had better quash that now. Do you understand?"

"I guess I misheard."

"You damn straight, you misheard."

Marcus heard all the ruckus at the far corner of the bar and also being pissed off because Amber would not serve him another drink, decided to go over to Cobb and Johnny. Marcus walked fairly straight for having a bad knee. When he finally made it to the table, he volunteered to help interrogate Johnny. "You know, Cobb, I can get him to talk. You just give me five minutes alone with him, and I'll have him squealing like a baby. I have a way with people. Or I could just knock the shit out of him?"

Johnny was surprised at his remark, "Marcus, I have bought you drinks. Why are you jumping on me? What the hell?"

Marcus, a little confused, looked again at Johnny and said, "Whoops, you can't buy me one now, that damn Amber got the booze locked tighter than that fat ass of hers."

Deputy Cobb got up and escorted Marcus back to the bar, and told Amber to get him a half-shot with mostly coke and to keep him there. Amber immediately objected and said, "You heard Roland, and I'm not doing it."

Doc, sitting at the bar, had jumped in, "Damn, Amber, can't you ever just be a little helpful? By God, this is Roland's deputy, and I'm sure if he says it's ok, it's ok. Quit being such a bitch."

This was just the fuel Amber needed to jump back at Doc, "Listen here, I told you not to cuss me. And you do not run this bar, I do. So you can just shut the fuck up."

Sparky chimed in, "Look who's cussing now. Give him the drink, Amber."

Three other customers told Amber to chill out, and finally, she backed down and gave Marcus a drink. And just as she handed it to him, Roland walked through the door. He immediately saw Amber handing Marcus a drink, and he mildly said, "What do you think you are doing? Didn't I specifically tell you not to give Marcus any more?" At that, Marcus stood up again to salute Roland, to which again Roland said, "At ease and sit down."

Amber defended herself and said, "It was your deputy, Cobb, who ordered me to serve him whiskey, and it was like mutiny on the bounty and the customers, jump-started by Doc. Doc is always starting trouble."

Roland absorbed what Amber said and then spoke, 'If my deputy said for you to do it, then you do it. I have complete faith in my deputies, or they would not be my deputies. As for Doc, y'all should kiss and make up." After that was said, everybody in the bar began to laugh. They all knew how much she disliked Doc. Roland went over to Cobb to find out what he was able to find out. It was slim and none. Roland decided to call off the questioning for the time being and stated it to the bar. He also told everyone he would be doing interviews at his office in Hope. This got the bar crowd murmuring under their breath with discontent. Again, Roland's radio went off,

"Sheriff, Ed Nixon is out here at the Parrish house and wants to talk to Evelyn. What do you want me to do?"

Roland was about to lose it, "You tell Ed he is to meet me in my office in thirty minutes and do not let him near Ms. Parrish. That's an order."

"But Sheriff, he's in his three-piece suit and stated he just wants to help with final arrangements."

"He's full of shit, Ann. You just tell him I'll talk to him in thirty. I also want you to write down everybody that comes to her house. Out." Turning around back to Deputy Cobb, Roland stated, "I want you to go down to the Hope PD and get the case files on the two other homicides I requested and bring them to my office."

"What if they give me trouble, Sheriff? You know how they can get."

"Then tell them I will get with Judge Spurlin and the county DA's office to force the issue. Tell them cooperation is in their best interest."

"They're not going to like it."

"Ask me if I care?" With that statement, Roland proceeded to leave the bar and go to his car, but he couldn't get to the door before Amber interjected, "What do you want me to do with Marcus? And for that matter, Doc, since he's prone to start all this ruckus?"

Roland was just about on his last straw with the stupidity of some of these people and responded, "Amber, how do you usually handle it with Marcus? I'm sure this isn't the first time you have gotten him drunk. And we all know his family picks him up. So that answers that. Now about Doc, you need to cut him a break. His family does positive things for the community, and his father works for the court on a referral basis. It might, just might, be time for you to back up a step. After all, how squeaky-clean are you? Last time I checked, shine is still illegal." With that, Roland and Cobb left in their squad cars, squealing off with rubber burning once the tires hit the asphalt.

The bar was quiet except for Doc telling Johnny he would talk to him later. Doc then proceeded to leave without saying a word to anyone else. Sparky was the next to leave, stating, "I think I have had enough excitement for one day."

Amber was steaming, but in a subdued voice, she said to Sparky, "You know that was not fair for Roland to be such an ass to me. He hurt my feelings."

"What feelings? Amber, you are as tough as nails. Don't play that card." With that said, Sparky left the bar.

Chapter 5

THE SUSPECTS

D oc left Fred's and got into his slightly dented 1999 all-white Mercury Sable. He was in a bit of a rush because he needed to cook for his parents. He had been drafted the caregiver by default with two older brothers and he being the youngest. Having a double-heart stent just last year had brought him home to the farm from Savannah, Georgia. In Georgia, he was a general food manager of a truck stop restaurant. In a way, he had been glad to be away from that job and to provide care for his aging parents.

The family lived on a 160-acre farm where they grew pine trees. They cut timber on forty acres every ten years, not a real profitable venture. The family also had a literacy center in the city of Hope. It was set up to provide literary training for those who fell through the cracks of the educational system. The center also had court-appointed anger management classes.

About fifteen minutes later, Doc pulled into the farm to park the car under the carport, an extension of the barn. His family home had two stories, a series of extensions to a single one-bedroom house. There were separate entrances to the upstairs and downstairs, quite a unique structure. As Doc entered upstairs, he went straight to the kitchen to start supper. His parents had been rousing from the bedroom about this time from an afternoon nap in time to see the national TV news, which they never missed. His mother, out on a walker, first asked, "Why are you so late?"

"There was a murder of a local girl from Willington, and I got stuck at Fred's."

"Why were you at Fred's? You know you can't handle your drink."

"Do you want to hear the story or not?"

"Of course, but wait till your dad gets up. "Then his mom yelled, "Jim, you up?" In the faint background, you could hear, "The news on already?"

"NO! Now wake up! Someone was murdered down the road." The next thing, dad hobbled out of the bedroom extremely disheveled: his gray hair standing straight up, one suspender connected to pants half-way up. And his face was matted as if ironed that way. He had a bit of an awkward gait as he attempted to walk straight. Meanwhile, Doc's mom was pushing her walker at a tortoise rate to her designated chair. A good five minutes later, the onslaught of questions began. First, his parents had to be in their chairs for the thought process to begin. The first question came from his mom; she was the true detective of the family. "So, what was her name?" she asked.

"Sheriff Roland said it was Sue Parrish."

"You haven't been with her, have you? You know how that could look."

"No, Mom. I do not even know her." He lied a bit to give her peace of mind.

Doc's dad finally spoke up, "What's for dinner? I'm starved."

His mom, raising her voice at his dad, said, "Haven't you been listening? A young girl was killed by a rapist."

"I didn't hear she was raped."

"Well, I had to get you to listen somehow. Oh, what are you cooking, Richard?"

He said, "lasagna." And that was the end of the conversation because the national news came on.

Ed Nixon was in his 2011 BMW on the way to Sheriff Roland's office as per the deputy's instructions. He could not see why he was not allowed to console and make funeral arrangements for Sue. He was always the first one on the scene, and that was why his business was successful. His father used to say, "Let sleeping dogs lie while you sneak in and get the bone." He never really grasped everything his father had said, but this little saying always stuck with him. Ed was not happy to have to go see Roland due to the fact he had an affair with his second wife or at least while he was divorcing his second wife. The irony of it was everybody knew about it before he did. They were separated, but it just stuck in his crawl. How long had they been seeing each other? Why did she get so disinterested in him so quickly? They were only together a year, and after that was when it started to fall apart. She would say to him, "Ed, you just can't satisfy me, and I can't live around all this death. It's creepy." He would just let it fly over his head, and maybe if he hadn't, they'd still be together. Oh well, he was over it in his mind. Or was he? He pulled into the parking lot to the sheriff's office. It was the old post office of Hope converted to a makeshift sheriff office. The building was made of brick and the front was a double-door main entrance. The back of the building still had the old loading docks for the mail trucks. Ed parked away from the other vehicles because he desired no dings on his beamer.

He walked through the front door of the sheriff's office and was greeted by Mildred, who handled most of dispatch. She let him know the sheriff was in his office and would be with him shortly. She also said he was talking to the Montgomery coroner. This information made Ed a little nervous because he thought that was supposed to be him, and he was cut out of the entire process. Mildred instructed him to have a seat on the other side of the counter away from her. Behind the counter were six desks, all with computers and what looked to be stacks of files. While Ed waited, Deputy Cobb walked in, holding a handful of files, and immediately said to Mildred, "Why, you'd think these files were made of gold the way the city was hanging onto them. Why, I had to go to the Chief of Police Bob Thorn for them to release the files to me. It was like they had something to..." Then Cobb noticed Ed sitting down and shut up with a quickness.

"He in his office?"

"Yes, go on back, he has been waiting on you."

Frustrated, Ed spoke up, "I've got to be somewhere. How long do I need to wait?"

Mildred attempted to be funny and quipped at Ed, "I don't think any of your customers are going anywhere, Ed." At that, Ed remained silent. Ed waited about twenty minutes and his temper started to get the best of him when Mildred's phone rang, Mildred answered and promptly replied and put the phone down. She then turned to Ed, "You can go on back now. Sorry for the wait. I hear people are just dying to see you." She started to giggle; he ignored her and walked back to Roland's office. As he opened the door, Roland was sitting behind a rather large mahogany desk with open files and pictures of what looked like murder victims. Cobb was sitting to the side of the desk, and they had a chair for him in front of the desk. As soon as Roland looked up and saw Ed, he rapidly started to put together the open files and put them off to the side of the desk. Accidently or not, he left out a picture of a previous murder victim that occurred back in 2009. The picture was quite gruesome. Ed could not help but notice it, and when Roland caught his eyes, he slowly put it in the file hidden from view. Roland told him to have a seat at the only chair available. As he sat down, his curious nature got the best of him, "What was that a picture of?"

As if waiting for the question, Roland stated, "We believe there is a link to this recent murder from some that have occurred in the past ten years."

"They caught that one."

"Or they framed the wrong man. Anyway, we are not ruling anything out. I asked you here to find why you went to Sue's mother's house so quickly? The woman has lost her only child and you're there in your three-piece trying to sell a plot? What goes through your head?"

Nervously, Ed said, "It has always been our, or my, policy to help with arrangements due to the family being distraught."

"You mean their only child being brutally murdered and head bashed in and body molested by a perverted shit. Is that what you mean by being distraught?"

Ed started to get on the defensive, "You know for the past twelve years I was appointed the temporary coroner for the city of Hope. It was a part of my job description until you decided it was not."

"Well, Ed, we do not need you in this. As a matter of fact, I want all records you have of the two previous homicides that occurred since 2005. And I would like them by tomorrow."

"You know I don't have that. I turn everything over to the city."

"Really? Didn't you bury and charge the city for all costs of embalming, caskets, and mourners? Mourners, really? Now that's a kick in the ass."

"You know those were all justified costs. I do not have to defend that. I did what I felt was right."

"Well, what I feel is right is that I want all expenses and procedures you did to the bodies. If necessary, I will exhume the bodies for physical evidence lost or not found during the shabby investigation."

"Roland, you're barking real loud. You have limited powers in this, and what you're requesting will not hold with the county judge, nor will the chief of police allow it. If I were you, I would just solve the case on hand. I will note my objections to the proper authority."

"Ed, you are a real shit. I have just gotten off the phone with Montgomery so that I would have no interference in investigating this case and the corruption of evidence of two prior cases involving this town and county. The state attorney is on board and backs me one hundred percent. You can bet that when I'm finished, the truth will be known. And about your little winnie, do not threaten me again!"

Ed paused to absorb what was just said. He felt very small indeed. Another thought came to him, "Ok, Roland, I see you like to play hardball. I do have some old files, and your deputies are welcome to them. Let it not be said I will not cooperate. I will help as best I can. I can make myself available tomorrow around nine."

"You will make yourself available now. Cobb will accompany you now to your office, and you will give originals, or you can give him copies. Are we like-minded, Ed?"

"We will never be like-minded. That's fine, he can come now. I really didn't appreciate the winnie remark."

"Shoe fits, Ed, shoe fits." Roland started to smile, but fought it back. "Oh, just one more thing, Ed. You know my late grandmother used to say that those who think their shit don't stink their farts give them away. Just a thought to carry with you."

"Thanks. My father used to say a few things too."

As Amber escorted Marcus to his sister's car for her to carry him home, she thought that he was a lot more agile today than usual. It just seemed to stick with her for some odd reason. Marcus' sister, Nadine, opened the door for Marcus to fasten him in the VW she had with the seatbelt, when Amber said, "He was not quite himself today. Thought you should know." Before Nadine could say something, Amber turned to walk toward her 1998 Chevy Silverado truck to go home. Her shift was over, and she was ready to get home. Once Nadine got into the driver seat and cranked up the bug, she turned to Marcus and said, "You didn't screw things up today, did ya?"

Marcus responded, "Let's get out of the parking lot before we talk, please."

Nadine finally got on Highway 54, and turned to Marcus, "Well?"

"They still think I'm crazy. Hell, I stood up and saluted Roland twice."

"Roland? You mean Sheriff Roland? What the hell was he doing there?"

"Apparently, Sue Parrish was murdered down on the old dirt road where we get some of the mushrooms."

"You were there last night, weren't you?"

"Yes, but I didn't see anything. She was probably dumped there. Anyway, we are still good to make a fortune. They all think I'm not much capable of wiping my butt. Everything is still on."

"Sue Parrish, she was a looker, and her mother had her at seventeen. I always had the hots for her mother."

"Stop it, Nadine, leave that cat in the bag. We just need to lay low for a couple of days, and it will all work out. I got to meet the people coming up from Florida in five days, so let's be cool."

"Ok."

Amber went up a rocky dirt road about fifty yards from the country road toward her home. She lived in an older model single-wide up on blocks that you could see from the road. You could even see the wheels were still on it; there was no skirting around it. Amber used to say she left them on for a quick getaway if needed. She was hoping her boyfriend Doug Rogers was there, and he was. She knew because his Harley was at the side of the trailer. As she went to the front door, he was there, and opened the door with an extremely worried look on his face. Amber being Amber, told him, "Git me a beer out of the fridge, this has been a hell of a day."

"I thought it was. I drove past Fred's to see two sheriff cars. Needless to say, I kept driving on."

"Yes, it was Sheriff Roland and his deputy, Cobb. Sue Parrish was murdered out on the old dirt road off 54."

"Big dog Roland himself, wow. This must be big. What he want?"

"Well, it appears he knows about my moonshine business because he made reference to it in front of the whole bar. Thank God I live in a different county. We will need to move the stockpile to a different location tonight."

"Shit. You mean, I will have to move it."

"You don't expect me to be out there where it is, do ya? Anyway, all you got to do is bury it out by the shed at Roy's. Ok?"

"Yes, I'll do it. I will need some loving for all this hard work. And I don't mean just a quickie."

"You know I appreciate you. Might as well get started, it's not going to move itself. I'll be here if you need me." Doug left right then, and you could hear his Harley crank up and leave the yard. Amber needed the privacy. Today had been crazy. She was totally unaware Roland was going to come to the bar, and how the hell did he know about her moonshine business? Amber had to re-think who she had done business with. She thought it was Doc, but he didn't know anything that she was aware of. Johnny liked her product. Was there a connection to Sue? Sue did ask about it, but she denied any knowledge of it to her. Then there was that night before she died and was at the bar. No questions had been asked about that yet. She thought certain people were going to need to get together to have the same story of the events that occurred. After finishing the first beer Doug gave her, she went to the fridge to get another, and the twelve-pack box was empty. That damn Doug drank all her beer again. She had been with Doug for two and a half months, and it was definitely not working. He was unemployed, and his sex was not that great. She thought he could be called the minuteman. Oh well, another one gone. She could still use him to get her business affairs in order. He was good at that, and he did have good connections for other items she sometimes needed. She sat back in her broken La-Z-Boy and closed her eyes to figure a way that she had no knowledge of Sue or her mother. As she sat there, she fell soundly asleep.

Johnny and Sparky were still at Fred's, and this was late for them. They were usually gone by four, and it was now 7 pm. They had been discussing every scenario that could have occurred today. They even mulled over suspects. There was an older man in cowboy boots in the bar that neither of them knew. He had been playing pool with several people. Johnny and Sparky didn't play pool because they both sucked at it. But they kept this elderly gentleman under observation. He was wearing old jeans and a checkered flannel shirt. He had put his Levi jacket over a chair while playing pool. His face had three-day beard growth. Sparky had narrowed down the suspects to Amber for jealousy, and just any pervert in Hope. Johnny was trying to be more scientific since he was the news at his AM station. In fact, he wasn't sure when Roland was going to let him get out any of the details. Feeling no pain, Sparky got up to tell the night bartender he was off to the house when Ed Nixon walked in the bar. Sparky immediately sat back down. Ed was not in his suit. In fact, he was in tight jeans with pointed toe cowboy boots and a heavy flannel shirt. He didn't notice Johnny or Sparky, and walked over to the older guy who had been playing pool. They stood there talking, which seemed forever, when Vicky, the night bartender, asked Ed, "Damn it, boy, you drinking or at a fashion show?"

Ed just laughed, and then noticed Johnny and Sparky. Walking toward the two, he said, "Just give me a Crown and Coke. Why hello, Johnny and Sparky. What a day for a drink wouldn't you say?"

Johnny spoke first, "Ed, I hear tell that Roland has been all over you. What's up with that?"

"He has never liked me, you know that, and I have no reason to like him after he got with my ex-wife. Let just say it's been semi-friendly war."

Sparky, eager at the bit, jumped in, "Did he pull his gun on you?"

"Why, hell no. Who the hell said that?"

Sparky retreated, "Just gossip. You know how it gets."

Ed, showing a little apprehension, "Well, I hope the gossip doesn't get too creative. I have a business to run."

Sparky got up again, yelling for Vicky, "Hey baby, I got to git. I've pulled overtime today. I'm glad you got to see me." Sparky then turned for the door to get in his 2011 Grand Marquis. Once Sparky was out the door, Johnny asked Ed who the old guy was. Ed, at first, tried to evade the question, and then said, "He used to live here a long time ago. I believe he was a mechanic by trade. He did some work for me on one of my hearses." After that answer, Johnny yelled down for Vicky to tell her he was gone and that he always enjoyed her presence. But before he could get in his jeep, Ed asked, "What you going to report on the radio tonight?"

"What can I report? The lid is quite tight except that Sue Parrish is dead from foul play."

"How do you know it was foul play? For that matter, how does anyone know what happened except Roland? I never seen him like this. He has broken all protocol. That's not the way to make friends in this neck of the woods."

Johnny looked directly into Ed's eyes and said, "I don't think he cares to make friends." He then walked to the exit, hopped in his jeep, and took off. Vicky was working the bar with her jovial self, and yelled to the bar, "Let's get some money in the juke box, this place is like a morgue. Sorry, Ed."

Chapter 6

T he roosters began to make their racket due to the oncoming
dawn. The three horses were already leaving the barn and
heading to the pasture adjoining the barn, while the four pigs just
wallowed in their pen undisturbed. The wind was brisk with a
typical forty-five-degree temperature. In the one-story log cabin
house, Sheriff Roland had begun to make his coffee. It was 5 am,
and he was bound and determined to get a good day's worth of
work accomplished today. He figured no uniform today and go
with jeans and a sports jacket to cover his weapon. He would
put his badge on his belt. His first call would be to Evelyn, the
victim's mother. He was very impressed by her, not only by her
composure but her demeanor as well. She was a very attractive
woman, and it was a pure shame the way her immediate neighbors
treated her since she had Sue out of wedlock at such an early age.
The hypocrisy just simply pissed him off. He decided to keep a
deputy there till her daughter was laid to rest. His second thing
to do was to meet with Dr. Price to discuss the X-ray taken, and
see if there were comparisons to the other two cases he pulled
from the city. Then finally, he could have the conference call with
Montgomery coroner to derive the cause of death and other evidence extracted from the body. After all this, he should be able
to narrow down who could have committed this crime. Now he
had to feed the animals. He loved his horses. He had one mare,
one pure breed for breeding, and then, of course, his sorrel, which

33

used to be a great cutting horse. The pigs were easy to feed. He thought the life of a pig was like some of the people he knew in Hope. Just throw slop to them and watch them wallow in their own shit. He got through pitch-forking some fresh hay for the horses and looked back at his home. He truly loved his log cabin. It was a two-bedroom and two-bath home with afull-size kitchen and a large living space with a huge fireplace. Then he thought of the failed relationships he was involved with, all of which tried to get his house through divorce and were unsuccessful. This he was grateful to the Almighty that no one got their slimy hands on what he had been building all his life. He knew there would be someone someday soon he could share this little piece of heaven with or least he has prayed as much.

Instead of taking his county vehicle, he decided to drive his Jeep Wrangler. The first stop was to Willington to see Evelyn Parrish. On second thought, he decided to re-visit the crime scene. Upon driving down that familiar dirt road, his mind raced as to the action that happened prior to the murder. What was in the conscious of the murderer? Why this road? Why, just why would someone take the life of such a young vibrant girl? He finally arrived to the spot of the taped-off areas and was glad to see it was not tampered with. Being so early in the morning, there was dew on the ground, which glistened from the early morning sun. He stopped his jeep and got out to look around the crime scene area. From a distance, he saw an unusual sparkle. It was like an object that didn't belong. It was only about fifteen feet from where the body was discovered. As he walked closer, he could see it was a cell phone. Not wanting to lose any possible prints or anything for that matter, he ran to his jeep to get an evidence bag. Once back to the phone, he carefully placed it into the bag. Attempting to turn the phone on, he soon learned the battery was dead. Again, he surveyed the area to perhaps see another bit of evidence. It was in Sheriff Roland's mind that he would not rest until this crime was solved and solved to his satisfaction. It was now time to go to Evelyn's. For the victim's mother, his emotions were mixed. Her neighbors were just wrong to judge her for having her child out of wedlock. It's not like they didn't have skeletons lurking in their closets. This just made Roland mad thinking about that side of Evelyn's life. To lose her only child made it that much crueler, he thought.

It was now 9 am as Roland pulled into Willington to go to Evelyn's house. When he got on the road where she lived, he spotted his deputy's car with Ann in it. As she saw him pull up, she exited the vehicle. Roland parked beside her and went up to her to find out what had transpired after he left. Greeting Ann, Roland said, "Have we had any excitement?"

Ann, being in full uniform, responded, "Been like a graveyard here except for when Ed cameyesterday. He sure didn't like me telling him he couldn't talk to Evelyn."

Feeling satisfied, Roland grinned a little and said, "I guess that's just tough luck for him. Anybody else try to come by? A concerned neighbor or any unusual traffic on this road?"

"It's odd. Nobody came by at all. I'm sure the word has gotten around. She has just been alone in there. I did leave to go home at 10 pm last night and came back this morning at 7 am."

"There's no need for you to pull any more hours here. I want you to go back to the station and tell Bob to come out here today. I think I've punished him on the desk long enough. Tell him to use an unmarked vehicle from the impound lot, but to be in full uniform. I want to keep a presence here for one more day. Also, tell him I want all cars and tags that travel this road noted. It shouldn't take you more than twenty minutes to get there, and I will be here till he arrives."

"Why not radio him in, Sheriff?"

"No need, I will be getting vital information from Ms. Parrish during the interim. She was quite upset yesterday, and I think now will be the proper time to dig a bit. Let Bob know to knock on the door when he arrives here. Thanks Ann."

"No problem, Sheriff. You got any ideas yet?"

"Too soon to say, Ann. Too soon. Oh, Dr. Price is scheduled to be at my office this am. If I'm not there, please radio me, and I'll get there ASAP."

"No problem, Sheriff. She sure does have a nice place. I met her once, and it just doesn't seem fair what happened to her child."

Roland looked toward Evelyn's home and saw her looking out from the doorway toward them. "Well let's get a move on, I see her now- and I'd better go ahead and talk to her." With that said, Ann got in her squad car and proceeded to drive toward Hope. Roland looked up and down the street, and it was true, Evelyn had the nicest yard and well-manicured landscape. As he walked to the front door, he could not help but to see what she was wearing. She had on sweat pants and a sweatshirt, with her hair pulled back in a ponytail. Even in this outfit, she was a vision of beauty in his eyes. As he made it to the door, Evelyn opened the door for him and invited him in. They proceeded to the kitchen area where there was a wood table with four wooden chairs. The kitchen itself was extremely clean and had the aroma of coffee brewing. Evelyn graciously offered him coffee, which he eagerly accepted.

"Do you take cream and sugar?" she asked

Roland looked into her eyes and saw them puffy as if she had been crying significantly, and said, "I take mine black, thank you." He saw his opportunity and decided to try as delicately as possible to get some background information. "So, how long have you lived here? I mean, your home is quite nice as compared to the rest on this street."

"Why, thank you. I have lived here since my mother died some fifteen years ago."

"Do you rent?"

"That's a waste of money to rent. No, I have a mortgage."

"I agree with you on that. Evelyn, I have to ask you some questions, and I do not wish to upset you, but there are some things I need to know so I can come to a quick closure to this, this horrible happening."

"I figured that's why you were here. I would like to thank you for posting that deputy here yesterday. I really did not want to talk to anyone. I'm still having major difficulty trying to believe my only child is dead." Evelyn's eyes started to water up again. Roland immediately looked around the kitchen to find a Kleenex box and spotted one by the sink. He got up with a quickness and grabbed the box, brought it to where Evelyn was sitting, and then returned to his chair. He looked at her with true compassion in his own eyes. There was silence for a while when Roland finally said, "What do you do for a living?"

Evelyn wiped her eyes dry and took a moment, then responded, "I work at the sewing factory in Hope. I have been there since I graduated from here. You see, I had a baby to support by myself. Her father went off to college, never to be heard of again."

"That must have been hard. I can only imagine. I hope they are giving you paid time off right now."

"Yes, my position is floor supervisor, so I have some built up time. Of course, those under me are all doing their regular gossip about me."

Roland showed his feelings, which was not unusual, and said, "Screw them and the dented car they rode up on!"

Evelyn did a half-smile and said, "Thank you."

"Well, let me tell you where we are. I will be getting a report from Montgomery this morning on the exact cause of death. Also, critical evidence as to who could have done this. I'm also going out of my way with a local, Dr. Price, to assist me with the areas I'm not smart in. And believe it or not, I'm also using Willy Barnes, the vet. These are people I trust and know they will shoot it straight to me. I believe the person who did this to your child has done it before and was not caught. I also believe he or she lives in the Hope area. There is compelling evidence that suggests this I cannot ignore. Now I need to ask you if you know some people I talked to. Do you feel up to it?"

Stunning Roland, Evelyn said, "Do I feel up to it? Do I feel up to it? You can bet your ass I'm up to it. As a matter of fact, I'll help kill the bastard."

Roland took a sip of his coffee and tried to regain his shock at this point, and admiration of her response, he began his questions. "Evelyn, do you know an Amber? She bartends at Fred's."

"I do not wish to be un-ladylike, but that bitch has lied and gossiped about me since I was in high school, and when I became pregnant at seventeen, she passed the rumor I was a whore. The fact is, he was my first, and I was so naïve. She went to the same school, and is older than me, but was always jealous the boys

37

liked me better till I got pregnant. She had a reputation of being easy and did drugs."

"Do you think she would do anything against you physically?"

"She's big enough to. But no." They both laughed.

"Do you think she is still into drugs?"

"What I heard is she got a still and sells corn whiskey."

"Do you ever go to Fred's or maybe buy packages to go?"

"No. You will not catch me there. I do not care for the patrons except one called Doc. His son graduated with my girl. He's an ok guy, a little crazy, but ok."

"Did you know Sue applied for a bartender job at Fred's and gave her application to Amber? Amber was quick to turn it down."

Evelyn turned red with extreme anger, "Had I known, I would have burned down that bar. Sue knew my feelings. I guess she was so desperate for a job because she lost financial aid at the technical school, and she had to come up with additional tuition, and I couldn't afford it. She kept things from me because, I guess, I would go off, so to speak."

"She also applied with Ed Nixon. Do you know him?"

"He's that guy that came here yesterday, right?"

"Yes."

"I didn't know she applied there. I can tell you that Ed guy tried to hit on me once, but he gave me the creeps."

Roland understood that completely. They continued to talk for about twenty more minutes, and covered most of the patrons that went to Fred's because Sue was spotted there that fatal night. Evelyn was very helpful, and painted the picture of what Roland was seeing from gut instinct. All of a sudden, there was a knock on the door. Evelyn looked surprised, but Roland got up and answered the door, where Deputy Bob Walker stood in full uniform. Evelyn walked up behind Roland and asked, "Who's he?"

"I told you I'm going to be looking out after you, and that was my word. This here is Bob Walker, and he will be outside in an unmarked vehicle. I want to know of any spectators or just idiots who visit. Besides, until we get Sue laid to rest, I want to be there for you. You deserve it."

Out of the blue, Evelyn turned Roland around and proceeded to hug him with strength. Roland turned all red, from either shyness or just embarrassment, paused, and then finally hugged her back. It truly felt good. He was falling hard for this woman, and it scared him tremendously. Bob looked on as they hugged and said nothing. When he and Roland went to their cars, Roland turned to him and said, "I want you to get tag numbers and stop anybody who goes to her door. Write all this down in a time sequence. Also, try to keep a low profile. If anything you think might warrant my attention, radio Mildred to tell me. I will be in the office most of the day. Ok?"

"You got it, Sheriff. You got any ideas yet?"

"Yes I do, and I want concrete evidence to convict."

"Yes, sir."

With that, Roland got in his jeep and proceeded to head for Hope.

Chapter 7

On the day after the morning of the discovery of Sue Parrish's body, Marcus was up at 8 am. He lived in Hope in a three-bedroom brick house with an unkempt yard. His sister lived with him. Today was the day they were to check on his illegal investment. It was a secluded meth lab. He figured on some quick easy cash. Waking up his sister, who was still soundly asleep, he yelled, "Hey, we got to go check and see if Ronnie has finished the product. So get your ass up. You know I can't drive out there. We have to take the bug."

Drowsy, Nadine responded, "Let me get dressed. Man, you act like you're still in the Army. What's the rush anyway? You know we have to go down that dirt road to get to the trailer."

"Yes, but I'm sure a lot of people are going down that road just for morbid curiosity. Hurry up, I got to know how much he has made." He walked to the front door and opened it to check the weather. There was a cool breeze, and he was cold natured. He closed the door and went to his room to get a jacket, and at the same time, he opened a drawer on his chest and pulled out a 44 semi-automatic. He checked the clip and it was full. He then shoved it down the back of his pants. He decided he wanted no surprises, and if so, he was prepared. He then put on his jacket to cover the presence of the gun. As he and his sister walked out to the car, his sister noticed the bulge from his back. She then knew he was carrying, and this worried her, for she has known him all her life.

As they got in the car, Nadine said to Marcus, "Either overnight, you have developed a severe case of hemorrhoids, or you're packing. And if you're packing, why?"

"Damn it, Nadine, you know this is a dangerous proposition, and I will not be caught with my pants down."

"Good God, Marcus, Ronnie is cool, he's not going to start anything."

"That's right, he's not." With that statement, Nadine started toward the site where they were producing the meth, which meant they had to go down that dirt road off 54 where Sue was killed. This gave her a queasy feeling in her stomach. As they got close to the turn-off of 54 onto the dirt road, she saw Sheriff Roland's jeep pull out and turn up toward Willington. She and Marcus saw this but said nothing. They just took notice, and their radar heightened. They made the turn down the dirt road. It was only about a mile when they saw the police tape-off area. They drove by slowly as if the body was still there. Marcus finally spoke up, "Come on and pick the pace, we got another mile to go." About a half a mile further, there was a large fenced-in cow field. This was where the youth of the area would go cow tipping and harvest mushrooms. It was well patrolled by the county. Another half a mile to the left was a locked gate. Marcus got out, unlocked the gate, and pulled it back for Nadine to pull through. After she pulled through, he locked the gate. This dirt road was a lot rougher, grass growing in the middle, and just two tracks to follow. It was like an old wagon trail from the West. It took ten minutes to finally get to the makeshift trailer that was shaded by a large oak, making it hard to see from the sky. There was one truck there as they pulled up. It was Ronnie's old beat-up Datsun. As they pulled up, Ronnie came out the front door with a gas mask on. He pulled the gas mask off and belted, "You're a sight for sore eyes."

Marcus, the first one out of the bug, yelled back, "Get over here and bring me up to date. I mean, do we have enough to ship? This area is getting hot."

"We are well ahead of schedule. I got the complete amount you need for Florida and then some."

"God bless you, Ronnie. I thought I was going to have to kill you." Ronnie looked extremely shocked and started to tremble a bit. Marcus noticed this and said, "Just kidding buddy, come here. I got two butane tanks in the bug. Why don't you take them out for me? My legs are bugging me today." Nadine got out of the car and was silent. Marcus spoke up again, "Well, I guess that means I can go ahead and get my stuff and conclude this transaction."

Ronnie leaned over in the back seat of the bug, pulling two five-gallon butane tanks out when he said, "There is a matter of payment, Marcus. It's a bitch being back in these woods, and it has not been easy. Hell, yesterday I thought we were busted, with all the sirens and all."

"We? You need to re-think that."

"Whatever, it scared me."

After Ronnie set down the butane tanks, Marcus walked up to him, reached inside his jacket, and handed him a brown envelope. "That's three thousand dollars cash as we agreed. Now, where is my product?" Ronnie then walked over outside the trailer, lifted a tarp, and under it, an ice chest, and brought it over to Marcus. He opened it, and inside were ten baggies of a white crystal-type substance. Lifting one out, he said, "Here, try it."

Marcus yelled over at Nadine, "Get over here, this is your part." Nadine walked over to look at the product, and then pulled out a pocket knife and put a little on the end of the blade and snorted it right there. Marcus, eager to know, "Well, is it or what? Damn it, girl, speak up."

"Damn, Ronnie, I think this is your best batch. This shit hits like a freight train. Wow, that was a blast. What did you do different?"

"Your brother gave me all his Sudafed he got from the VA. Hell, they shipped him a ninety-day supply. I had 360 pills to work with."

Marcus got back to business, "Nadine, put the ice chest in the bug. Ronnie, it might be wise to shut down for a while until the heat blows over."

"Damn, Marcus, I got five more pounds working."

"After that, shut it down. Ok. You got it."

"Yes, no problem. What do you want me to do with the extra?"

"Consider it your bonus. But so help me, God, if you get caught selling or you get busted, you do not know me or Nadine. Do you understand?"

"Of course."

"I mean, do you understand?" Marcus pulled his gun out and pointed it at Ronnie's head and said, "I will kill you. Now, do you understand?"

Ronnie shook and said, "I will never cross you. You have my word."

Marcus put the gun up and looked around the area. This was a perfect place. "Alright, close her down. Nadine, get in the car, we need to be drinking by twelve, or I need to be drinking by twelve at Fred's." They left.

Roland had only been gone one hour from Evelyn's when a shiny BMW pulled up in front of Ms. Parrish's home. Deputy Bob immediately got out of his unmarked car, which was parked across the street, and walked up to Ed Nixon, who was starting to get out of his beamer. Bob intercepted him before getting to the front gate of the yard. Ed was dressed in his three-piece suit again. Ed saw Bob, and started to get steamed, saying, "Not again."

Bob kept his cool and merely replied, "Is there something I can help you with, Ed?"

"Yes, Bob, you can get out of my way so I can see Ms. Parrish."

"Why don't we see if Ms. Parrish wants to see you first? You stay right here and I will go ask. Will you accept that?"

"I guess I have no choice. I will be right here. You know this is getting ridiculous."

Deputy Bob walked up to the front door and rang the bell. Evelyn came to it rather quickly. Bob asked to come in, and she let him in. She looked over Bob's shoulder and saw Ed waiting at the gate, and then shut the door behind Bob once he was in. Being rather disturbed that Ed was here again, she asked Bob, "What is he doing here again? Can't he take a hint?"

Bob replied, "I'm to ask you if you wish to see him? Normally, I wouldn't bother you, but he was being persistent."

"No, Bob, you keep him away from me, please. He gives me the creeps, and always has."

All of a sudden, Mildred came over Bob's radio, "Deputy Bob, we have a situation. The TV media from Montgomery and Dothan are here wanting to report the murder for the five o'clock news. They are here in Hope at the station. The sheriff is sending Ann out there to you to keep them away from Ms. Parrish if she wishes. Ask her if that is ok."

Bob responded, "Give me one moment, Mildred, I got Ed Nixon out here too."

"Roger that. I'll tell the sheriff."

Bob looked at Evelyn, "Well, I reckon this had to happen sooner or later. What do you want us to do?"

Evelyn rubbed her head, and her eyes welled up a little. She was quiet for at least a minute. She finally spoke up and said, "I like the way the sheriff has been handling this whole deal. I'm not prepared to speak to anybody. Why can't people just let me mourn my loss privately? All I have is me and maybe two close friends. You tell Roland to handle this for me the way he seems fit. Of course, I'll let you know my friends so you can let them see me. It's bad enough the loss, now all this other crap. This is my business and mine alone. Get rid of that prick outside, and I'll be in here waiting to hear from Roland. Ok?"

Bob got on the radio, "Mildred."

"Go ahead, Bob."

"You say Ann's on the way out here?"

"Roger that, and she will be in a squad car. Roland said she was to park it in front of the home, and for you to keep the same position. He also told me for you to tell Ed the media is here and it's his time to be a star."

"Thanks, Mildred, I'm sending Ed away now. I will keep position and keep making note of drive-bys per the sheriff's instruction. I take it we are to keep the reporters away from Ms. Parrish and no comment from us."

"You hit the nail on the head, Bob. Ann will be there shortly. Out."

Bob turned to Ms. Parrish, "I'm so sorry for this. I will make sure you are not disturbed other than your friends."

"Thank you, Deputy." She watched him go out the front door. and she immediately shut the door behind him and locked it. She thought to herself why she was calling the sheriff *Roland*. And why was she so confident in him? She was always self-sufficient. Why now was she dependent on a man? She felt very comfortable around him, and maybe that was it.

Bob walked up to Ed, and was beginning to tell him to go when Ed spoke up, "You sure was in there long enough. Shit. I was just going to help her with arrangements for her daughter's burial."

"I really don't care, Ed. Roland told me to tell you that, as we speak, the TV media from Dothan and Montgomery are at the sheriff's office, and are now going for the story. He said this is your time to become a star. Reckon you better git."

"You mean I can't see Ms. Parrish?"

"Ed, Ms. Parrish doesn't want to see you. It has nothing to do with the sheriff. Drive safely."

"Well, hell. Don't think I won't talk to those reporters on the way this whole thing was handled. I'm the damn coroner, and I was not in the loop at all. I'm heading to y'all's station right now."

"Tata, Ed. I wouldn't speed, you might get a ticket from Hope PD." With that said, Bob cracked a smile and turned his back to Ed. Once Ed took off, Bob got back on the radio, "Mildred."

"Bring it on, Bob."

"Ed is fuming and heading your way. He can't wait to tell his side of the failed protocol. Be sure to tell the sheriff."

"He's on top of it, believe me, Bob. That man is one smart cookie. Out."

Chapter 8

W hen Roland pulled into the station, Dr. Price had pulled in at the same time. And behind Dr. Price's car was Willy Barnes, the vet. They had planned to meet this morning. The timing worked out perfectly. They all walked through the front to see Mildred's smiling face, then they all said "good morning" to her and proceeded to the sheriff's office. Roland turned back to Mildred and said, "Hey, could you get me that stand-up dry-erase board in the storage room and bring it to my office? I need to set up a crime and evidence board. Thanks."

Once in the office, they all proceeded to sit down. It was a rather big office, so there was plenty of room when Mildred brought in the big dry-erase board. She set it off to the left side of the office so all could get a good view. She then turned to the sheriff to see if he needed anything else. All he needed was that, and she preceded to go back to her desk. Roland looked at Dr. Price and saw he was carrying a package and said, "Is that what I think it is?"

"Yep, it's the X-rays. I wish I had a light board to show you better, but we can use a flash light."

Roland wouldn't have known what he was seeing, so he said, "Why don't you just tell me what you saw."

"Well, it was a deep trauma to the occipital lobe of the brain. I would say close to two inches deep. The striking blow came over the top of her head in a straight down motion right in the middle of right and left lobes of the brain and down the middle of the of the occipital lobe. It almost split the cerebellum. This kind of impact was forceful, with a strong downward motion."

"Could you tell what kind of instrument was used? I mean a hatchet, or sword, or what exactly?"

"Well, the bone fragments suggest a serrated edge. Perhaps a saw or something of that nature."

"Willy, what do you think?"

Willy thought for a moment and said, "There was no animal molestation of the body. I think your deputy got there before that could happen. As for the markings on the body, they were man-made. And I concur with Dr. Price's findings on the X-rays. This type of blow was very precise. Whoever did it had a calculated hand. And I believe the body was dumped there. She had to have been killed elsewhere."

Dr. Price jumped in, "Oh, the body was definitely dumped, just like those two others."

"You mean the Black girl in 2009 and the White girl in 2005?"

"Exactly what I mean. It's no coincidence that their cause of death was head trauma too."

Roland felt a sense of validation knowing that this had to be true, and it was his gut instinct at those times they arrested the wrong man. He turned to Dr. Price, "I got those files right here. I had to argue with the police chief to get them, but here they are." He handed one to Willy and to Price. "Look those over and tell me if we have a serial killer."

As they read, Mildred buzzed the sheriff, "We got a problem out here! The TV stations from Montgomery and Dothan just pulled up. Somebody has leaked out what happened."

"When they get in, stall them. Call the Hope police chief and tell him to get over here. Also, send Ann out to Ms. Parrish's home to back up Bob."

"Sheriff, I got Bob on the radio."

"Find out what it is and then tell me immediately."

A couple of moments later, Mildred responded, "It's that damn Ed Nixon again. He's out there at the Parrish place."

Roland looked as if he was going to have a stroke. "Calm down, Roland," said Dr. Price, noticing how Roland appeared.

Roland took a few breaths and told Mildred, "Tell Bob to tell him TV is here. He can become a star now. What a prick. Sorry, Mildred."

"No problem, it's done. The TV folks are just setting up their cameras outside. They have those big antenna trucks."

Roland looked flustered and said, "Well, shit." Dr. Price had a bag to his side along with the package of X-rays. He rummaged through until he found a pill bottle and pulled out two pills. "Here, Roland, take this now. I will not take no for an answer."

"What is it?"

"Swallow, damn you." After Roland took the medication, Price told him what it was. "I just gave you 1mg of Xanax. Now just get your game face on and chill out."

"You're right, Price. I want y'all to study the cause of death in those files. Also, where they were buried. I have a strong idea who we are looking for. Call it gut instinct. See if there was any forensics done on either one of them to determine evidence of foul play."

While they looked at the files, Mildred came over the phone again, "Sheriff, I got the Montgomery coroner on the phone, line two."

He thanked Mildred and picked up on line two, "This is Sheriff Roland."

"Good morning, this is Tom McGruder, chief coroner and CSI investigator. Let me tell you one thing, you really sent me a doozy here. Who threw up all over the body?"

"Do you mind if I put you on speaker phone? I have two doctors present that were with me for the discovery of the body."

"No problem. You know I just have a preliminary report."

"Tom I'll take whatever you got. I believe this is the third murder of a serial murderer, and I need every bit of evidence you can gather."

"I did not know that. Thanks. Well, let's start. Cause of death: head trauma was the cause of death. It was a serrated saw of some nature that penetrated the skull three and a quarter inches, causing immediate death. Prior to death, she was raped. We did a full rape kit, and this poor sucker left DNA. I do not have results of the DNA yet. It takes a little longer. I will have the results in the morning or sooner. Besides the rape, there is evidence there was a second person involved. The bruising indicates someone was holding down the victim during the rape. The marking and superficial scratching of the body on the torso and legs were done post mortem.

The weapon is the problem. You need to be looking for a serrated-edge saw-like instrument that has a bit of weight to it. I'm at a loss on the weapon."

Roland interrupted and said, "Do you think it could be one of those old antique bone saws used in amputation during the Second World War?"

"Well, that's interesting. I do believe it would probably be a perfect fit. I think we have one somewhere up here. I will test that theory. Also, whoever had the emetic event on the body, please tell him or her they have a bleeding ulcer. We found traces of blood in the vomit."

"Figures. Hey, Tom, I got two TV stations outside my front door here. If we could match that DNA to a suspect here, would you say he or she was the murderer?"

"Yes, definitely. The victim was not a virgin, but was not sexually active also. The attack only showed one set of DNA."

Dr. Price got the curiosity bug and asked, "Mr. McGruder, from the bruising of the second person involved, what are the chances of fingerprints or hand print outlines, or for that matter, a hair that might produce a second set of DNA?"

"As I said, this is preliminary report, but you are right, there is a chance."

"Tom, this is the sheriff. I need your help. I have already contacted the state attorney, and he is aware of this case. What I need is a subpoena to exhume the bodies of the two prior victims I believe were done by the same person, one killed in 2005 named Kelly Foster, and in 2009, a Sharee Washington."

Dr. Price interrupted, "Make it just one for Kelly Foster. From the file, Sharee Washington was cremated."

There was a pause on the phone, then Tom responded, "So you're inferring this is part of a serial killing?"

Roland was eager, "You damn, Skippy. And besides, was your office ever notified of the other two victims mentioned?"

"I'll have to check, but offhand I have been here twenty years, and to my knowledge, this is the first body I ever received from Hope. Kind of freaked me out. Y'all always seem a rather peaceful area."

"Do you know Ed Nixon, our assigned coroner?"

"Yes, actually, I authorized him. You know he is also a medical doctor. He passed his boards back in 1999. That's why I assigned him."

"I didn't know that. I thought he was just a mortician. He owns the funeral home in the area."

"That's what made him perfect. Oh, well. I will call the state attorney and get your subpoena. I should have the DNA results too. I understand you bypassed Ed completely through this process."

"I sure did. That doesn't break change of custody, does it? We are not going to have a legal loophole, are we?"

"No, you're good, the change of custody was perfect to me. You did exceptionally there. I will be in touch with you this afternoon, around three or so, with the results."

"One more thing, the mother of the victim wants the body released to White's Funeral Home in Elba. Do you know when that could be?"

"I only need the body one more day. After that, they are welcome to pick up."

"Thanks. Till three, then."

Right then, there was another call from Mildred, "Sheriff, the chief of police is here."

"Send him back. Thanks."

There was a slight knock on the door and the chief walked in the office. He looked surprised to see Willy and Price there. Roland greeted Bob, and then said, "I'm sure you know Dr. Price and our vet, Willy Barnes."

"Sure do. What's going on Roland? You got a lot of TV folks out there."

"Looks like it. They are here about the murder out on the dirt road off 54. I need you by my side on this. I'm going to compliment your cooperation in this matter. What do you say?"

"Well, what can I say? Of course I will be by your side. I would look like a moron if I wasn't. Do you have any leads?"

"Yes, as a matter of fact, I do. I will reveal to the cameras shortly."

With that said, the chief sat down with the rest of them to wait for the call to go outside.

Just like it was on schedule, Mildred came on the phone again, "Sheriff, two reporters are out here and they want to ask you questions about the murder off County Road 54"

Roland knew the intercom was loud enough the reporters could hear his response, so he said, "What time is it?"

"Its 11:30 am, Sheriff."

"Please tell them I will be more than happy to issue a statement and answer a few questions in the front of the station in fifteen minutes. Thanks."

Mildred turned to the reporters, and they had already gone outside to set up. She peeked out the front window and saw Johnny right in the middle of them. They put up a stand with four microphones on it. She was figuring to herself where the fourth microphone came from. Two reporters, then Johnny's from the radio, and that left one open. As she surveyed, she saw Ed Nixon walk to the front door. Knowing Roland, she figured she had better walk back to the office to tell him, but before she could turn to walk back, Ed busted through the front door. "Why, hey Ed, what can I do for you?"

"You can tell the sheriff I'm here and will let my feelings be known on how this whole debacle was handled."

"I'm sure he will be glad for your participation. Take a seat. I have to go to his office, and I'll let him know you're here." Ed said nothing and sat down.

As Mildred entered the sheriff's office, it looked rather crowded. "Well, Sheriff, it looks like show time. Ed just made it and is sitting up front. They put up a microphone stand on the front steps. There are four microphones on it. From what I gathered, one is Johnny, one is Dothan, one is Montgomery, and there is a fourth one I don't know."

Roland looked at Mildred with appreciation. She was a keeper. She was always loyal, and damn good at her job. Plus, she was tightlipped. "Mildred, what would I do without you?"

"Oh, you would do just fine."

"Well, gentlemen, I guess it's time. Chief, I would like you by my side to show unity, and Doctors, if you would stand behind us. Everybody, please, kind of crowd out Ed from the microphones. If he starts something, I will be quite abrupt, so be prepared. Are we good?"

Everybody responded affirmatively. Mildred was the first to walk out of the office, followed by Roland, then the chief, Price, and then Willy. As they reached Ed, he looked as if he just seen a ghost. He turned white as a sheet. Roland looked at him and said, "You ok?"

"Of course. Where do you want me?"

"Out of the way, naturally." That being said, they all proceeded out the front door.

The microphones were at the center of the front steps where Roland and the chief took their places. Then Price and Willie flanked to both sides, leaving nowhere for Ed, so he went to the far end to the right with a disgusted look on his face. Roland spoke out to the waiting reporters, "Well, how do you want to start this shindig? I do have an opening statement that might answer most of the questions you might have if y'all are ready."

"Just a moment, Sheriff." One reporter walked up to the microphone stand and proceeded to turn on all four microphones. He then got in front, saying "test, test," and finally got a thumbs-up from all involved.

"Well, first of all I hate to even be out here on such a negative event happening here in the Hope area. Beside me is Chief of Police Bob Thorn. And to his right is Dr. Price, and to my left is the best vet in the country, Willy Barnes. On November 15th at approximately 7:00 am, Deputy Bill Boyd found the body of a young woman brutally murdered on a dirt road off of Highway 54. We have ascertained her name and cause of death. I will not release the name out of respect for her mother, who is grieving this most tragic loss. The body is with the Montgomery coroner, and Tom McGruder is conducting the autopsy. I have not heard from him yet, but when I do, I expect to be able to apprehend the culprit or culprits within 72 hours of the coroner's report. Again, this community is sickened by this crime being committed in our area. The body will be released after the autopsy to White's Funeral Home in Elba for proper burial. At this time, I will take a limited amount of questions due to this being an open and sensitive investigation."

Johnny chomped at the bit and burst out, "Sheriff, why didn't you go through local protocol and use Ed Nixon, our local coroner"

"Good question, Johnny. It's simple. Ed runs a funeral home. This was a brutal murder. An embalming table was not the place for this victim. I needed the best forensic science available so that I would have the opportunity to catch this freak."

The Dothan reporter jumped in, "It was brought to our attention that you just cut out the local police. Is that true?"

"I'll let the police chief answer that."

Not sure as to what to say, Bob had never been put on the spot like this, with cameras running, no less. He took a deep breath and said, "Well, you're wrong there. The sheriff came to me that same day to get files in my possession that might shed some light on the nature of the crime. We have vowed to work together to catch this criminal."

"Sheriff, Tom Walker with Action News. There is a rumor that the girl was only 25, and that Hope has had two other murders of girls in that age frame dating back to 2005. My question is, do you think there is a connection?"

"Well, Tom, I do not know where you get your information, but I can't deny nor affirm that rumor until all evidence has been collected."

"Sheriff, Tom Walker again. Just a follow-up question. Don't you think that it is a little arrogant of you to say you will have an arrest in 72 hours?" Are you Superman?"

Roland thanked Price for that Xanax. He even turned toward him and winked. "To answer your question, Tom, it is Tom, right?

I mean, you only mentioned it twice. Perhaps a third, I'll get it. Anyway, the culprit left behind very incriminating evidence, which narrows down the suspect pool. This makes my job and the job of all the deputies a lot easier, hence my boast. Thank you everybody for coming, and Tom, check me on those 72 hours, would ya?" Roland then turned to go inside. He looked to where Ed was standing, and he was nowhere in sight. He guessed he didn't want to be on camera.

As Roland entered the building followed by the doctors and the chief of police, they all heard him say to Mildred, "Mildred, where is Cobb?"

"He's on patrol, Sheriff."

"Get him on the radio and tell him to get to Ed's Funeral Home immediately and bring Ed in for questioning. And if he is not there, go in and check that museum box he has there of the old medical instruments to see if anything is missing. Tell him to also take a picture of it on his phone. After that, get Judge Spurlin on the phone for me. Got it?"

"I'm on it, Sheriff."

Everybody looked at the sheriff with puzzled faces, especially Bob Thorn. Roland requested all of them to his office. Once everybody was in the office and the door closed, Roland turned to the police chief, and said, "Tom, you know Ed has a heavy-looking curved bone saw. I believe it might be a match to the murder weapon used on Kelly Foster in 2005 and Sharee Washington in 2009 and now Sue Parrish 2014."

Bob looked rather shocked and said, "You know that makes a lot of sense. The reason I say that is because the two previous victims he ruled head trauma as cause of death, and they were not sent to Montgomery. His findings were all we used. Do you want me to put my boys out looking for him?"

"Not yet. I think he has an idea he might be under suspicion, and I do not want to lose the murder weapon. You could send an officer to meet Cobb at the funeral home. That would show solidarity. By the way, thanks for your support in front of the reporters."

"From what I'm seeing now, it's the least I could do."

Dr. Price raised his head up from the 2005 file he was given and stated to Roland, "This file is incomplete. There were no X-rays or forensics to validate head trauma as cause of death."

Willy spoke up, "It's the same here on the 2009 file."

Roland was silent for a moment, and then scratched his head. "Damn it, Tom, change that. Put out an APB on Ed Nixon."

"You got it. Should we cuff him and bring him to you?"

"No! Just bring him here as a person of interest for questioning."

"I see. Smart thinking. Let me get over across the street to my precinct and get this going."

Tom Thorn left the office with a quickness and was gone. Roland followed behind him and went up to Mildred. "Mildred, go out there and give directions to the murder scene for them to get some film. Tell Johnny to help them out. We want to be shown as cooperative. A lot of things are going to start happening now. Did you get the judge?"

"He's in session."

"Who do we have working the court today?"

"Bill."

"Call him to get the judge on a recess so I can get a telephonic search warrant, or have Bill get it on paper and get it straight to the funeral home. He will have to talk to me prior so I can give him the reasonable cause. Reporters first, then Bill or the judge. Got it?"

"On it, Sheriff."

Chapter 9

D oc, (Richard McClusky) drove from where he did volunteer work, and being noon, was headed for that beer at Fred's. It wasn't just for the beer; it was to catch up on current events. He knew the regular crew would be there. Just as he made a right on 54, his phone rang. It was his son who lived in Jacksonville, Florida. He was happy to hear from his son. He pulled over to the side of the road so as not to be distracted. They talked for about five minutes to catch up on what was going on with his son, when Doc mentioned, "Thomas, you know just yesterday Sue Parrish was murdered on that dirt road just off 54 going to Fred's?"

"Sue Parrish and her mother being Evelyn Parrish?"

"Yes, I think that's her name. Did you know her from Willington High?'

"Hell, Dad, I dated Sue three time. She was the prettiest girl there. Everybody wanted a date with her. And her mother was just as pretty as she was. Who killed her?"

"They are looking into it now, Sheriff Roland is handling it."

"Thank God, he is. You know how the Hope police are."

"Afraid I do. Wow, I forgot you dated her."

"You couldn't keep up, Dad. I hope they hang whoever it is. You know that Amber woman was always a bitch to her mother."

"What do you mean?"

"Well, when I went out with Sue, she would start rumors on her mother and such. Amber's daughter was ugly as mud. And her kid did meth. Messed up all her teeth. Nobody much hung around her."

"Wow. Doesn't seem quite fair she would talk about Evelyn when she had problems like that."

"Dad you are so naïve. Everybody talked about everybody. They had nothing else to do. But what Amber did was just cruel. They both graduated from Willington. Amber first, she was older, and uglier, if I do say."

"I realize these people gossip, trust me. I have been at the center of a lot of it. So tell me, did you get any?"

"Dad, that is so wrong to ask. No. She was a very nice girl at the time, and she was fun to be around. Her mother worked real hard at some sewing factory, and we had a lot of time alone, but she held true to her virginity. I admired her for that. Most of the other girls were a bit easier to go around the bases."

"I guess that says quite a bit about her."

"You bet it does. I really hate to hear that. She was such a great person. You should go see her mother and give my heartfelt condolences. Her mother lives on 1695 Carver Lane in Willington. Easy to find, there are only a few streets there."

"You know, I think I will before I go to Fred's. Love ya, Son. Bye."

"Love you too, Dad."

Doc thought that it would be the proper thing to do. He got back on the road and headed toward Willington. It only took ten minutes as he passed Fred's on the way. He took one left turn, then a right, and he was on Carver Lane. He could see down the road a sheriff's car with two officers outside and two news vans to the far side of the house. He eased in behind the sheriff's car and saw Deputy Ann right off. As he got out, Ann walked up to him, "What the hell are you doing here, Doc?"

Doc had known Ann for a while. They went to nursing school together. He always liked Ann, but she never expressed any interest. "Looks like you got an unwanted party here. My son asked me to drop by and see Ms. Parrish to express both of our condolences, and to offer any assistance she may need."

Ann just looked at him with questions in her eyes, "What do you mean your son?"

"He dated Sue when they were in school together here."

"Oh. I'm sorry, this whole thing has been crazy. Let me go ask Evelyn if she wants to see you. I will signal you from the door to come up if she says yes. In the meantime, wait here. Ok?"

"Yes, ma'am."

The other deputy, Bob, held the TV reporters at bay. They had cameras out and were ready to catch anything. Doc was nervous as to the right words to say. And to walk in front of TV reporters was the last thing he wanted. Doc looked toward the porch with anticipation, waiting for Ann to give him the high sign. While he did that, the TV reporters watched him and his every move, with cameras at the ready. Ann walked out on the porch and motioned Doc to come in. Doc immediately did a quick pace to the door while cameras were running. As he got to the door, he saw Evelyn there dressed quite nice in a pantsuit and her golden hair down to her shoulders. As he entered the door, Doc said, "Evelyn, you have my son's heart and mine." At that statement, Evelyn gave Doc a gentle hug. While this was happening, Ann slipped out the front door, and closed it, staying on the porch.

Evelyn was the first to break the silence, "They call you Doc, is that right?"

"Yes, it's a stupid nickname I got when I was a nurse. I told my son what had happened, and he told me to express his condolences. He had an extreme amount of respect for Sue, and you, for that matter. You see, I was a single parent with him due to a nasty divorce. And I understand you were a single parent. I tell you what, no one understands the difficulty of being a single parent no matter how you become a single parent."

"Your son was Thomas?"

"Yes."

"Well, I must say, you did well by him. He was the only boy I would allow in this house with Sue if I was not here. He showed respect, and his manners were impeccable. This whole thing has hit me hard. Roland has been a Godsend."

"Well, thank you for the compliment. And as far as Roland goes, you got a good man there. A lot of people talk bad about him, but they know he is the best man for the job in this area. I would not be surprised if he wraps this up pretty quickly with the culprit caught."

"You haven't heard?"

"Heard?"

"He got an APB out for Ed Nixon, for questioning, of course. I think he knows who and is just waiting on lab results."

"You sure are being exceptionally strong during this. My hat is off for you. I don't know what I'd do."

"I have had to be strong all my life, Doc. And now the page turns once more. It's how we handle life's obstacles that define us as human beings."

"My God, you are so prophetic. I truly love the way you are coping. Is there anything I can do for you at all?"

"Maybe, Doc. Leave your number. I'd be honored if you would attend the funeral. It will be conducted by White's Funeral Home of Elba."

"Count me in, I'll be there. When you get a date, I will call Thomas and see if he could make it, with your permission, of course."

"Of course, he could come. As a matter of fact, I would like to see the man he has grown into."

"You honor me too much."

"No, I don't. You may not realize we wear the same moccasins. One day I will explain that."

"Believe it or not, I think I understand you perfectly. It's been an honor to be here with you and for you. I had better leave, we don't want the zoo outside talking crap."

"Bye, Doc, don't be a stranger." With that said, Doc walked outside to the porch where Ann had been waiting. She escorted him to his car while the media hounds tried to get him to talk. Doc got in his car, did a U-turn, and headed for that well-deserved beer.

It was 12:45 pm, and Fred's bustled with business. Amber was working and she was her usual dry self. Marcus, Molly, Sparky, Johnny, and many other regulars were at the bar. Two people were playing pool, and the door opened with Doc making his entrance. Sparky turned around, saw Doc, and said, "What's up, Doc?" he then started to giggle as well as others. Even Amber cracked a grin.

"I just got back from seeing Ms. Parrish."

With that being said, Johnny told the person sitting next to him to move, and offered Doc his chair.

"Sit here, Doc, by Johnny boy."

Sparky jumped in, "That's it, I'm jealous, I thought I was the only one."

"Sparky, you know you are the only one." Amber, being aggravated by the conversation, gave Doc a Budweiser as he sat down next to Johnny. There was some small talk about the weather, and then finally, Johnny turned to Doc and asked, "What's going on out there?"

"Well, you would think they are making a movie. There are two TV trucks and two deputies keeping things at bay. Hell, I had to be escorted by Ann to see Evelyn."

Sparky jumped in again, "Bet that's a first."

Doc took a long look at Sparky and then turned to Johnny, "Somebody leaked all this out to the TV stations."

Johnny looked at him like he was a fool, "Of course, Sherlock. It was me. How else could I get any information? Roland was keeping his lips tighter than a virgin." At that statement, Amber looked aggravated as she always looked, and said, "Watch the language."

Sparky was at it again, "Damn it, Amber, you are no school teacher. Let us kids have a little fun, would ya?"

"I have standards, you know."

Doc had to jump on that one, "You're right, Amber, you do. And when you find them, please let us know what they are because they seem to change frequently." The bar got silent until Marcus broke it with, "I want to marry Molly."

Molly yelled, "Oh, hell, no! You probably can't even get it up."

"They got pills. Hell, I put a splint on it for you, baby."

"You need to romance me first, you baboon."

The conversation between Marcus and Molly took off the attention of what Doc said to Amber, and the steam that came from her started to settle down. Doc and Johnny whispered so that it was a semi-private conversation. Johnny told Doc about the news conference and how they were looking for Ed, which Doc already knew, but said nothing. Johnny mentioned that Roland boasted he would have an arrest within 72 hours after getting the coroner's report. He then turned to Doc, "Do you think he knows who did it?"

"You bet your bottom dollar he does, and he is taking care of everything concerning the burial of Sue."

"Who did it?"

"Come on, Johnny, you know. Who are they looking for?"

"Well, I guess you are right." Johnny turned to Amber, "Another Crown and Bud, please."

Amber just looked at the both of them. Then she went to get their drinks. As she set them down, she said, "Y'all could be nice to me. I haven't done anything to y'all."

Doc turned a little red and said, "And I suppose you have been an angel to Evelyn Parrish."

With that said, the front door opened, and Vicky walked in. She went behind the bar and took Amber's place while Amber stormed out the door.

"Something I said?" commented Doc

Johnny spoke up, "I think she is worried about her moonshine business. I'm a good customer. Hers is the shit."

That made sense. Then Doc looked over at Vicky, who wore a low-cut shirt, almost revealing her breasts, which caused everyone to take a second look. Vicky walked over to Doc, "Need another beer?"

"Yes, I just all of a sudden went parched."

"Doc, the answer is still no."

Sparky came to the rescue, "Boom, crash, and burn, once again. Maybe one day, Doc."

Again the door opened to Fred's, and this time it was Paul from the local police. He walked to Johnny, "What a way to blow things up, buddy."

Johnny angrily responded, "It's news."

"Anywho." Then Paul turned to everyone in the bar, and raised his voice to be heard, "The authorities are looking for Ed Nixon for questioning only. If anyone runs across him, you are to contact the police or the sheriff's department. Does everyone understand?" Everybody nodded their heads. Paul then turned and walked out.

Johnny looked at Doc. "Well, that's no rumor or gossip."

Chapter 10

R oland got off the phone with Judge Spurlin, and he approved
a search warrant for the funeral home and Ed's residence.
Roland told Dr. Price and Willy to put what they thought was
important from the files on the evidence board and call it a day.
He thanked them for their help and was off to his jeep to go to the
funeral home with the warrant.

Roland pulled up to the funeral home to see Cobb in the front.
As soon as he got out of his jeep, he went to Cobb and asked, "Why
aren't you inside?"

"Doors locked, Sheriff."

"Where is the local PD?"

"Paul came and I sent him off to Fred's and other places to
spread the word we were looking for Ed."

"Good idea, Cobb. Now go get that battering ram out of your
car, and we shall gain entrance."

"Not necessary, Sheriff. I can pick it." Cobb pulled a leather
kit from his back pocket that contained various tools, and he proceeded to use them on the lock. Within one minute, they were
through the doors. Roland looked at him with a new sense of
amazement, and said nothing. As they entered, they split up.
Roland knew exactly what he was looking for. It was that old
museum case that contained old surgical instruments. Ed was so
proud of it. He found it was moved to where they prepared the
bodies for the caskets. As he peered through, he saw what he was

looking for. Roland immediately yelled out for Cobb. As Cobb came to where he was, he pointed out where it was in the case. What they both were looking at was an 1820 old shiny steel saw with deep serrated teeth they used for the amputation of limbs. It was used extensively during the Civil War. Roland stared at it and said, "That's our murder weapon. Cobb, can you pick the lock on this and get it into an evidence bag? We got to send this quickly to Montgomery for testing."

Before Roland finished speaking, Cobb opened the case. Roland turned to Cobb, "Damn, Cobb, I'm glad you're working for our side." Cobb just laughed. Roland continued, "After you bag this, I want you to go to Ed's house and look for boots, any and all. Bag them all." After that was said, Mildred came over the radio, "Sheriff, we got a tip that a beamer turned down that dirt road off 54, and it has yet to come out."

"Thanks, I'm heading that way."

Mildred came back on the radio sounding concerned, "Sheriff, don't you think a little backup is warranted?"

"I got it, Mildred. I'll radio if I need anything. Thanks."

With that said, Roland headed off to his jeep. Cobb remained there and bagged the evidence. Cobb kind of felt left out. He wanted to go with the sheriff. But he knew Roland, and he would have none of it. What made Cobb feel ok about it was he knew how good Roland was with his weapon on a draw. Hell, he should have been Wyatt Earp. Cobb had seen the way he handled his gun on the gun range numerous times. He had that old western-style holster with a single loop over the hammer, and when he drew the pistol it was not slow at all.

Roland turned down the infamous dirt road and drove very slowly. Passing the murder scene and seeing the tape marking it off still intact gave him satisfaction. He kept going. He passed the cow pasture when he noticed up to the left a gate with a chain and lock on it. As far as he could remember, there was never a gate there. He stopped his jeep fifty yards from it, and got out to walk up to it. As he walked, he noticed tire tracks turning into the gate. The tracks were new. He continued to approach the gate, when he started to smell a chemical substance in the air. It was a very odd smell. Then it came to him that was the smell of a meth lab. He ran back to the jeep and got on the radio. "Mildred."

"Yes, Sheriff."

"You were right, I need back up. I need you to get Riley Jenkins from the ATF out here to the road. Tell him it's a mile past the crime scene on the left. There will be an open gate because I'm going through. Tell him there is a full-fledged meth lab running out here."

"Sheriff, it will take him twenty minutes to get there. Shouldn't you wait?"

"No. I'm going in, get him here as quickly as he can make it, and tell him not to spare the sirens."

"Ok, Sheriff, on it now. Be careful, those kind of people ain't right."

"Thanks, Mildred. Out. Oh, radio silence till you hear from me."

"OK. But you be careful, Roland. Damn it."

"Why Mildred, I didn't know you cared."

"I don't. I just do not want to have to break in a new boss. Out."

Roland smiled. He went to the back of his jeep and pulled out his bolt cutters and proceeded to cut the chain off the gate. After this was done, he opened the gate as wide as he could get it. He then got back in his jeep and very slowly proceeded down the rugged road. As he traveled about a half a mile, he came into a clearing where he saw the trailer, and right in front was Ed's beamer. He stopped and surveyed the area to see anybody lurking around trees or any sense of an ambush. It looked like they must have been in the trailer. Roland then edged up in the jeep about thirty yards from the trailer. He then opened the jeep door wide as possible to provide protection. He then slid the loop off the hammer of his pistol. He removed the pistol from the holster to check the load, and it was good to go. He then replaced his gun into his holster. As he stepped out of the jeep, Ed opened the front door of the trailer and stepped down with a long barrel pump-action shotgun. He had the shotgun facing down, held in the crook of his arm. As he reached the bottom step, he yelled out to Roland, "Why, if you aren't the nosiest bastard I have ever met. Not only did you screw my ex-wife, you are now ruining all my plans."

"Ed, you don't have to do this, you know. I'm sure an insanity plea will do you good."

"Why the hell do you think I'm insane?" He stepped a little closer to where Roland was. They were now only about 30 feet apart. Roland stepped out from behind the jeep door facing Ed.

"You'd have to be. With what you did to those young girls and all."

"They deserved it. All they were was sluts. Besides, I gave them what they deserved."

"Why did you have help on this last one? You couldn't handle it yourself?"

"She volunteered to help. I couldn't deny the offer now, could I?"

"Ed, I'm going to have to bring you in."

"No, you aren't. If you notice, I have a twenty-gauge shotgun here, and you with that tiny, but pretty pistol. All I have to do is point in your general direction and you're dead."

"Well, I suppose you are right there, Ed. Why don't you try to raise that shotgun, you short-dick bastard." When Roland said that, everything went in slow motion. Ed started to raise the shotgun to finally kill the one he had hated for such a long time. As his shotgun became level, the only thing he saw was a flash of light that came from Roland's direction, and a red spot that spread on his chest area. He tried to pull the trigger on the shotgun, but when he did, it shot straight down in the dirt. He was unable to hold it up. His eyes were wide as he fell to his knees. He tried to speak, but the words would not come, for he was shot directly in the heart. He then fell over face first in the dirt dead. Roland holstered his gun and then yelled, "If there is anybody in that trailer, I suggest you come out now, or I will start shooting into it. And we all know how volatile the substance is in there."

With a plea from inside, "I'm coming out unarmed. I do not believe in guns, please don't shoot. I'm just an innocent bystander."

"Then let me see you now, or I shoot randomly."

The door opened fast, and Ronnie ran out of the trailer, not noticing Ed on the ground, and tripped over his body, and fell on top of him. Ronnie screamed and got up as quickly as possible, and noticed he had Ed's blood on him, so he stripped off his shirt. "What the hell, you killed him."

"He was going to kill me. What could I do?"

Ronnie searched his mind and could see no other result. "For some reason, he knew y'all would face off."

"Ok, Ronnie, you seem like a nice guy in the wrong place. Who's all in this with you? And I suggest you not lie to me."

"It was Ed, and that's it."

"Come here." As Ronnie approached him, he placed handcuffs on him, then leaned him on his jeep. Roland went inside the trailer. This outfit was set up for mass production. There had to be more people involved. At the end of one counter, he spotted a full quart-size baggie full of meth. He got another empty baggie and put it in there and carried it outside. As he stepped down the steps from the trailer, he heard the sirens. About time, he thought. He took that bag and showed it to Ronnie. "This is all you made here?"

Ronnie, being put on the spot, said, "Yes."

Roland flash-drawled his pistol again and pointed at Ronnie's head. "I can kill you as a matter of self-defense. You going to come clean or dead?"

Ronnie then pissed himself, which became obvious to Roland that he was scared, but he did not back down. The sirens were coming very close. "You now have two seconds."

"Stop, stop. It is Marcus; he has a big load at his house or in that bug of theirs. He made me do it. Ed was the startup money. I was just the cook, nothing else, I swear. Marcus said he would kill me if I mentioned him. I'm going to need protection. Please." Roland flicked open his spent chamber and replaced the bullet. He was always taught to never have an empty chamber. As he completed that, the ATF pulled in with three cars. Riley was the first one out, and he looked around. As his six agents got out, he informed them to set up a perimeter, inspect the trailer, and call Biohazard out to clean the site. He then walked over to Roland and said, "Just couldn't wait, could you?"

"Riley, you just passed the sickest murder scene I have ever witnessed. And if you think I was going to let that bastard see the light of day, you would be wrong."

"Yeah, I heard about it. News had fun with it. How do you want to handle it here? I mean, looks like you got a dead body over there."

"Why don't I make your day? You give me Ed, and I give you the largest meth bust in the county."

"I like the sound of that. I get front page billing for the meth."

"Sure, and I caught a serial killer."

"Serial killer?"

"Yep. This Ed feller has killed three that we know of. There might be gravesites on this land alone. This was one sick cookie."

"What a sick fuck."

"Well, do we have a deal?'

"Deal. Who has the bulk and dealing it?"

"Marcus, and he should be at Fred's right now. Ronnie down there, with the wet pants, named him a co-conspirator. And on my hood is five pounds of meth. Is that good enough?"

"Well, if you had a silver plate, that would be nice."

"I guess we are through here?"

"You know something, Roland, you are all right, sometimes."

"Well, let's call Mildred for someone to pick up the body I shot."

"For what you're giving me, Roland, we will take care of the body and justify the shooting. By the way, how many shots did you take?"

"Why one, of coarse." Then Roland smiled and got in his jeep to tell the good news to Evelyn. But he thought he better call in to Mildred. She was his right arm. "Mildred."

"About time, Sheriff. What's up?"

"You did well with the ATF, they are here now. Call off the APB on Ed. He's dead. Tell Cobb I need those boots at Ed's house tagged and bagged. Have you heard from Montgomery?"

"No, Sheriff. It's only two-thirty."

"I'm going to Willington to give the news to Ms. Parrish."

"Be careful, the TV folks are out there."

"Got it. Thanks"

Roland got into his jeep and headed out. He felt a major sense of relief. Now he had to figure out the other person involved, and according to Ed, it had to be a woman. Hopefully, the forensics from Montgomery would make it easy to get the next one. He was now on 54 and headed for Willington. As he pulled up behind Ann's squad car, he saw the two news vans. He debated going in first or just going straight to the TV guys. He made up his mind he would tell Evelyn first. As he went past the TV vans, they yelled out various questions, which he tuned out. At the front door, he knocked gently, and the door opened immediately, and there was Evelyn. She was radiant in his eyes. She let him in, and he suggested they sit at the table again. She had a worried look on her face. He looked her straight in the eyes and said, "It's over, Evelyn. I killed the one who did it. It was Ed Nixon. He will no longer hurt anyone else." She started to cry again, this time, with relief showing on her face. The Kleenex was on the table, and she helped herself. "I must leave you now, and try to get the TV guys away. I'm still leaving a deputy because there is one more person involved we must apprehend. I will also let you know when the funeral arrangements can be made. I hope I have been of help for you because you have struck a chord in my heart."

Evelyn got up quickly as Roland got up, and once more gave him a deep hug, and he responded without hesitance. After that tender moment, Roland teared up a bit, but he fought it back and went outside to the TV reporters. That dick, Tom, was there, and he wanted to talk to him first. He told them he had the news they wanted. They gathered the cameras around him and were ready.

"As you know, Tom, I boasted that I would apprehend the culprit of this heinous crime within 72 hours. Well, I lied. He has been apprehended now. The murderer was Ed Nixon, and he tried to avoid incarceration with a shotgun. He left me no choice, but to return fire, and Ed Nixon is now dead. It would appear that Mr. Nixon was a serial killer. We are now trying to determine how many people died at his hand. And trust me, Tom, we will find out. I would also like to thank the ATF who has helped in a joint venture on this investigation. That's all I have, no questions, please. Now could y'all please show some respect to Ms. Parrish and leave here before I have my deputies move you? It's the right thing to do, guys. Please."

Roland told Ann and Bob Walker to hang around until further notice. He headed back to the station. As he drove down 54, up ahead was Fred's, and he saw three ATF cars there with Marcus in tow in handcuffs, being loaded into the backseat of one of their cars. Roland thought, *Why, that sly old bastard.* He had everyone hoodwinked. For some reason, he did not know why he decided to pull in. "Hi, guys, what you got here?"

Riley Jenkins spoke up and smiled from ear to ear, "Why, we got a dealer here. And believe it or not, he had a gun on him."

"The hell you say. Keep up the good work, guys."

Everybody in the bar looked out the windows and crowded the door. Roland went to the door and then split the crowd, like Moses parting the Red Sea. Roland went to the bar with all eyes on him.

Vicky came up to with her pretty smile and said, "What will it be, Roland?"

"A double Crown."

"Coming right up." Roland turned to face the crowd and asked, "Where's Amber?"

Sparky, saw his moment and belched, "Why, Doc over there ran her off with his wit."

Vicky delivered Roland's drink and said, "That's not true. She'd asked me to cover for her because she had an eye appointment."

Roland turned to Doc and asked, "What the hell you say to her?"

Doc responded, "I had just got back from Ms. Parrish's home, and I did not care for her opinion whatsoever."

Roland pounded down the double and walked out the front door, then turned to Doc, "Do follow me, will ya?" Once outside, Roland walked over to his jeep far enough away from the eavesdroppers and asked, "What's your relationship to Ms. Parrish?"

"Me, none really. It's my son; he dated Sue three or four times while they were in high school together. When I let him know what happened he told me to go there to give his condolences. He also told me that Amber was always stalking and spreading malicious gossip about Ms. Parrish. I felt it was the least I could do."

"You're right. You did good. You know why I had to ask."

'No. Not really."

"Ed Nixon has been caught. Well that's not true; I killed hm. But there were two involved with Sue's death. Can I count on you not to mention the second part of this? I don't care if you tell them I killed Ed."

"Yes, sir, you got my word."

"Thanks, Gotta go."

When Doc walked back in the bar, everybody crammed around him, Johnny the closest, "Well?"

Doc stayed quiet for a spell, enjoyed the moment, then finally as the suspense was at its peak, he said, "Sheriff Roland shot down Ed Nixon and killed him dead!" Everybody at the bar rushed poor little Vicky and ordered another drink.

Chapter 11

R oland pulled into his office when he saw that Dr. Price's car was still there, but Willy's was gone. As he parked and entered through the front door, Mildred was there to greet him, "Well, somebody has had an eventful day."

"You could say that. Is Dr. Price still here?"

"You bet he is. He's been in your office working like a Trojan. When Cobb brought in all that evidence, it gave Price a second wind."

"Well, let's see what they have figured out."

Roland walked back to his office to see him and Cobb at the board Mildred set up. As he entered the door, they turned to him, and Dr. Price said, "Did you really kill Ed?"

"He pulled a shotgun on me. I had no choice."

Cobb interjected, "You drew on him, didn't you?"

"Yes. What have y'all got?"

Dr. Price turned to Cobb, "You go first."

Cobb took a deep breath and faced Roland, "I don't know how you figured all this out unless you own a crystal ball or something of the kind. The saw was consistent with the head trauma, and the boots I retrieved matched perfectly with the plaster molds we took at the crime scene. And the phone had three sets of prints. One being Sue, another being Amber, and the last, Ed. And the ATF lifted the trunk of Ed's beamer, and there was hair in there and what they think are bloodstains. Don't say it, Roland. I have already sent the car to Montgomery, along with the bone saw for forensics to analyze. All right, Price, it's your turn."

"Well, I agree with Cobb on the crystal ball stuff. All the files on the previous victims are incomplete. There was no rape kit done on either of them. As a matter of fact, the 2005 case was ruled accidental. And the 2009 case was ruled murder by a blunt undetermined object. It's a shame she was cremated. There is little hope we can reverse the conviction of the guy they convicted. Now, there might be some hope. If Ed did not clean out his trunk good or completely clean that saw, Montgomery might find some trace evidence."

Roland spoke up, "You guys rock. Here is the problem with the phone. Even though Amber's prints are on it, we can't place her at the scene." Mildred came over the intercom, "Montgomery coroner on line two, Sheriff."

Roland picked up the phone, "Tom, do you mind if I put you on speaker?"

"No problem, Sheriff. It seems I'm always on speaker to most of the people I speak to. Anyway, I hear you are sending me the murder weapon and a BMW. I knew you liked me, but the car is a little much."

They all laughed, and Roland said, "You know how we all love you. Now give me some good news."

"Well, Ed is your man. His DNA was on file, and it's a complete match. And as for your second party, we were able to lift prints from the shoulders, and they came back to an Amber Woods. She was in the system for a DUI. All you need to do now is apprehend the suspects. You have a great court case and should have a solid conviction."

Roland jumped in, "Tom, Ed is dead. He pulled a shotgun on me."

"Oh, I see. Well, I guess that is good. Save the taxpayer some money. Then all you have to get is Amber. What do you want with the beamer?"

"I need you to look for any possible evidence of multiple victims ever being placed in that trunk. I believe an innocent man was convicted of a crime Ed did."

"You realize the deterioration of evidence over time will make it very hard to produce anything solid?"

"I know, but it's the least I can do, Tom."

"I'll go over it for you."

"When can you release the body?"

"Hell, this case is about over. Today, we have retrieved everything necessary for a conviction."

"Thanks, Tom. I'll notify White's Funeral Home to go up there now. The mother has been very distraught."

"I'm sure she has. Hey, Roland, I like the cases you send me. Not much work or guessing. Makes my life easier and we get the bad guys. Thanks."

"Just wish we didn't have to use you. Let me know about the beamer."

"No problem, Roland. Bye."

"Well, guys, where do you think Amber is? Do you think she knows we are on to her?"

Mildred came over the intercom again, "Sheriff, Ann and Bob says Amber is at the Parrish home, demanding to speak to Ms. Parrish."

Roland fumed and said, "Tell them to apprehend her immediately and Mirandize her for murder. I want her cuffed and booked within the hour. Once she is in custody, tell them to notify me."

Ann and Bob both got their instructions over the radio, and Amber heard it, and started to run to her truck, however, she was not as fast as Bob. He body-tackled her as she reached the door and slammed her to the ground. Ann was right behind him, and she assisted in putting on the cuffs. As they stood her up, Ann began her Miranda rights and informed her she was being arrested for accessory to murder. She screamed that she had done nothing. Evelyn watched all of this from a window of her home. It took both of them to get her in the back of Ann's squad car, and as soon as the door was shut, Ann flick on the siren and floored it to the county jail. Meanwhile, Bob went to the door of the home, which Evelyn already had the door open, and she asked, "What was that about?"

Bob responded, "It's over, Ms. Parrish. Everybody involved with your loss has been caught. I'm sure the sheriff will call you and let you know all the details. I've been called back. Still, keep your door locked, and if anybody you don't know comes by, call us immediately."

"Thank you so much." And with that said, she shut the door and locked it. As she stood behind the door, she thought to herself. *'Over' he says. It will never be over. I will live with this for the rest of my life. How will I survive? How can I carry on? Sue was my life, and she was brutally taken away. How am I to go on? I can't live without her.* With that last thought, the phone rang. She went to pick it up; it was Roland. "Hello."

"Yes, this is Roland, and I want you to know your daughter will be in Elba this evening. Also, I want you to know I'm here for you. I will drive you there in the morning if you wish. You have been very strong; please stay strong like you have been your entire life. This is not the end. Do you understand me?"

Evelyn began to cry again, and she fought it back to say, "Yes I'll take that ride in the morning." After she said ok to the ride, she hung up the phone, collapsed, and cried.

Chapter 12

Two days later, it was a closed-casket service in Elba, with few in attendance. Sheriff Roland was there with half his deputies all in squad cars, which were all cleaned and waxed. Doc and his son sat by Ms. Parrish along with her close friends she had, which were few. Roland had furnished an honor guard to carry the casket to the hearse. Sue was to be buried in Willington in a small graveyard where she had purchased plots a long time ago. As the casket was placed in the hearse, the guard got in their squad cars, a total of five, with only two cars of her close friends to follow. Evelyn rode in a limousine with Doc and his son. As they left the church, she felt so alone.

Roland had planned the route and told the Hope police about it ahead of time, and the newspaper. From Elba, he would go through the main street of Hope, then up 54 to Willington, and then pull into the small graveyard she had chosen. They left Elba with Roland in the lead and two squad cars behind him, then the hearse, limo, friends' two cars, and three squad cars that followed behind. As they left Elba and began to enter Hope, Roland got on the radio, "Ok, now, boys." With that said, they all turned on their sirens on low, but audible. As they hit the main street of Hope, people by the hundreds lined the street, and as the limo passed by, they lowered their heads out of respect to Evelyn. When she saw this, it took her breath. It was like this all the way to 54. She was in complete disbelief. Then the local police began to follow, using their sirens in a subdued sound. The line of cars that waited at the beginning of 54 to join was over a mile long.

Evelyn saw the cars and began to cry. Doc and his son both put their arms around her to comfort her. As they made it to Willington, the entire town must have been on the streets. They pulled in where Sue Parrish was to be buried, and it was the most elaborate scene ever. Flowers encompassed almost the entire graveyard, and the spot where Sue was to be buried was completely carpeted. The town folk did not enter the graveyard, they just made a perimeter around it with their heads held down out of respect. All of this overwhelmed Evelyn. And she was weak to the knees; Doc and his son held her up and to her chair for the graveside service. You'd have thought a president had died the way this was handled. Evelyn lowered her head and whispered, "Thank you, GOD!"

Chapter 13

R oland was in his office early that morning. He looked at the murder board they had constructed. He thought strongly this wasn't over. What about the other two girls? How was Dixon allowed to sign off on their death certificates as accidental deaths? Were they accidental deaths? And was one of the victims cremated? And where did all this meth production get involved? He decided he would leave this board up until he found the answers. Suddenly, over the speakerphone came a voice, "Sheriff, District Attorney Adams from Montgomery is here, and demands to see you."

"Send him back."

Adams was all slicked up in a suit and tie while Roland was casual with jeans and holster and his famous pistol. "Well, Mr. Adams, I feel honored to get a visit from you all the way from Montgomery. Hope you a had a pleasant trip?"

"Roland, I'm here to inform you there will be a formal investigation of what happened here in Hope. Also, we cannot have some Wild West show of a shootout at the OK corral."

"You wait just one damn moment. Dixon was holding a shotgun on me, and it was him or me!"

Adams reluctantly replied, "So you say. Anyway, I have been instructed by the state attorney's office to see just what happened down here, and to also limit your powers until we have a full understanding."

Roland, became red around the neck and said, "What you going to do, arrest me?"

"Not yet, we are going to see just what happened here." Roland paced up and down several times and then finally thought out carefully what he would say.

"Well, Mr. Adams, you do what you got to do, and I will do what I got to do to see the truth gets out. That includes the corruption and falsifications of legal documents, paid-off officials, and not to mention how in the hell did the DEA not know of such a large meth production lab in their backyard? And lastly, Mr. Adams, you can kiss my lily-white ass!"

CORRUPTION IN L.A.

Chapter 14

R oland did not want to get out of bed, but he knew there was too much to be done at the office. His brain was a flurry of ideas of where to begin. First, he needed to follow up on suspects in lockup. He also needed the autopsy report from Montgomery. Today, he decided to dress in uniform and wear his traditional gun belt, as he always did. He was not going to change his routine for anybody, not even the assistant DA. Departing from his house after feeding his livestock, he got into his jeep.

As he drove, Roland turned his radio to the local channel his friend, Johnny, owned, a source of gossip and sometimes information. Johnny had been doing his morning commentary, "As I was saying, our community has been crime-free for some time until this recent and heinous act occurred in our community. I'm talking about murder in the worst sense. On a desolate county road, a young female just beginning her life was snuffed out before it had really begun. I believe we are lucky that the county had jurisdiction. If the case had fallen under local jurisdiction, there would have been a different result. Sheriff Roland Smith should be commended for his quick professional actions. He not only found the suspects, he also discovered a drug ring in the mix. Out of fear for his own life, he was forced to shoot the prime suspect, Ed Nixon, while he was holding a shotgun on our sheriff. DEA and ATF were on the scene, and will corroborate all the facts. So, why has the assistant DA suddenly sparked an interest in this case? Hell, he didn't even know about a drug ring, or did he? This sounds like a conspiracy to me. I hope all of our citizens will support our sheriff and let him do his job. Maybe, just maybe, some light might be shed on questionable convictions of the past." At this point, Roland turned off his radio. He pulled into his office.

This would be a very busy day for Roland. As he entered the front door, his assistant Mildred greeted him a little differently today, "Looks like someone is a celebrity." Everybody, including the deputies, started to applaud. Roland, not really prepared for this, made a hasty retreat to his office and closed the door. Deputies Randy Cobb and Bill Boyd looked at each other and just shook their heads. Finally, Bill spoke up, "What's up with him, ya think?"

"He was never much for attention. Besides, the assistant DA didn't help matters by saying he was going to look into the shooting."

Bill retorted, "He needs to go to the shooting range and watch Roland shoot that cannon, and he would have another opinion. I know what I have seen, he is just fast, I mean really fast."

"I know. It's like he belongs in a different time. I think there is a lot more going on, and Roland knows it."

Roland still had his whiteboard handy with all the evidence and a circle of suspects. He decided this would stay within reach until he could investigate and connect the previous two murders of young girls, even though it was a city issue. *I believe all three are connected, and I am going to need some help.* His real name was Richard McClusky. "Doc" would do. His son had dated the murdered girl. Besides, Doc knew the mother and Roland had taken a fancy to her at first sight. Roland buzzed Mildred, "Mildred, get me Doc on the phone, please."

"Dr. Barnes?"

"No! You know Doc, that McClusky guy that hangs out at Fred's." Fred owned the local pub where everyone met and socialized, meaning, gossiped.

"Yes, sir, right away." It was only a few minutes, and the phone rang. Mildred buzzed back, "Doc's on line one, Sheriff."

Roland picked up line one, "Doc, old buddy, I could use your help on a matter of importance. Can you meet me in my office this morning?"

Doc was stunned. He had always like Roland and considered him a friend, but this was the first time Roland had called him for something like this. "Why sure, Roland, I can be there in, say, about forty-five minutes?"

"Perfect, see you then. Oh, by the way, let's keep this under our hats for the time being. Ok?"

"Will do, see ya in a bit." There were all types of people in this county, and Doc was a stand-up guy. He would never back down about ideas he believed in, and was dismissive of people who were either prejudiced or narrow-minded.

This has got me wound up tighter than a drum. I need to take five... Hard to believe I have to deal with so many different groups. The Baptists have a firm grip on people, politics, and gossip. The Methodists are Methodists just to say they aren't Baptist. The Methodists are a little more progressive and tolerant than most. The poorer people, those who don't go to church, well, they are just talked about in an unflattering way. Of course, you have other religions like Jehovah Witnesses, holiness types, and so on. They aren't taken seriously, or just considered weird. These mixtures of people create a unique dynamic.

Roland was proud to serve this community. He loved his job, and the people must have liked him; he had been re-elected five times every five years. He never singled out Blacks or Hispanics, or anyone for that matter, just because of their race. He considered profiling mostly inaccurate and used to place blame by a crafty criminal.

Suddenly, he was up against it. For the first time in his career, he was being singled out and did not like it. He was going to have to deploy alternative means to get to the bottom of the two previous murders, one of which was determined accidental by Ed Coroner Dixon, the dead suspect of the third murder. A Black man was found guilty, murdered shortly thereafter, based on circumstantial evidence provided by Nixon. There was that huge meth lab that had operated right under everybody's noses. Somehow there had to be a connection, definitely payoffs.

Roland was grateful for the catnap. He decided to put the pictures of the victims on the whiteboard. One was killed in 2005, and the other in 2009. Both had similar injuries, and both were young girls. He was not going to put the board to bed until he had some answers. At the bottom of the board, he wrote, *METH LAB*. Mildred came over the intercom, "Doc's here, or is it McClusky? You want me to send him back?"

"Yes, thanks, Mildred."

As Doc entered, Roland spoke up, "Shut the door, please."

"Well, Roland, I must say, you are always full of surprises. What you got going on now?"

"Take a seat, and would you like some coffee?"

Doc was distracted by the whiteboard, and did not hear the question. Roland spoke a little louder, "Doc, you want some damn coffee or not?"

Doc started laughing. "Wow, Roland, you need to quit being wrapped so tightly."

'I guess you're right. Well, let's git straight to the point. I need your help on the down low. I would like you to go to this Homerville Funeral Home and find if this girl's body was cremated as stated in the file. I will give you a gas wage and a per diem for expenditures. The reason I'm asking you is because I know you will be tight-lipped. Can you do this for me? Oh, I will deputize you so you will have the authority of my office."

Doc just sat there for a moment and looked at the whiteboard and the pictures of all three victims. He took a deep breath and said, "You really think this was done by the same person, don't you?"

"Yes, and I think I may have shot the wrong guy."

"Wow, you bet I'll help. I always thought those deaths were fishy, especially when one was declared an accident. They pushed that Black guy through the legal system like a freight train, crazy stuff there. Point me in the right direction, Roland."

"I can't thank you enough. I have limited resources, and your involvement is our little secret. Tell no one, and I mean no one. I do not know how deep this goes."

Doc realized he was going to be in this up to his neck. "Well, come to think of it, I'll take that coffee now." Roland laughed a little, got on the intercom, and told Mildred to bring in two cups of coffee. Mildred interrupted, "Sheriff, there has been a killing at the county jail in Andalusia. It's that kid, Ronnie, he was cooking the meth where you shot Nixon. The locals are rushing in to investigate."

Roland's face flushed, and Doc could see the fury in his eyes. "Mildred, dispatch three deputies, I'm on my way. Let them know the crime scene is not to be disturbed. This is my rodeo, and the local PD had better be advised not to corrupt the evidence. Do it right away!"

Mildred responded, "Yes, sir, Sheriff, on it now."

"I think you can see how convoluted this is. From now on, we will communicate on burners. Go get one. I have one just for this. You still good to go, Doc?"

Doc looked Roland straight in the eye, "Damn straight!'

Chapter 15

M r. Adams, the assistant district attorney for the state of
Alabama, was mostly involved with internal affairs and
ethics. Police corruption was his primary responsibility, and he
enjoyed that part of his job.

Adams, neatly dressed in his navy-blue suit complete with a
red tie and US flag tie tack, sat on a couch in US Senator Alex
Bodacious Jackson's office in Washington, DC. It was quite a large
suite compared to his tiny office. Several people were waiting to
see the senator. His receptionist diligently worked on her computer. *I wonder why he wants to see me.* After all, his caseload
really had nothing to do with the senator except for his well-
known stance against marijuana. The current case he had been
investigating was the Hope murder and subsequent shooting of
the suspect. Then there was the discovery of a major meth production lab.

The receptionist finally asked him to come back to the senator's office. He walked through the door and the receptionist asked
him to have a seat. He was amazed at how ornate and clean the
office was, fully carpeted in a deep blue color, the desk was the
largest he had seen in a while. The hardwood desk gleamed; he
could see his face in its reflection. There were multiple college
degrees and pictures of the senator, one with President Reagan,
President Bush Sr., and Bush Jr., and off to the side, there was a

picture with President Clinton. Adams was quite impressed, to say the least. *This man is a career politician.*

A few minutes later, the senator entered through a side door toward the back of the office. He was not a tall man, about 5'6", and thin, around 135 lbs., but he had a full head of gray hair and large pronounced ears.

The senator started the conversation. "Well, Mr. Adams, my full name is Alex Bodacious Jackson. And about my middle name, I think my parents had maybe one too many mint juleps." He cracked a small smile, and when he did, Adams noticed that the senator had rather rosy cheeks, an indication that he was probably a drinker. The senator continued, "Long trip up here, I imagine? Would you care for a drink?" He opened a drawer and pulled out a bottle of Black Label Johnny Walker with two glasses in tow.

Adams, kind of shocked, replied, "Why, Senator, it's only ten am."

"Hell, boy, you know it's twelve o'clock somewhere. Grab 'em." He started to pour the two glasses, shoving the second glass over to him. "You don't have to call me senator. Call me Alex. Now, what the hell is going on down there in Hope? Hell, it's been reported to me that there was a large meth lab and a cowboy sheriff who gunned down the coroner. Is any of this true? And if so, what are you doing about it? It is embarrassing to me, that's my backyard." Adams attempted to gather his thoughts, but was interrupted again, "Look, boy, I do not like being surprised by large-scale media events. This is sure to go national, and when it does, I need to have containment. Do you understand me?" Not waiting for an answer, the senator polished off his scotch and poured another. "I hope you've talked to this sheriff, and had a come-to-Jesus with him, so he realizes all the people who will be affected by this?"

Adams saw his opportunity and jumped in, "I have met with the sheriff; by the way, his name is Roland Smith. I have him under formal investigation for the shooting. To his credit, he has ATF and DEA backing him up on the events that led up to the shooting. DEA was given credit for the meth bust, but that was a gift from Roland because he was the one who discovered the operation. The suspect, Ed Nixon, was the local coroner. The sheriff is investigating two previous murders to see if there is a connection."

"Well, I'll be a horse's ass. What can we do with this guy? We cannot have some country sheriff poking into something that's happened in the past. This will stir up a shitstorm. What can you do to tie his hands?"

Perplexed, Adams responded, "Senator, he has been elected sheriff five times by an overwhelming majority. The people like him. He is cleaner than Mr. Clean."

"I told you to call me Alex! This guy must be dirty. Hell, I know he has four failed marriages. He might be some sort of pervert. I have been in politics too long not to know there is some dirty laundry somewhere on everyone."

"Why not let him just do his job?"

"You have got to be kidding me. There are far-reaching implications if he suddenly starts finding payoffs or even other possible suspects. We convicted a man on one of those things, didn't we? Shit, we can't start releasing wrongfully convicted people. It sends the wrong message. Hell, I knew Ed Nixon. And I'm telling you right now I cannot and will not publicly or otherwise admit to any affiliation. We need this to go away. Are you the man that can do that, or do I need to look elsewhere? And do not think I don't have shit about you when you attended college. Do we understand each other?"

Adams suddenly realized the game had changed, and he was not going to be tossed off this case. *This guy is a real asshole!* He picked his words carefully and said, "Alex, I'm a team player. I will do as you instruct. I will also get to the bottom of it and put out the fires. As you so bluntly put it, this *shitstorm* will never happen."

"Now was that so hard? Drink up." They both saluted, and Adams downed the scotch in one gulp, choking and coughing a little. Alex gave a belly laugh, "Adams, my boy, you need to learn how to drink your scotch. Keep me informed, but be careful. I will give you a contact who will let me know what's happening on my end."

The phone rang and Alex picked it up. He listened for a spell, and finally said, "Good, good. Stay on target."

The senator turned to Adams and said, "Well, looks like our problem is shrinking. The meth lab cook, Ronnie, died in jail."

"That is the worst thing that could have happened. Now Roland will be all over it. That's a county lockup. It's his responsibility. He will be on top of this like stink on shit."

The senator continued to smile, "That county lockup is out-sourced through the state, giving the state ultimate authority. I suggest you grab your water hose and get down there before that pit dog, Roland, starts sniffing too hard. Good-bye." The senator got up, pushed a button on his desk, and left through the same door he'd originally used, almost running.

The receptionist opened another door to escort Adams out, but it was not the same way he'd come in. He asked her why the different exit, and she just said, "It's best this way, Mr. Adams. Good day."

Chapter 16

F red's Pub and Package boomed with a nearly-full bar and four people playing pool. The regulars were there in force, and hoped to gather information about the recent murder and Sheriff Roland. Johnny, Sparky, and Molly sat at their normal seats. The only thing different was the bartender, Vicky. Amber had been arrested and held in county lockup without bond. It seemed like everybody had been smoking; a thick haze surrounded the bar. Heads turned as Doc walked through the front door. Johnny jumped up and yelled, "Over here, Doc. We need to talk."

Vicky sauntered up to him, "The usual, Doc?"

Doc didn't miss a beat. "Oh yes, Vicky, and I must say, it is good to see you."

"I imagine it is. You and Amber were cause for a good argument, if nothing else."

She opened a beer when Johnny spoke up, "Did you hear my commentary on the radio this morning?"

Doc thought about it, "Why no, are you riling folks up again?"

"Hell, no, I'm just speaking the truth. I did a piece on Roland and how the state attorney is after him for shooting Ed. It all smells of a cover-up. And by the way, I saw your car at the sheriff's office. What's he got you in there for?"

"Funny you should mention that. Hell, I reckon I could never sneak around this town. Anywho, he wanted to ask me about my son's relationship with Sue. I had to tell him that was over four years ago; I think he's just trying to figure out all the loose ends and come up with a timeline of events. I must say, I wasn't very helpful."

Molly saw her chance to jump in, "He ask about me? You know at one time I think he liked me."

Sparky did not miss his chance and chimed in, "Hell, Molly, everybody has liked you, and some still do. Poor Marcus, we'll miss him. He was always good for a joke or fart."

Molly reflected and said, "You mean a fart." With that statement, she cracked up.

Doc turned his head and noticed an older, strange man that used to work for Ed. Doc elbowed Johnny and directed his conversation toward the gentleman, "Hey! Didn't you say you worked for Ed as a mechanic?"

All eyes were on the stranger. He waited about a minute, and said, "Yep, sure did. That was like ten years ago. I decided to move here and start my own mechanic shop. In fact, I'm looking at Ed's place now since it seems to be available."

Everybody seemed a little perplexed. Doc jumped back in, "What was your name again? I'm sorry, you might have said, but my memory is for shit."

"Never gave it. But Joey Michaels is the name and engines is my game. Haven't found one I couldn't fix."

"Cool, nice to meet ya. I guess you know Molly, Sparky, and the rest?"

"I'm making my rounds, thanks, it's nice to know you folks. I like this place. It's so quiet and peaceful."

With that comment, everybody in the bar began to laugh. Doc had to speak up, "We'll give you time to learn the curve."

Vicky came up to Doc and Johnny and asked, "Do you think they will ever let Amber out? I mean, I like working this shift and all and would hate to lose it, you know?"

Johnny spoke first, "Vicky, from what I have gathered you're good to go for at least 25 years."

Pretending to be shocked and happy at the same time, she said, "Oh my, that's just terrible."

Sparky couldn't hold back, "Yea, right."

Doc had forgotten about Ronnie being murdered in the county jail, and waited to see who would find out first. Apparently, nobody knew, and this was odd. The phone rang and Vicky went to answer it. She listened intently. Johnny, Sparky, and Doc looked at each other and waited with bated breath. Vicky gasped, "Are you sure? Oh, my God...In jail? How the hell could that happen?" While they all listened and watched, their new acquaintance slipped out the front door. Finally, she hung up the phone, "Ronnie is dead! Somehow, he died in jail; nobody is saying how, or they just don't know."

Johnny piped up, "Well, shit, Doc, you could have told us."

"Hell, I didn't know. It must have happened after I left Roland's. Holy shit, this just keeps getting deeper."

Molly felt her whiskey and yelled, "Bet Marcus got him for ratting him out!"

Sparky tried to make sense of the whole thing and said, "You know, guys, Ronnie was just a kid. He was probably working for some people who didn't want to be known. He was at the wrong place at the wrong time. That kid was okay. Well, except for the meth and all."

Johnny was quick to respond, "You make a good point, Sparky. Well, I'm out of here. Got to go to the jail and find out just what the hell they will tell me."

Doc looked at Vicky, "I'll have another beer for Ronnie." After that, the rest of the customers stormed the bar and chanted, "For Ronnie! For Ronnie!"

It was then Doc saw Doug Rodgers, Amber's live-in boyfriend. As Doug bellied up to the bar, Doc said, "Hey, Doug. How ya been and all?"

Doug looked at Doc for a moment, "Well, it sure has been peaceful with Amber gone and all. I must say, I kind of miss her yelling at me."

"Yelling at you? Wow, I thought I was the only one who received that honor."

"You're not so special, Doc. She spread her ill will around like Mardi Gras beads. Must say, though, I kind of miss her, never realized she was mixed up in all that shit."

"Well, good luck with ya all the same."

"Thanks, Doc." Doug leaned over to whisper to Doc, "Know anybody who would want a little shine. Amber never gave me the customer list. Got quite a bit to git rid of. You know what I mean?"

"Sure, I think Johnny can help you, as well as Sparky. It's not much of a secret."

"Thanks, buddy. To Ronnie."

Doc looked at Molly, a portion of her right breast had been protruding from her sleeveless blouse. He poked Sparky and whispered, "Look at Molly's right sleeve, casually."

Sparky peaked over at Molly and noticed. He immediately spoke up, "Damn Molly, your bra broke again? You got an escapee right there."

Molly looked to her right and stuffed her breast back in. She was quite large. Molly looked at Doc, then Sparky, "No freebies, gents. I can't help it if I was born blessed." Sparky's eyes widened, and Doc elbowed him in the ribs, saying nothing.

Doc wondered who had called Vicky, so he asked her. She took a long hard look at Doc and said, "Well, I have been dating Paul at HPD. And he knows how I liked Ronnie like a brother. He was just doing me a courtesy by letting me know."

"He had to know you would tell us."

"He has no idea who's here, and anyway, what's the big deal?"

Doc thought about it, she was right. He asked her, "What's the best way to get to Homerville from here?"

Vicky looked at him strangely and responded, "What the hell have you lost in Homerville? Hell, that's mostly a community anyway. Oh, I know what you want. You heard about that whorehouse over there."

"What? You're kidding me, really? I mean what? They don't call them that anymore, do they?"

"Boy, you sure got your dander up. Cool, I like that. When you get there, tell them I said howdy."

"Well, I wasn't going there exactly. Where is it in relationship to the town hall?"

"Hell, it's a block over. Funny, don't you think?"

"Amazing, you still didn't give directions."

"Use MapQuest, fool. The back roads would only get your ass in trouble."

"Vicky, I'm no tenderfoot."

"Let's put it this way," she began to whisper, "that meth lab Ronnie was running wasn't the only one."

"How the hell do you know?"

"I'm a bartender, ain't I? Besides, that's none of your business. Amber knew about them both. I believe she might be the next one heading for the bone yard. People do not like loose lips. If you tell anyone I said anything I'll call you a liar. You want another beer?"

"No, thanks, Vicky, but I will take your advice. I appreciate it. I'll see ya when I get back."

"Bye, Doc."

With that tidbit of information, Doc went to his Sable and proceeded to get that burner.

Chapter 17

The sun began to crest when Joey got out of bed. The day would be a busy one. *I sure hope those guards I paid off were reliable.* He stayed in a garage apartment owned by the deceased, Ed Nixon. So far nobody had made the connection. He proceeded to shower and get ready for his trip to the county jail. After his shower, he laid out a vial and an insulin syringe after getting dressed in a pair of Levi's and a dark hoody. He picked up the syringe and withdrew 50 CCs of the chemical, a compound that simulated a heart attack, and capped it. *That should do the trick.* He then proceeded to get dressed.

Today, he decided to ride the Harley. Besides, he was dressed for it. It was only twenty-five miles to the county jail. Prior to getting there, he had to make a call to one of the guards to make sure the video surveillance was down. It was supposed to look like a routine procedure.

He dialed the number given to him on his burner phone. A man answered, "Hello?"

"This is the mechanic. Are the vehicles in place?"

"Everything is in order. I will meet you at the south gate. Walk toward it, but do not use the parking area. Those cameras are fully functional. They are on a different circuit."

"Will the cameras capture me as I enter the area?"

"I have taken care of that. They will be roaming elsewhere when you arrive."

"See ya in thirty." He put the syringe in the hoody's hidden pocket. He thought about how he would proceed, was satisfied, walked out of his apartment, cranked his Harley, and was off.

Everything seems to be falling into place. I keep thinking about that girl, Susan. She died on that dirt road. But what a stupid mistake. He might have been my boss, but he never should have molested that young girl. That was his downfall, but what a sicko. But the money was good, who am I to say what's right and wrong? I can't think about this shit now.

He arrived at the jail in short order, parked as instructed, and walked to it via the sidewalk. It was a rather large octagonal building with razor wire surrounding the facility. The cameras were pointed away from the south entrance. Joey pushed a button and was buzzed into the gated trap area for an ID check. Moments later, a uniformed guard walked from the building on a sidewalk bordered by more razor-wire fence to unlock the second gate and allowed Joey to enter the main building. Once through the gate, the guard said to Joey, "I had Ronnie moved to the lawyer's conference room. There is no surveillance equipment there. You have ten minutes; after that, all cameras will be back up."

Joey handed him a brown envelope, "Here's a bonus. I was never here, delete my ID check."

The guard stuffed the envelope in his back pocket and escorted Joey to the room. It was small, with a metal table and two chairs at opposite ends. Ronnie was seated in one of the chairs. "I will be right outside the door."

Joey went in and got closer to Ronnie so he could whisper, "Ronnie, we are breaking you out. Open your hand." Ronnie complied. Joey handed him the syringe. "Now put that in your pocket. It simulates a heart attack. When they transport you to the hospital, we have people there that will put you on a plane bound for Jamaica. When the guard takes you back to your cell, inject yourself, all of it, between your toes. Break the syringe in half and flush it down the crapper. It should only take about three minutes to take effect. Do you understand?"

Ronnie had already placed the syringe in his pants. He looked at Joey, "Wow, I surely do appreciate y'all. I would never make it in prison. Are you sure this stuff is safe?"

"It's perfectly safe. I have used it numerous times. It works like a dream." *I don't think I'll tell him about the four that died after I injected them with it.* "Ok, I have to slip out. You know what to do. We will be waiting for you at the regional airport. You will be ok, Ronnie."

Ronnie grabbed him and hugged him, "Thank you so much, Joey. I knew y'all would take care of me."

"Stop it, you are going to get me all teary-eyed. Guard." The door opened, and the guard escorted Joey out the same way he had entered.

At the fenced gate, Joey said, "Get him to his cell immediately and monitor him. I'm out of here." The guard mentioned, "He's going to be ok, isn't he?"

"Of course, we are just faking a heart attack. He will be fine. And remember, I was never here. Understand, and when you search him, you find nothing."

"Yes."

As instructed, the guard took Ronnie back to his cell. The jail had surveillance in every cell. It was a prototype, constructed to cut down on in-house violence. As Ronnie sat on his bunk, he noticed the red light on the camera pointing toward his cell. Pretending to urinate, he removed the syringe, cupped it in his hand, and proceeded to remove his shoes and socks. He rubbed his foot and uncapped the syringe and injected himself between his toes as instructed.

He put his socks back on and was going to flush the syringe. Ronnie stood up, but fell instead, and the syringe slipped from his hand, sliding to the back of the toilet. The drug acted too quickly, and Ronnie started convulsing violently. He yelled, scared to death.

The alarm sounded, and the people behind the surveillance cameras unlocked his cell. Guards responded, including the one who had escorted him back to his cell. Ronnie convulsed on the floor, as if he was having a major seizure. The corrupt guard noticed the syringe and instructed the others to get a stretcher.

As they left, he bent over, picked up the needle, and put it in his pocket as if he was getting ready to administer first aid. The other guards came back with a stretcher. Ronnie foamed at the mouth as his eyes rolled toward the back of his head. By the time they had him on the stretcher, he had stopped breathing.

There was a moment of silence that seemed to last forever. Finally, the head guard spoke up. "Everybody, leave the cell, lock it down. We need to get the local authorities and the sheriff's department over here. Nothing else we can do for him."

The guard with the needle spoke up. "I got to go to the head."

One the other guards laughed a little, "Weak stomach, huh?"

"You could say that."

The bathroom was vacant; he went into a stall, broke the needle in half and flushed it down the commode. The needle would not go down. The guard, George, cussed out loud. He reached into the toilet and retrieved the broken syringe, broke off the needle, wiped it thoroughly, and placed it in the bottom of the trash can. He thought about the envelope in his back pocket and opened it. *Five thousand in hundreds!* He took the money and stuffed it into his pocket. *Was this all worth it?* He returned to the other guards.

Joey pulled up to his apartment with a strange feeling in the pit of his stomach. *Ronnie actually hugged me?* He decided to go to the local bar and feel out the community's response. *What next? Leave Hope or stay?*

Chapter 18

D oc had just bought a burner phone at a local gas station. Out of curiosity, he decided to check out what Vicky called a *whorehouse*, the one in Homerville.

The sign was there plain as day, *Aunt Vickie's Boarding House*, along with a vacancy sign. *Well, you know what they say, curiosity killed the cat.* As he entered the front door, he was impressed with the woodwork of the upstairs bannisters. The foyer was quite spacious, a dining room and reception room to the left. To the right was a desk, behind it were boxes and key hooks with some keys missing. The gray-haired lady stood there looking quite distinguished, well kept, one might say.

Before she could say anything, a rather portly man came in from a door toward the back. He was dressed in a sheriff's uniform and was fastening his gun belt. The lady hesitated, "How may I help you, Mister uh?" This was quite a bit to take in, Doc attempted to let it roll off his back as if he had seen nothing.

"I saw you had a vacancy and was wondering what your rates were?"

The sheriff, after getting his gun belt on, butted in, "Well, that depends on what amenities you want?"

At that moment, a very attractive woman poked her head out from the back, "Don't be a stranger, Sheriff. CoCo loves visitors." She shut the door as he began to chuckle.

Stern-faced, the woman interrupted, "You will have to excuse Bradley over there.He thinks he owns the joint."

"Hell, I might as well, since my wife kicked me out."

"You know all well and good that was your fault, you and your wandering eye. Oh, I'm so sorry, you was wanting to know the rates? Well, they vary. Will it... just be you? Do you plan on having companionship? Before I forget, name's Vickie."

Bradley saw his moment to jump back into the conversation, "I'm the sheriff hereabouts, and around here, there will be no *hanky panky*, if you get my drift. We run a law-abiding community."

Vickie jumped back in, "Now, there is no need to scare him off, what's your name, sugar?"

"They call me Doc, but my God-given name is Richard McClusky."

"You Irish?" asked the sheriff.

"No, I'm afraid not, though, there might be some Scottish down the road."

"You don't wear those damn kilts, do ya?"

"No, Sheriff, you are safe there. The thought of it kind of scares me."

"Well, praise the Lord. What brings ya here? We don't get many visitors, unless it's for a few hours, if you catch my meanin'." The sheriff had a smile on his face big as Texas.

Vickie knew it was her time to jump in, "Well, the room rate is $25.00 a night, and if you have a companion, the rate goes up."

Doc, tried to act innocent and asked, "The rate varies? What if it's just me?"

Vickie gave him a long hard look, "Then I guess you'll *get off* cheap."

The sheriff decided it was time to get down to brass tacks, "Why are you here exactly?"

"Well, I believe I'm going to have to speak to you in private. Do you know where the crematory is located?"

"Now you're talking. Old man Wilson owns that monstrosity. He also has a small graveyard. It was too small for him to accommodate enough bodies to make a profit, so he built this gigantic marble building that can hold over 200 bodies. That is, if you want to be above ground. Personally, I like the idea better than being worm bait. I think they call it a mausoleum?"

Doc was fascinated by Bradley's description. "Can you show me the way?"

"I'll do ya one better. I'll take you in the squad car. It will make ole Wilson think he got some business."

"Bradley, you can be such a dick sometimes." Doc laughed to himself. The sheriff just glared and walked out.

Doc got in the car; it was the most unkempt car he had ever seen. "Does the radio actually work?"

Feeling a little insulted, Bradley bellowed, "Works as good as this Smith & Wesson on my hip." Doc remained quiet till they arrived at Wilson's.

As they pulled up, Wilson was walking out the front door of the mortuary. At the back of the mortuary, Doc saw a large marble structure with columns; it looked quite impressive. Wilson noticed Doc looking at his mausoleum; he couldn't wait to get his impression. "Well, what ya think? Pretty fancy, huh?"

"It leaves me speechless. Have you sold many spots?"

"Hell yea, people like the look of it. Makes 'em think they are emperors. What a joke. Anyway, who are you, and why is Bradley bringing you here?" Bradley began to get a little restless.

Doc decided to show them his deputy badge. "You guys know Roland Smith, he deputized me to look into some things, kind of private, if you catch my drift."

Sheriff Bradley spoke candidly, "Catch ya like a tidal wave. What's up?"

"Well, there was this Black girl brought here back in 2009, and I need to see the records of her cremation. That is, if you have them?" Wilson looked at Bradley and started to shake his head. "Told you there was something fishy going on back then, didn't I?"

Bradley looked him straight in the eye, "I told you first it was fishy and for you to use that dead dog."

"First, like hell, and that dog had a name, Spike. No man had a better dog. I loved that dog. Reckon he got a pretty good send-off since I was going to dig a hole for him."

Doc was totally confused, "Uh, hold on guys! I'm not here about a dog. Ed Nixon brought a young female here to be cremated, right?"

Bradley was the first to speak up. "Heard ole Roland got him with one shot dead center. That true?"

"Yes, one shot center mass, killed him instantly."

"Boy, howdy, now that's what I call some shooting. Always had respect for Roland and that gun of his."

Wilson could not contain himself, "Bradley, we got to invite him hunting."

Doc lost his patience, "Guys, the girl. Ed, the body?"

Bradley bellied up, "Wilson, you want me to tell him or do you want to since Spike was a big part?"

Wilson took a little time before answering and finally said, "Oh hell, you go ahead, Bradley. You probably can tell it better than me anyway. But you be sure to mention Spike's part." Doc decided to sit on the hood of the sheriff's car. This would probably be a long story. As he waited, Bradley paced and tried to gather his thoughts.

"Ok, as we mentioned to you, this whole thing was fishy. For one thing, Ed came down here alone with a body in a bag for cremation. He convinced Nelson over there to take the body to the crematory to be cremated right away. And he had one thousand dollars in hundred-dollar bills. Well, if I had not been summoned as a witness, I never would have seen this. Now here is where Nelson had a stroke of genius."

Nelson jumped in, "Thank you, Bradley. I know it was quick thinking."

"Anyway, he told Ed he had to prepare the body and heat up the oven; it would take about an hour or so. He suggested Ed grab lunch at Vickie's boarding house. She has the best chicken and dumplings ever." Doc remained silent. He knew not to interrupt.

"Well, once he left, we both unzipped that body bag and noticed this poor young Black girl had been bludgeoned to death. It was as if someone had tried to crack her head open from the back. Nelson and I knew this could be used as evidence. So, we prepared the box for the oven, except we put Spike in it instead of the girl.

Nelson had one of them newfangled preservation bags, so he put the girl in it and sucked out all the air. You know, like those ones you see on TV. Well, anyway, we took the body and stashed it in the mausoleum. She is still there. When Ed came back, we had the box in the oven flaring up over a 1000 degrees. Ed took notice. So, when it was time to scrape out the bones and such, he looked for teeth. It was all torched up good cause ole Nelson had cooked it to nothing. Ed left here satisfied as a tick on a hound. Sorry for stealin' your thunder, Nelson."

"That's alright. You told it better than I could have."

Doc took a moment to soak it in. "You mean to tell me you have the body here, still preserved?"

Nelson spoke proudly, "You're damn straight. As we said something was..."

"Fishy, right, I got it. You might just have the key to a long-time serial killer, boys. So, just where is she right now?" Nelson walked toward the mausoleum, "Follow me, boys, and be amazed."

As they walked toward the monstrosity of what he called his mausoleum, it was truly impressive. It was all open air. There were four columns supporting an ornate roof. Once entering the hallways, you could see individual plaques of where people were placed. At each placement, there was a shelf for flowers. Doc was amazed at the time it must have taken to construct this place. Nelson stopped at a placement and said, "Here she is." The sheriff, Doc, and Nelson all just stood there in silence for what seemed like an eternity. Finally, Doc spoke up, "Well, I must commend you guys for having excellent foresight. I'll have to get with Roland and see how we can get this body exhumed legally. Can we keep this just between ourselves for the time being?"

Nelson and the sheriff spoke at the same time, "Hell, we have kept it quiet for eight years. What do you think?"

"You guys are awesome. Sheriff, can you get me to my car? I have some calls to make."

Bradley looked at Nelson with a smug smile as Nelson looked back at Bradley with another smug smile. Bradley looked over to Doc, "Hop in, daylight burning, and I'm hungry."

Once in the car, Doc casually mentioned what was told to him about another meth lab being in this area. As soon as he finished that statement, Bradley screeched on the brakes and pulled the car over to side of the road. "What the hell you trying to say, boy? You had better come clean. Are you trying to infer something going around here I don't know about or even worse, a part of?"

"I'm sorry, Sheriff. It's just a person told me to watch out which dirt road I took over here. I'm not suggesting a damn thing. As a matter of fact, you and Nelson have been a tremendous help. I just thought you might want to know."

The sheriff got back on the road to Vickie's and said, "I'm sorry, I do not know why that pissed me off. It's just that I thought y'all got the meth lab, and from there to another one in such proximity, and me not knowing, well, I was taken aback." They pulled into Vickie's Boarding House and the sheriff mentioned one more thing to Doc. "You know I'm a good ole boy, but I will not tolerate major violations of the law. Now, I think you might think something goes on here at the boarding house, and I want you to know for a fact that nothing illegal goes on here since the 1700s. These are some of the eldest of professions practiced around even today I feel that does not hurt anyone. And if there is no harm, I call it no foul. Do you get me?"

"Sheriff, I'm of the same opinion."

"Then we shall get along fine. I will consider this meth thing. You just took me off-guard, and I do not like that."

"No problem, Sheriff. It was an honor to meet you."

"Well, boy, I guess you'll do in a pinch." With that being said, Doc got in his car and drove off, knowing he had to get with Roland and soon.

Chapter 19

R oland pulled into the jail complex. He entered through the gate. He looked around the parking lot and noticed three cameras on light poles, all facing away from the jail itself. He found that to be odd. Then he saw two state trooper cars, two local police cars, one ambulance, and three of his deputy cars. Seeing his cars made him proud. He knew they would contain the scene. As he looked at the building, he saw a second entrance to the side, lined with a razor-wire fence. Roland never recalled that being there. He continued to enter through the main entrance. As he went through the main door, he was greeted by one of the nine guards on duty. There was no trace of the troopers or local police. He made note of this to the guard, "Hey, where are all the other troopers and police?"

He responded, "They are all arguing with your deputies about who is in charge."

"Well, I can settle that rather quickly. Take me to them."

As the guard took him through secure locked doors, he explained to him how it was set up. "We are set up on a three-tier level system. Women are kept on the bottom tier, and ones awaiting trial, tier two, and ones awaiting transfer, on three. Now, each cell has video surveillance 24/7, except today, for about thirty minutes." Roland burst in abruptly, "What the hell do you mean 'today'? Now, isn't that a little convenient?"

"Sheriff, it's no conspiracy. Every three months, the video system is purged and files are sent to the home office. Unfortunately, during this time, we must shut down part of the system and re-boot. It takes about thirty minutes. We have never had a problem before, and absolutely no one knows when it's going to happen. We just get notification from the home the day it's to be done, and we do it."

Roland, not satisfied with that response, said, "Well that's just fucked up!"

Roland entered tier two and saw his deputies with relief on their faces when they saw him, and they turned all heads of the local police and troopers to look at Roland. The guard told Roland, "Well, I'll have to leave you with them. I have to return to my station on tier one."

"Wait, Where were you when all this went down?"

"I was on tier one, handing out breakfast to the female inmates."

"Who was monitoring or screwing with the surveillance?"

"That would be Charles Gun, Roland. May I go now?"

"Yes, but I'm going to have more questions." Roland proceeded to the cell where everyone had been congregating. There he noticed some foam around Ronnie's mouth. Roland looked to Deputy Cobb and asked, "Did you get a swab of that around his mouth?"

Cobb, taken aback, stated, "No, sir. The troopers said they got this." Roland became red around the gills, and Cobb knew what this meant; he headed toward the body with an evidence bag to swab the contents around the mouth, when a trooper stepped in front of him. At that precise moment, Roland grabbed the trooper by the arm and slammed it behind his back and cuffed him to the outside railing. Roland then said, "Continue, Cobb." One trooper was incapacitated. The other placed his hand on his weapon, and Roland said, "You don't want to do that!" Then Roland turned to the local police and told them they could go. Needless to say, they did not hesitate to make their exit. The other trooper was as mad as Roland, and fists were fixed to fly when both their phones rang.

Roland was the first to answer, and it was Mildred on the other end. "Roland, I just got a call from that guy who is after you. You know, the assistant attorney. Well, he is apparently jetting from DC to Andalusia to meet with you. He said specifically for you to stay where you are at until he arrives, which will be in about two hours."

Roland, did not know what to make of this and responded, "Inform him I will be here." He looked over his shoulder saw the trooper getting his ears burned by someone. Finally, the trooper said to Roland, "I think we got off on the wrong foot here. I'm Doug Jones, and my rank is Sergeant of Investigation. The man you hogtied is my partner in the said investigations. He has equal rank. I would appreciate it if you would release him. And my boss has instructed me that you are to take the lead and we are to assist. I disagree with the decision to have some hick sheriff take the lead, but I have my orders. Oh, my partner's name is Roy Smith."

Cobb took out his camera to take pictures of the body and nearly dropped it when he heard the term "hick sheriff." He was scared as to how Roland would respond.

Roland put a huge smile on his face, paused, then said, "This hick sheriff could fuck your world up, so I would choose my words a little more carefully." Roland instructed his other deputy, Boyd, to release Roy.

Now Roland could concentrate on the scene. Why was he on a gurney? What chemical would cause foaming at the mouth? How was it administered, and by whom? Roland turned to his deputies and the two troopers. "Nobody leaves till they have been interviewed by us. What is that side entrance for?"

Trooper Doug couldn't help himself, "That's where the lawyers come to meet their clients. I thought you would have known that." He started to smile.

Roland turned to him, "Well, jackass, that was the entry point for the one who assisted in this murder. That was where the killing agent was introduced to Ronnie. And I bet he arrived when the cameras were down. We need to interview very closely that guard who escorted whoever in. Let's take the tier two guards down to the interview rooms and see what we can find out. Also, I want a search of the guards' bathroom's trash for anything that might look like a delivery device of a toxic drug. Is there any confusion, people? Let's start moving."

Roland's burner phone rang. He knew he had to take this in private, so he said, "Let's get moving, NOW!" He then walked away to the phone, "Tell me you have some good news."

Doc was on the other side, bursting at the seams, "Roland, they never cremated the victim. They preserved her body and put it in a crypt, so to speak. They gave Ed some dog remains, and he was none the wiser. And did you know there is a prostitute house here in Homerville? And also, there is supposed to be another meth lab somewhere on the back roads."

Roland was happy and confused, "Damn, Doc, I sent you to find out about the body, and all this surfaced. Wow. You missed your calling. I'll get with Judge Spurlin about exhuming the body. About the other, we will have to sit on it for a bit. You are not a disappointment. I'm going to be here for about three hours. We need to meet. How about that JR Food Store in Hope, say around four?"

"The one where that fruit loop works?"

"Fruit loop?"

"Yes, his name is Andy, and rumor has it he been with some of the local police here."

"The hell you say. Is there anything else I should know?"

"I thought you knew. He doesn't hide it. In fact, he's quite proud."

"Whatever, see ya around four." Roland hung up the phone. He decided to get down to the interview rooms with Trooper Doug to assist with the interviews. He was going to leave no stone unturned. But before he could start moving that way, Deputy Boyd came running up to him with an evidence bag in his hand. You could see the excitement all over his face. Roland looked at him, "What you got there?"

Boyd bursted with pride and said, "I found this at the bottom of the guard's trash can in the bathroom. It's an insulin syringe." Things came together quickly. Roland looked at Boyd, "Good job. Put that with the other bags, and call CSI and the coroner in Montgomery. Tell the coroner I'm sending him another case that needs to be handled delicately, and one that is eight years old."

"Another one?"

"Don't you worry about it. Use that ambulance for transport, and tell them not to spare the siren." Just as Roland was moving toward the interview rooms, he heard a. "Psst, Psst." He looked into the adjoining cell, and an inmate was trying to get his attention. Roland went up to his cell, "You want to say something?"

The inmate said, "Sure do. You need to come here more often. These guards have free rein. Drugs, sex with females on tier one, and your boy was taken down to the interview room, and now he is dead. This place is not safe."

Roland took this in and asked, "What's your name?"

"John Doe."

"Well, thanks, Mr. Doe. I'll look into it." With that being said, Roland started again toward the interview rooms. Once there, he saw that Trooper Jones had already started the interviews. This got under his skin. However, Cobb was outside, which made him feel better. Looking at Cobb, Roland asked, "How many?" Cobb just turned to him and raised one finger. With a big smile on his face, Roland said, "Well, let me in, big boy." Once in the room, he spoke briefly to the guard and then to Jones. "Thought we were together on this?"

Trooper Jones, a smug look on his face, replied, "But of course. This is the guard that handles the video for the facility. He has brought down his laptop to show what he's got for us."

Roland went over to sit with Jones, grabbed the computer, and looked at the time stamp and what areas he wanted to see. At 8:30 am, all the parking lot videos moved to show the back-parking spaces, away from the building's view. Then all interior video went to fuzz. "Randy, can you explain why the outside cameras changed location while the inside ones went to shit?"

Randy was what people called a *techy*, and he tried to explain the process. "Well, when we start sending the image data to the home office, this is standard procedure. We move outside cameras and re-boot all inside cameras. Then we get on a secure feed and transmit all data. It usually takes about twenty-five minutes."

Roland did not like this and asked, "How often is this done and who knows when it's being done?"

"It's supposed to be done every ninety days, but this time it was requested around sixty-five days."

"Why the change?"

'We just get the email and do it when they say. I'm sorry, I do not know why."

"Have they ever done it this early before?"

"No, not since I've been here, and I was here when we opened."

"Do you have any video when Ronnie was back in his cell or when the cameras came back on?"

"Yes, let me queue it up." Roland and Jones watched the screen intently. The video only showed his cell. He had apparently been taking off his shoes and socks on one foot. Then he got up to use the toilet. He appeared to be massaging his foot. He then proceeded to put his sock back on, but before he could get his shoe on, he started violently convulsing. You could tell he was screaming in agony. At that moment, the chief guard, George, ran to the cell and opened the door. It was odd that he didn't go to Ronnie immediately, but to something by the toilet obscured from the view. He then reached into his pocket and pulled out nothing. This was odd. He then moved Ronnie's head to the side and started first aid. Then two other guards rolled in a stretcher. Roland interjected, "Back it up to when he was standing up and go slow-mo." Randy did what he was told. And as Ronnie was standing, there appeared to be something in his right hand that was tossed violently toward the toilet. It was very difficult to see. Roland looked to Jones, "You see what I see?"

Jones looking closely at the video said, "It's so damn hard to make out."

"Keep rolling the video slowly, now see, when George goes in, he goes directly to where the object was thrown." Jones now looked intensely. "I think I see what you're getting at."

Roland yelled out at Cobb, "Cobb, get this guy out of here and get Chief Guard George down here. He is next."

Randy felt relieved and said, "Then you are through with me?" Roland responded rather quickly, "Not by a long shot, buddy."

As Randy exited the room, Jones looked over at Roland, "You know, I think I would have missed that. I didn't mean anything by that hick statement."

"I didn't care. Now, how do you want to play this? He is our man. He escorted him to these conference rooms and escorted him back. We need to know who he met. That will be our murderer."

"You don't think that it could be George?"

"Hell, yes! He's a pussy. We will have him crying in here within twenty minutes."

"Oh yea. I'll take that, say, fifty dollars?"

"It's a bet. Don't welsh. I like being the bad cop. Will that be ok with you? And you start off the interrogation."

Jones felt a little more included, and started to see why his boss wanted Roland to take the lead. "I'm good with that."

Roland joked, "I'll bet you're a real sweetie."

"I consider that the payback for the hick comment."

Cobb escorted George into the room where Roland and Doug Jones smiled like Cheshire cats. Jones was the first to speak up, "Have a seat, George. We just have a few questions to put this matter to bed. It should not take too long."

George was scared, and that money in his pocket didn't help matters. As a matter of fact, Roland noticed the bulge in his right pocket, but said nothing. The first thing George said was, "Do I need a lawyer?" Roland looked at Jones, and they both shook their heads. Jones spoke up and said, "Why do you need a lawyer? You're not being charged with anything. We are going to ask everyone where they were so we can find out what happened here. Are you ok with that?"

After a moment, George finally said, "I want to help out as best I can. Go ahead and ask your questions."

Jones started with, "I believe it was you who let in a lawyer to visit with Ronnie this morning?"

"Yes, we received a call from the Wilkerson law firm out of Montgomery. They arranged for him to visit his client. I was to escort him to the interview rooms to meet inmate Ronnie."

"Did you watch this interview, or did you see them exchange anything?"

"We are not allowed to eavesdrop. Lawyer-client thing. And Ronnie was handcuffed to the table per protocol."

"Did you frisk Ronnie after the meeting when you took him back to his cell?"

"It's required. Yes, I did."

"Well, it all looks like a routine job. I have nothing more. You, Roland?"

George sat there with a feeling of relief. He thought, *Thank God, this was it*. Then Roland spoke up, "Stand up, George!"

George's feeling of well-being disappeared. Looking confused, he asked Roland, "Why?"

"Just stand the fuck up, or I will lift you up."

"There's no need for all that."

George stood up. Roland walked over to him and put his hand in George's bulging pocket. George attempted to fight him off. Roland then slammed George's head down onto the interview table and forced his hand in the pocket. He pulled out a wad of one hundred-dollar bills. Jones had to scoot back when George was thrown to the table, but said nothing. Roland continued to pull out hundred-dollar bills until the pocket was empty. He then pushed George back to his seat while he gathered up all the money. He winked at Jones. Jones took the hint, "My God, Roland was that necessary? I'm sure there is a logical explanation for that money. Right, George?" Roland continued to count and sort the money.

George spoke up, "That's mine. I was going to buy a used car after work. Give it back."

"There you go, Roland. What did I say?"

Roland took his time and methodically arranged the bills. Finally, he said, "What bank did you get this from?"

George didn't expect this. "I've been saving up over time for another car. Mine has been breaking down."

Roland looked him straight in the eye. "Are you going to stay with that lie?"

"I'm not lying."

"Then maybe you can explain to me why these one hundred dollar bills are new and have consecutive serial numbers?"

George realized that he was in a real pickle. Roland continued. "We also found a syringe in the guard's bathroom at the bottom of the trash can. I would say you botched this thing up pretty good.

Also, I feel it's time you come clean, or you will be charged with murder or conspiracy to commit murder. Ronnie was a good kid. I knew him and his family. He did not deserve this. You are no better than the lowlife who prepared the poison. I will personally make it my mission that you will do hard time. And I will make sure you will be the bitch of the prison."

George started crying hysterically, and Doug Jones cussed because he just lost fifty dollars. Roland continued, "George, it's time to come clean. We know this guy you let in paid you off. We also know you picked up something, like the syringe in the cell, and disposed of it in yall's bathroom. It's up to you how bad we can make it for you. Doug, do you think we can cut him a break if he cooperates?"

Doug, already pissed because he lost the bet, said, "Well, if he tells all, I'm sure I can talk to the assistant state attorney into lesser charges. That is, only if he comes clean completely."

Roland looked at George, who continued to cry, "Well, boy. You care to play or do we lock you up now?"

George started to wipe his nose, "They said it would be like a fake heart attack, and they were going to bust him loose at the hospital. I swear, I never knew it was poison. I did not know it would kill him."

"Who was this lawyer?"

"I'm not sure. They just called him the mechanic. He was wearing a hoodie. First time I met him. He's older, with some gray. I believe he knew Ed Nixon. Maybe he was called Joey, but I cannot be sure."

"Holy shit." Roland got up immediately and yelled to Cobb, "Open the door. Doug, watch him. I have to make a phone call. Be right back." Cobb opened the door and Roland burst through. He used his burner phone to call Doc. After four long rings, Doc answered. "Thought we were going to meet at four?"

Roland cut him off. "That guy that was friends with Ed. He was at Fred's, right?"

"Sure, he said he was. He said he was a mechanic. Just talked to him today at Fred's. Said his name was Joey Michaels, and that he's going to open up a mechanic shop."

"Not in my fucking county." Roland hung up the phone. He went up to Cobb, "Radio Mildred to put out an APB on a Joey Michaels. Tell her to contact local and state police on this. We also need to locate all of Ed's property; he might be living on one of them. Do it now!"

Cobb spoke up, "You know, Ed had a garage apartment. The reason I know is that I almost rented it. It was pretty nice."

"I love you, Cobb. Have some of our local backup go to that residence now. If they find him, he is to be considered armed and dangerous. Got all that?"

"Yes, sir. On it right now. You still want me here?"

You bet your sweet ass I do. We are at the tip of the iceberg." Roland then leaned over and kissed Cobb on the cheek, something he had never done. He went back into the interview room. Cobb stood there, just dumbfounded for a moment, and finally radioed in Roland's request.

Roland looked over at Doug and said, "Can you get out an APB ASAP on a Joey Michaels?"

Doug looked at Roland and said, "Watch this; Dispatch, this is Sergeant Doug Jones. Authorization bravo, echo, Wyoming, 286, I need an immediate APB on a one Joey Michaels, middle aged with grey hair, possibly riding a Harley Roadster. He is armed and dangerous."

The response came back. "You're verified, and it's out state-wide as of now. 10-46." Doug turned to Roland, "Well?"

Roland just turned to Doug and responded, "Y'all sure are fancy. I'd forget those codes as soon as I was told." They now both focused their attention on George. Best not lock him up now. He had become a little too valuable. He would check with the assistant state attorney. Roland looked to Doug and then to George and said, "It looks like we have to read you your rights to you now, but we are not going to arrest you. You will be detained under our protection until a decision has been made."

"You said if I cooperated there would be consideration. Besides, I'm not the only one, and I will definitely need protection."

Roland was beside himself, and Doug's mouth just dropped an inch. Doug jumped in this time, "What do you mean?"

"Why do you think the video went down? And where do you think that order came from? And did you know that Amber was transferred to the women's prison in Montgomery so you could not get to her? And lastly, I cannot even tell you where Marcus wound up."

Doug and Roland both said, "Spill it!"

"No way, until I get something in writing and y'all get me out of here. If I stay here, my life is not worth spit."Roland gestured Doug into the hallway. He banged the door to be let out, and he and Doug told Cobb to keep George on ice.

Chapter 20

T he Lear jet cruised the flight path into Andalusia Airport. The
runways were long enough for small jets. It was built for local
training for a nearby military base. In no time, the jet landed, and
Mr. Adams knocked on the flight deck door. Once opened by one
of the pilots, Mr. Adams inquired about what he saw out of his
window. "Did y'all see that fire?"

The chief pilot mentioned, "You bet, it was a doozy. I would
guess it was around Homerville." The other pilot jumped in, "It
had to be on the outside of Homerville. I'd say closer to the out-
skirts of the woods. I could see about three fire trucks. Looked
like they were containing it. Had to be a trailer or old house the
way it was burning."

"Thanks, guys, I was curious."

"Boss, should we wait here or go back to Montgomery?"

"Go back to Montgomery, and thanks for a smooth ride." The
administrator of the county jails waited in a Lincoln to take him
to the county jail. His name was Jacob Sweeny. Jacob walked
around the car to shake Mr. Adams' hand. After the greeting, he
asked, "Well, how do I get the honor of a DA meeting me here?"

Adams, a little pissed, responded, "I'm not a DA. I'm the assistant State of Alabama attorney. I represent the state's interest, and
right now, you have a dead inmate under your watch."

"Well, you have all the law enforcement at the facility. I'm sure
they will get to the bottom of what happened."

"Let's pray so." Then Adams got on his phone. One minute later, he was connected to the FTA supervisor. "Rob, there was a fire over near Homerville, and I want you to take a crew over there. I have a strange feeling you will find remnants of a meth lab. I want you to keep what YOU FIND UNDER WRAPS AND REPORT ONLY TO ME!" Rob was a little taken aback at these instructions. This was the first time Adams had ever given him such orders. He took a moment and responded, "Is there anything I should know about this? People will be wondering why I'm there, especially that nosey sheriff."

"I'll handle that. Just refer any questions to me. Ok?"

"Yes, sir, on my way." Right after Adams got off the phone, Jacob jumped in. "It would appear you have a lot of irons in the fire."

"It would appear you need to realize what you hear and what you do not hear. And, if my memory serves me, I have made no phone conversations in this car. Do you understand?"

"I must say, I spoke out of turn. I never saw you on the phone." As they drove to the jail, there was an eerie silence in the car. Finally, Adams asked Jacob, "How many jails are under your supervision?"

"The company assigned me three. Andalusia, Atmore, and a small one outside Montgomery. Why do you ask?"

"I understand you are the boss; who runs the jails while you are running around?"

"We have a management structure in place with me being the last one called in an emergency. For example, chief of guards, then chief's assistant and numerous privates. Oh, we also have a technical director who runs the new surveillance."

"When were you told about the death?"

"I was notified by the chief's assistant ten minutes after it occurred. We then put in place the state-mandated protocol. We also notified all respective authorities to investigate the occurrence."

The car pulled into the jail facility. The first thing Adams saw was Roland's jeep, as well as the state trooper cars. It looked like a convention to him. Even Jacob spoke up, "Wow, I hope there is no crime elsewhere. Looks like everybody is here." Adams ignored what Rob had to say. He exited the vehicle and started for the entrance to the jail. The first person he met at the door was Deputy Boyd. Boyd spoke up, "Who are you? There will be no visitors for a while. So, I suggest you just turn around and ske-daddle." Behind Boyd was Roland, and he began to laugh. Adams looked at Boyd and said, "Do you know who I am?"

Boyd, felt emboldened and said, "I really do not care. I have my orders from Sheriff Roland himself. You could be God, and I would not care. You will not enter!"

Roland, feeling satisfied with Boyd, butted in, "Boyd, this is the assistant state attorney for the State of Alabama, and he is spearheading this inquiry. I think you can let him and Jacob in. Good job, Boyd."

Boyd, extremely embarrassed, lowered his head, moved out of the way, and allowed them to pass.

Adams ignored what just happened, looked over to Roland, and gestured him to the side. "There was a major fire on my way flying into here. It was around Homerville. I instructed Rob from ATF to investigate the origin. I feel it is connected."

"You damn, Skippy, it is. I have it on good authority it was another meth lab. I think someone is on a massive cleanup. We have a guard here paid off with brand new one hundred-dollar bills with consecutive serial numbers. And if that is not enough, my witnesses have been killed to look like an accident or transferred out of my jurisdiction. I am pissed off."

"Roland, we can't talk here. Tomorrow at your office at 9:00 am, ok?"

Roland acknowledged him with a nod, and then entered the jail complex. Before they entered the complex, Adams phone started to ring. "Roland, I got to take this. "Adams…what? Who ordered this? Don't you have anybody to do what I asked? Then who do you suggest I get to investigate the fire? The fire chief!" When Adams disconnected the call, he had turned red like Roland, and Roland was observant of the fact. "I take it you got some bad news?"

"Well, you could say that. I ordered the FTA to investigate the fire over there at Homerville. There was no problem until my boss got wind and re-directed them to Birmingham for a suspect weapons stash of a cult group. Which, by the way, is a pile of shit. I considered that group, and they are harmless. There seems to be power play here by people who do not want the truth to be told. I do not know who I can trust, except you."

Roland was taken aback a bit, not sure if that was a compliment or not. Either way, Roland jumped in, "No need to worry, my boy, Roland is here to your rescue." Adams became angrier and angrier. He then watched Roland get on his phone, and listened intently.

"Charlie, my fishing buddy and best friend of all time…Well, I need your help and I need it on the down low. Do you think you can do that? No need to cuss…It seems someone is pulling the ATF strings and hampering my and the state's case on a meth lab production ring and disguising it as serial murder…I knew you would see it my way…Over in Homerville, there was a trailer or house fire of some size and we need a professional analysis of what's left in evidence bags, and a chemical analysis…Yes, you get all credit for the meth. I just want the serial killer. I might be able to swing some pot busts your way…What do you mean you don't want them I agree, opioids are the killer…So, you'll help? Love ya, baby…Ok. That was not necessary. Bye." Adams waited with bated breath. Roland turned to him and said, "DEA will be out there in thirty."

Adams thought about this for a moment, and voiced his concern, "DEA is federal, and I have no jurisdiction. This could get a little messy."

Roland turned to him, "Charlie and I are childhood friends, and there is nobody else I would trust. He is operating on a reliable informer he has used in the past. That opens the door for both of us. You might want to keep it under your hat. I would say you have a massive leak in your department." Adams had always suspected payoffs in his department, but was unable to prove it. Another case getting washed under the rug was not going to happen under his watch.

Cobb was still outside of the interview room guarding their best informant. Up came Roland and Adams. Doug and the other troopers interviewed the other guards on tier two. Roland spoke first, "How's our boy?" Cobb finally felt involved and said, "Well, he did get one visitor, which I did not let in, the video guy. Other than that, very quiet." Cobb let in the both of them and shut the door. George was fidgety as a mouse in a snake's cage. Roland introduced Adams and proceeded to inform him he would be taken to a safe house of Roland's choosing. He also explained he would need a lot more answers than what he had so far. At this point, Adams spoke up, "Is there anybody you know of in my department that has donated funds or moved prisoners from here?" George took his time, and then responded, "Where do you think the transfer orders came from. We are servants to the contract signed by your boss. We do not ask questions. And I tell you; here recently, since that girl got killed on that road, it's been tense around here. Like there was a bigger boss or something." Adams listened intently. He looked over to Roland, and he shook his head as if they needed to protect this guy.

Adams finally spoke up, "What do you want for your testimony?"

"Well, I think immunity is not a far stretch since I led you in the right direction." Adams looked again at Roland and saw him shaking his head yes. "Ok, I'll write it up. Roland, get him out now before anybody else gets wind."

Roland called out for Cobb, and instructed him to take George to a house they both knew that had been used before to hide people. He also instructed Cobb to take Boyd to help on the guard duty. Roland assured Cobb that Boyd was the perfect person. With no further conversation, they proceeded to escort George from the jail to Cobb's car, and Boyd would follow. Roland then called over his radio to Doug that his end had concluded, and he and Mr. Adams were going to his office. He also asked him if he could share his notes there tomorrow at 9:30 am. Doug was agreeable and fifty dollars lighter.

When Adams got into Roland's jeep, he asked if they had a hotel in Hope. Roland found this amusing, and said that he could stay in his barn. They both laughed. "You know, Roland, I was ordered by my boss to investigate you. I had heard of your reputation and saw no need. But, my boss was emphatic as if you were a major criminal. I had never seen him act that way before. I am sure someone was pulling his strings, and when we find that out, we will have our culprit. The only problem will be physical evidence." Roland just turned to Adams with a big fat grin on his face, waiting for him to say something, which he did. "All right, I give. It's obvious you are enjoying something and it must be good, like sweet potato pie."

Roland, a disgusted look on his face, said, "I hate sweet potato pie. But I will keep you in suspense no longer. We have the body of the second victim intact and preserved in a mausoleum. It was supposed to be cremated, and it wasn't. Two concerned citizens found it to be quite fishy for Ed to do such a fast cremation. So, they cremated a dog and gave it to Ed, and he was none the wiser. They put the body in a vacuum-sealed bag, like you see on TV, and sucked all the air out of it to keep it preserved."

"Well, I'll be a horse's ass. This is unprecedented. I know of no case law on this. I am going to have to research how we can legally exhume the body that legally doesn't exist. I won't lie to you, Roland. This could be a nightmare. I'm sure without a doubt that that body will have the evidence of our culprit. Wow, this is big. Who knows?"

"Just the two who put the body there and a deputy assigned undercover by me."

"Can you trust this so-called deputy?"

"More than I trust you and your sweet potato pie. As a matter of fact, I got a meeting with him in about forty minutes."

"I want to be there."

"Let me put it to you this way: no way in hell. Since you have been involved, I have another dead body, and missing, presumed dead witnesses, and a contract killer on the loose. Is there any more I need to say?"

"Roland, I know it looks bad. But I have been played, and I'm not a happy camper either."

"Not happening! Here you are, Days Inn. I will have a deputy drop you off a car so you can get around. Of course, you will tell me and ask me where you will be going. You cannot trust the local police, nor the police chief. And be careful which troopers you talk to. And when you are on your official phone, consider it bugged. See you tomorrow."

"You sure do make one feel safe."

"Adams, the safest person around right now is George. Bye."

Chapter 21

J oey Michaels drove down County Road 72 to Mississippi in his newly acquired Ford Ranger. Joey Michaels was no longer Joey Michaels. He was Earl McSweeney, with red hair and an Irish accent. All his IDs matched his new identity. This proved to be advantageous because he rapidly came up to a roadblock at the Mississippi State Line that he knew nothing about.

Earl thought of Ronnie and those piercing innocent and trusting eyes he had when he handed him that lethal syringe. He even thanked him for his help. This struck a chord deep inside of him. For the first time, he felt a sense of remorse and the need to get as far away as he could from his involvement with his now-former employer. Sure, he made good money, and this was his line of work, but Ronnie changed all that for him. Ronnie could have been like a son to him. His feelings for that child were strong, and his guilt immense. It was time to go back to New Orleans and resume his old way of accepting contracts. The old way being usually despicable people with no emotional connection. Things were different now for Earl.

While his emotions had their way with him, he rapidly approached a roadblock by state troopers, looking for the person he used to look like. At the top of the two-lane road, he saw flashing lights and cars being stopped and checked. It was too late for him to turn around. He proceeded to the roadblock and was two cars back. This road was seldom traveled; therefore, there was light traffic. He got his license and registration ready as he inched his way toward the troopers. There were no cars behind him, and it was now his turn. The trooper approached his car and asked for his license and registration, which he produced. The trooper looked at the picture on the license and then back at him several times. The other trooper circled his truck, taking notice of his tag number. Finally, the trooper spoke up. "You from Alabama, Mr. McSweeney?"

"Oh no, I'm originally from Louisiana."

"You have business here in Alabama?"

"You could say that. I come over to buy vehicles. They are so much cheaper over here."

The trooper just nodded his head and excused himself to the squad car to call in the license. The other trooper was at the vehicle and kept an eye on him. They had two cars at the block, and were prepared for anything. He realized there was little room to make a break for it if he had to try.

This trooper was very observant. He noticed in the picture of Earl he had red eyebrows. The man in the truck had gray eyebrows. He had just keyed in the data from the license and registration and waited for a response. While he waited, he went back to the truck and asked Earl about this to see how he would react. Earl was cool, calm, and collected. He did not frazzle easily. He noticed when the trooper came back to him. When the trooper arrived, he asked, "Could I get you to step out of the vehicle?"

"Is there something wrong?"

"Standard procedure. You wouldn't happen to have any weapons in the truck?"

"Yes, in the glove box, I have a registered pistol in a lock-box-unloaded. I also have a permit for it."

"May I inspect your glove box?"

"Wow, y'all must be looking for someone dangerous?"

"Why do you say that?"

"I have never in my whole life been through such a rigorous check. I thought it was some sort of DUI check point or something else. I have no problem with you checking the glove box. I want to cooperate completely."

The other trooper opened the passenger door and checked the glove box. Sure enough, there was a locked gun box there. He took it out and laid it on the seat. The other trooper at the passenger side asked for the key. Earl had just a tinge of nervousness and asked, "Have I broken a law or something? I thought it was legal to have a firearm, as long as it takes five steps to shoot."

The trooper ignored the comment and asked again, "May I have the key?"

Earl tugged into his pocket and produced a small key. He handed it to the trooper. The opened box revealed a 9mm Glock in excellent condition. The clip was removed and there was no bullet in the chamber. It was also very clean and oiled. The trooper commented, "You know how to take care of your weapon."

"My father taught me to take firearms seriously and to never use one out of malice." With that statement, both troopers looked at each other. The radio came on in the squad car. The trooper who had the license responded. On the other end of the radio, an all-clear was given. He didn't like it. He felt something was off. He had nothing for which he could detain him. He told his partner to lock up the box and put it back where it was. He returned the license and registration and asked, "Why are your eyebrows gray and your hair red?"

Earl realized that he was in such a hurry to get out that he forgot to dye the eyebrows; such a rookie mistake. He was pissed at himself for such an error. "Well, I guess my secret is out. My vanity gets the best of me sometimes. You see, certain women like red-headed men of my age and origin, being Irish and all. I forgot to dye them. I try to make it look as natural as possible. Whoops!"

The trooper took all this in and handed him his papers. "Have a safe trip home, Mr. Michaels." The trooper had hoped to catch a glimmer of recognition of that name, but he got neither. Earl said, "Who? The name is McSweeney."

"Sorry, sir, had someone else on my mind. Drive safely."

"I always do. Thanks." Earl got in his truck and drove to Mississippi. It struck him how smart that trooper was for him to say the other name. It had to be the sheriff, Roland. Roland was the only one he had respect for. Everyone else could be bought, and most by his employer. He realized he would have to watch his back trail and lose the truck as soon as possible. He was certain that the trooper would report the tag and name. And he was positive Roland would get the information. He was very glad of his decision to leave. One more hour in Alabama would have been his demise.

Chapter 22

R oland pulled into the JR Food Mart where he would meet
Doc. As he arrived, he noticed Doc's car was nowhere to be
seen. He checked his watch, and he was right on time. He thought
about what Doc had told him about the cashier being gay and all.
He also said he had relations with some of the Hope PD. This
tidbit of information aroused his curiosity. He wondered which
one, and how many. He really didn't care because that went into
the realm of privacy, and Roland was a firm believer in people's
right to privacy. Having thought all that, he still had to go in and
meet this guy and check him out. Doc wasn't here, and he might
as well be sociable. The first thing he had to do was wipe the fat
smile off his face.

There were only two customers in the store, and they checked
him out. Roland decided to get some coffee. They had quite a
setup for coffee, and it was close to where the cashier was. Wow,
four types of coffee. There was Columbian, House, decaf, and
special blend. Roland always liked a stout coffee, and he went for
the Columbian. As he poured, he noticed the last customer leave.
It was the perfect time to inquire a bit. "So, you're the famous
Andy I've heard about."

Andy, taken by surprise by this unknown person, noticed the
badge and the rather distinctive gun on his side. "I don't know
what you mean by famous?"

"Well, I have been told you do a killer drag."

Andy smiled and responded, "It's good to know some people in this godforsaken town recognize talent. Who are you?"

"I'm sorry, Roland is the name and being sheriff is the game."

With a very surprised look on his face, Andy replied, "Oh, you're the one everybody talks about. The local PD don't not like you too much."

It was just the opening Roland had looked for. "The local PD, huh? The way I hear it, you have been quite intimate with a couple of them."

"Boy, the word sure gets around. What's your interest? I haven't committed no crime."

"Oh my goodness, of course not. I was just curious. What you do on your time is cool with me. As long as you don't break the law, that is. I'm happy for you to be honest. People in this town can be so judgmental."

"You got that shit right. Besides, what's wrong with a little dick now and then? Well, with me it's more now than then." He laughed at his own remark.

Roland smiled, "So tell me, which officers have you been with? I promise I'll keep it to myself."

"You might as well know, it seems everybody else does. It's Jacob and Charlie. They weren't that great, if you know what I mean."

"Not sure if I do know what you mean."

"You know, like if a woman just lays there. Well, these guys got a lot to learn. I do not have the time to teach. Besides, I only got with them because I was bored. There are slim pickings in this town. You aren't trying to hit on me, are you?"

"Oh. God, no! I mean, if I was that way, doesn't mean I wouldn't try. I mean, oh hell, I don't know what I mean. How much for the coffee?"

"It's free for the cops. I guess you're a cop. You ain't bad for your age. I might have had a rumble with you when you were younger."

"Thank you, I guess. Well, it was nice talking with you. Got to go." Right then, to his delight, Roland's burner phone rang. He ignored anything Andy said as he put the phone to his ear and walked out the door. "Roland here."

"Roland, it's me, Doc. The Hope PD has arrested me and is trying to get me to blow the breath analyzer. They pulled me for no reason, and are holding me at the police station. I could use your help."

"Don't do anything, I'm three minutes out."

Meanwhile, at the police station, the officer who brought him in was Paul Smith. Paul had been instructed by the police chief to bring him in on a DUI charge. Police Bob Thorn had gotten his instructions by a phone call from a concerned citizen that Doc had supposedly been driving drunk. Paul knew how to rig the breath machine to show the results he needed to make the arrest, and he had made the adjustments already. Paul, a little upset, asked Doc, "Now, why did you have to go and call Roland? He is not going to be able to help you. You know you have been drinking and you were at Fred's. We got you fair and square."

"I might have been at Fred's, but that does not mean I'm drunk. Besides, who called you from Fred's? You know that is illegal and a setup."

Chief Thorn walked in. "He called who? Roland? What the fuck, Doc? What pull do you have with Roland? Don't think he can help you. Now blow into the analyzer."

"Roland advised me I was to wait till he arrives before I do anything."

The chief turned red with anger, "Roland's coming here? This is a local matter, and I will not have it."

Just then, Roland walked through the door. "Were you looking for me, Chief? Glad to be here. I realize I'm late, but better late than never." Roland walked over to the breath analyzer to check for his tag of calibration. It only took a moment to see it was removed. "Glad I got here. You cannot use this machine till I calibrate it. Aren't you glad I'm here? You see, there must be a recent calibration tag by the sheriff's department for your readings to hold up in court. Now, let me get this done really quickly so you can continue with Doc here." Paul looked over to the chief to see what to do, and the chief threw up his shoulders. The chief knew that Roland was right, and there was nothing he could do but watch. Roland had been certified on this particular machine ever since he had been in office, and had continued to educate himself on every upgrade. He had, more than once, overturned a couple of DUI convictions due to calibration issues. The chief had no ground to protest, and it pissed him off. Meanwhile, Doc showed some relief on his face. He knew he was set up, but by whom he did not know. Everybody in the room watched Roland as he worked on the machine, whistling to aggravate all. Roland took his time, and it took about forty-five long minutes. Finally, he mentioned to Paul, "Please hand me that box marked certifications." Paul complied, and Roland finished up and tagged the machine. "Now, Doc, if you will please come over here and blow into the machine, let's see if you are legal."

Police Chief Thorn, fed up with Roland, interjected, "Now, wait a minute. Paul can do this. It's his job. Now back off." Roland said nothing and backed away from the machine. Paul proceeded to have Doc blow into the machine. As the machine calculated the results, Roland spoke up. "What violation did Doc do to get brought down here?"

Paul, pissed off, responded quickly, "We had it on reliable information he was driving drunk and we responded to the call."

"So, some person called it in?"

"What about it?"

"Seems funny to me. That's all."

The machine printed out the results. Paul was the first to see and his face showed he was not happy. This pleased Roland. He jumped over to the printout and said rather loudly, "A .02. My goodness. I probably stay at .02 all the time. I guess you will be releasing Doc?"

Chief Thorn spoke up, "Yes, he can go." He left the room and slammed the door behind him. Paul took the handcuffs off Doc and nodded that he could go. As they walked outside of the building, Roland turned to Doc and said, "Your cover is shit." Doc thought about this and recalled in his mind his steps and if anyone had followed him. He also remembered the bartender being curious about where he was going, and was dating Paul.

He shared this information with Roland, and they both agreed his cover might still be intact.

Doc looked over to Roland and said, "I'm going to need a ride to where they left my car."

"Where did they leave it?"

"Grocery store parking lot."

They both got in Roland's jeep and headed toward Doc's car. During the trip, Roland brought Doc up to speed as to what was going on. "I'm afraid, since the fire over at Homerville, I'm going to need you to stay at that boarding house and keep an eye out. I can't have anybody find out about the body over there. That is our ace in the hole. In the morning, the other body has been approved to be exhumed. I am meeting with Trooper Doug; Mr. Adams and I should be getting a preliminary report on Ronnie at my office."

"Wow, big day tomorrow. I hate to say this, but I'm a little low on funds."

"No problem, come by the office when we get you to your car. I will give you some front money. I figure around 500.00."

"What, I will not need that much."

"I thought you said they offered amenities."

"Well, they do, but…"

"But hell, might as well join the locals. This will make them trust you more. We can't have you looking from the outside in, now can we?"

"Ok, this will be a first for me."

"It's time you break that virginity streak anyhow." Roland then busted into a big laugh. He reassured Doc not to worry about doing anything that made him uncomfortable. He also let Doc know how important the other body was, and it was crucial nothing happened to it.

Thirty minutes later, Doc was five hundred richer, and Roland headed home.

Chapter 23

D oc was extremely nervous as he pulled into Vickie's Boarding House. The thoughts that crossed his mind were vast and many. He entered the building to see the sheriff was not there. Vickie was behind the desk. "Thought I would be seeing you again. Just couldn't stay away?"

Doc said rather nervously, "I was hoping you had a vacancy for about three days?"

Vickie gave him a serious look and said, "For you, no problem. I will have to put you at the end of the hall upstairs. It's a little quieter there. Will that be ok?"

"Sure, although I wouldn't mind any amenities you have to offer. If that's ok?"

"Room and board is $25.00 a night, which includes breakfast. You are on your own for lunch and supper. We serve both, but at our restaurant prices. There will be a two hundred deposit on the room. Can you handle that?"

Doc pulled out the roll of one hundred-dollar bills and peeled off two to Anne. Anne noticed the other money in his pocket. She mentioned that CoCo would see him to his room, and then rang a bell. After the bell ring subsided, CoCo entered from the side entrance in tight shorts and a low-cut t-shirt, leaving nothing to the imagination. Doc's eyes were transfixed at Coco's breasts. CoCo took one look at Doc and said, "My eyes are up here."

"Oh, yes of course. Excuse me, I just like the t-shirt. I went to that concert."

"You went to a KISS concert? Never would have pegged you for a fan."

"You better believe it."

CoCo escorted Doc to his room upstairs at the very end of the hall. She opened the door with the key and entered the room with him. "Over here is the bathroom. You're lucky. All the other rooms share a community bathroom except downstairs. I guess you could say you have the suite."

"Well, I feel privileged. Thank you."

"If you need anything, and I do mean anything, do not hesitate to call on me. The other residents are always busy up to four times a night, while I limit myself. Catch my drift?"

"Sure do! Besides, I find you quite attractive and polite."

"Well, here is your key. Be sure to keep your door locked. A lot of cleptos around here." With that being said, CoCo left the room and gently closed the door.

Doc leaped on the bed and discovered it was a box spring mattress, and he was slightly gouged by a spring. He decided he'd better restrict movement on this bed. It was obvious this bed had seen its fair share of action.

Meanwhile, Roland headed home to get a good night's rest. But before he went to his farm, he decided to go to the safe house where deputy Cobb held their witness. As he pulled into the shack, he saw light from the window. He exited the jeep to hear Cobb challenge him, "Who goes there?"

"Sheriff Roland."

"Advance."

Roland entered the door and saw George eating supper. All seemed quiet and peaceful. "Boyd set up to replace you?"

"Yes. He will be here at 11:00 pm."

"George, you have anything to tell me?"

"One thing. You are dealing with someone who commands a lot of corruption and payoffs. But now the meth production has been limited; the income is sure to dry up. The only hint I can give you is to follow the owner's property where illegal activity was being conducted. No more till I get my immunity papers."

"Don't worry. It's in the works. In the meantime, do not leave here or even peek out the window." Roland whispered a few things to Cobb and left to go home. Roland was only two miles from the safe house. As he approached his farm, he noticed a solid black car parked across the street from the entrance to his farm. *Now, who the hell could this be?* Without hesitation, Roland gunned the jeep and blocked in the other car so it could not escape. He got out of his jeep in one motion, his gun drawn, and walked toward the vehicle. He yelled, "Hands! I said, hands!"

None were produced. Roland said, "No more fucking warning. Hands, Goddamn it!"

Almost immediately, two hands came out of the windows, "Please don't shoot. I'm FBI." Roland slung the car door open, and trained his gun on the man's head. "With your left hand, toss your weapon. Now!" The officer complied. "Now some ID. Now!" The officer complied and handed Roland his FBI credentials, which were in order. "Go get your gun."

The FBI agent, quite shaken, asked, "Is this how you treat all you neighbors?"

"You're no fucking neighbor. What are you doing here? And do me a favor, no bullshit answers."

"Well, it appears you have stumbled on a cold case in the FBI files until now. It was a serial killer who abducted over fifteen young girls, and their bodies have never been recovered."

"Well, asshole, you could have been a man and joined our investigation instead of lurking in the dark."

"You're wrong. This goes way up the chain. The reason it's a cold case is that when we get close, something catastrophic always happens, and we are derailed. Not this time. I have too much time invested."

"Ok, I haven't seen you. Here is my burner phone number. If you can contribute or shed light, please use it. And remember, its a two-way street. Now, will you leave my humble territory?"

"Sure."

"Wait a minute. I am having a strategy meeting in my office at 9:30 am. Be there and bring your file and all relevant data on these past murders. Maybe there will be a common thread. And if I find you are a mole or working for any guilty party, I promise you your body will never be found."

"Are you threatening me?"

"No. I'm promising you."

Roland got back in his jeep and went home. Before he ate, however, he had to feed his livestock. This had been his routine for years. Once in the house, he thought, *FBI, this case just keeps getting bigger.* Boy, did he stick his foot in a big hole. Tomorrow would produce a lot of results. One, he would have the body exhumed in that other county with two of his deputies present. Dixon had ruled it an accident, and Roland knew that had to be bullshit. Second, he would have the troopers and state assistant lawyer coming to his office. He still had his crime board up, but now there was a lot more to add, like the mechanic who disappeared. Local police and one of his deputies found the garage apartment he was living in. It was wiped so clean and bleached it was impossible to get trace evidence. He would get a plumber tomorrow to check the drainpipes for hair to get DNA. It was obvious he was a professional, and a high paid professional at that. Throwing a TV dinner in the microwave, Roland was ready to eat and go to bed. There would be lots to do tomorrow; and poor ole Doc at the boarding house. He wondered how his night would go.

Doc slept soundly in his room. He began to have a very vivid dream when he was awakened by what he thought was a woman in distress. Once fully awake, he determined the screams were of a different kind of distress.

A woman's voice from the next room over, "Oh, my God, you're so big!"

A man soon replied, "Who's your daddy?"

"Oh, you're my daddy. Hey, not in there or it's going to be extra."

"Whoops, sorry. It slipped out and I misfired. How about this?"

"Oh! Hell, ya, that's the spot. Give it to me!"

"You bet I'm going to give it to you. Take it baby."

"Oh, my God. You're such a man."

"That's right baby, take it, take it all."

"Oh, dear, I'm trying."

After he heard all this commentary, Doc threw his extra pillow over his head and tried to get back to sleep. It took a while, but eventually Doc went back sleep.

Morning could not come quick enough for Doc. He was downstairs at the dining room table and waited for breakfast. Three other women were at the table with him. They were all scantily dressed. This made Doc a little nervous. Soon CoCo came in with scrambled eggs, sausage, bacon, biscuits, and sausage gravy. Doc looked at all this food and was amazed. Coffee and juices were already on the table. There was little talk as people piled on their plates. CoCo asked Doc if everything was ok and he was quick to respond, "Fantastic!"

Doc couldn't eat fast enough, and was on the road to the mausoleum to see Wilson. It was a short drive, and soon he pulled into Wilson's place. Wilson walked out of the crematory to greet him with that wide smile of his.

"I was wondering when I was going to see you again. Just the other day, right after you left, another person came by, asking about the same girl you asked about. I found this to be quite fishy, and I told him that ole Ed had the remains, and I didn't know anything past that. He seemed quite satisfied with the answer, so I paid it no mind." Doc looked at Wilson worried-like, and Wilson sensed how Doc was feeling.

"Look, you got nothing to worry about. Follow me." He took Doc to a different part of the mausoleum; away from the area he showed him the last time. "You know, in today's world, the only one you can trust is yourself. With that in mind, look up, there to the upper left-hand corner of the vaults." Doc acknowledged the spot Wilson pointed to. "That is where your girl is. You see, I don't even trust the sheriff, not that I can't. I just figured I'd be on the safe side and let this secret stay with me." Doc was amazed at Wilson's ingenuity. Wilson proved to be the perfect guardian over this girl's tragic end. Doc pointed it out and said how proud he was of Wilson. At this point, Wilson interjected, "Heard you stayed over at the boarding house last night? Wondering if you heard any ghosts?" Wilson then laughed.

Doc replied, "I tell you one thing. They were very satisfied ghosts." Then they both began to laugh. When the laughter subsided, Doc asked, "That fire y'all had. It was a doozy, I hear?"

"You bet it was. It was more like an explosion from what the sheriff told me. It was an old trailer home. That's where the sheriff is now. Some guy from the DEA came here to check it out."

"How long after that guy asked about the girl did the explosion happen?"

"Well, son of a bitch, same day. Now that does seem a bit fishy."

"Fishy hell. I'll bet 100 to 1 it was related."

"Don't think I'll take that bet. You know the property was owned by one of the oldest families in Alabama. Or it was at one time. The Jackson family used to own over two and one half thousand acres. Hell, they still have an old plantation house close to your county. It is in a state of disrepair. From what I hear, though, it's impressive. Two to three stories with long columns in the front. And it still has the old slave quarters close to the house intact. They were one of the richest families in Alabama. Might still be."

"Interesting bit of history. Can one go look at it?"

"No. The family has fenced it off and has a chain lock on the front gate. It's a shame. I would love to check it out."

"Do they still own it?"

"You bet they do, and some 800 acres around it."

"Must be nice to have money."

"I don't know about all that. From rumors and gossip I hear, some of the family was not right in the head. You know, like crazy. Oh, one of the family members has been a senator for Alabama for twenty years. He's up there in D.C. now."

"Really, which one?"

"Alex B. Jackson."

Chapter 24

A s the sun crested on the horizon, Roland finished up feeding the livestock. He got little sleep that night due to all the developments that had occurred the previous day. He looked forward to everyone coming to his office to get a solid bearing on the next step of the investigation. The one thing that bothered him the most was the FBI's newly acquired involvement. This opened a lot of questions in Roland's mind. The secrecy alone was disturbing. He entered his house to cook a rather large breakfast for himself: bacon, two OM eggs, and cheese grits. He would have a full stomach and be prepared for whatever fell his way.

Once in the jeep, he followed his routine and turned on the radio to listen to what his friend was broadcasting today.

"Well, the saga continues. Ronnie, a beloved local, has died in jail under questionable circumstances. Everyone in law enforcement has been tightlipped. Even a reporter, attempting to get at the sheriff's office, was turned away abruptly. Its appears there are multiple law enforcement agencies involved in this investigation, state troopers, as well as state attorneys, DEA, and prison officials. It is the opinion of this humble reporter that this situation goes up the food chain. How far it goes will be brought to you as soon as I know. And now for the weather."

Roland, as usual, turned off the radio. It would appear ole Johnny was doing his due diligence, and Roland respected him for his relentless pursuit of the truth. He pulled into his station. He was exceptionally early. It was 7:45 am. When he walked through the door, he was shocked to see Mildred at her desk. She had her head down and had been going through what looked like old land deeds. Roland could not help but ask her, "My God, Mildred, what brings you in so early?"

"Sheriff, I really do not know what you would do without me. You have been bouncing around everywhere, and I knew it was just a matter of time before you would direct me to find out who owned the land where these meth labs were. By the way, Charlie at the DEA phoned to tell you the site of the fire tested positive for meth and cocaine. So, you see, I wanted to be one step ahead of your requests."

"Damn, Mildred, what would I do without you?"

"Good question, Roland."

"Well, what have you found?"

"Roland, it a crossword puzzle. One thing I do know is that the land was originally owned by the Jackson family. Since then, various real estate development companies have divested, and the properties are a cluster fuck of ownership. It's a paperwork jungle. But, fear not, I'm on it."

"Mildred, you are my angel." With the end of the conversation, Roland proceeded to his office to bring his crime board up to date. He wanted all events correlated and posted prior to the arrival of his guests. He made a call to the deputies that would be present at the exhumation of the body, whose death had been declared an accident. He was sure this would lead to the original murderer of several young women.

He dialed up Head Deputy Anderson, who would supervise. "Good morning, Anderson. Roland here. How soon till they start digging?"

"Wow, Sheriff, didn't expect you to call so soon. They are delivering the backhoe as we speak. Should only take an hour. They are a little skittish, if you know what I mean."

"Fuck them. Call me with what you find."

Roland then arranged his crime board. At the top, he put up a blank picture and marked it as person of interest. This person would be the one he wanted. He got ready to call Mildred for his coffee when she walked into the office with a pot, a pumping Thermos, and five cups. She placed them on the side table and said, "Decided not to hear you bark for coffee this morning." After that, she walked out of the office. Roland just smiled. He sat in his chair and stared at the crime board, and hoped it would talk to him and point him to right direction. He now waited for his guests. The wait was short-lived. The FBI agent came bursting through the door, followed by Mildred. Mildred stated, "This rude ass just ran past me and proceeded to your office, Sheriff. Care if I whoop his ass and cuff him?"

The agent turned toward Mildred with a surprised look on his face; a look of disbelief. Mildred took his left arm and swung it behind his back and applied pressure. He screamed, and while he screamed, she cuffed both his hands. Roland laughed at the expense of the agent. "Do you mind giving me your name now so I can have Mildred check you out?"

Frustrated, he answered, "My name is Trent Mathews, and I work out of the Montgomery office. Been there twenty years."

"Mildred, take his ID and match it up with his credentials. Oh, by the way, I guess you can take the cuffs off now." Mildred did as she had been told with a slight smile on her face. Trent looked at Mildred and said, "For a Black woman, you have amazing speed." Mildred took another jump at him. He nearly fell over himself and had tried to get away. She had only faked the move. She said, "Calling me a Black woman was unnecessary. What if I were White? Would you say the same thing? I swear you men are so stupid and prejudiced." After that last comment, she started toward her desk until Roland interrupted her. "Remember, Mildred, about the property assignment I gave you."

"On it, Sheriff."

Trent attempted to gather his composure and looked at Roland with a sense of admiration. "It's nice to have loyalty."

"Comes with the job. I would have it no other way. You see, we have no leaks here. I thought I told you 9:00 am?"

"I'll be right back." Trent left the office and came back with two big file boxes and placed them by Roland's crime board. He took the lid off the first box and Roland interjected, "Wait a minute. This all must be in chronological order, as to date, time, and location."

"This is not my first rodeo. Box one begins with 1989-1995, and the second box is from 1996-2014. All cases occurred in Alabama, and all cases were abductions and missing persons fitting the MO. You were our first break with a body and an autopsy. The only other was cremated by Dixon, who declared it an accident. We are waiting with great anticipation on the body to be exhumed for the evidence it will contain."

"Well, I'll be damned. Little ole me has opened causes and motives on two boxes of potential victims of a sadistic serial killer. Somebody up the chain had to know something. I mean, really. How many victims are we looking at?"

"Hold on to your hat: 26."

"Holy shit!" Has no one, and I mean no one, given a damn about these people?"

"Well, most of them were from broken homes, had low economic status, or were drug addicts. The state attorney considered them low priority till now."

"So, you're telling me these people didn't count till I stumbled over a real person whose death was neglected and covered up. Well, you can tell that son of a bitch when I find out who did this, I'm coming for his sorry ass." It was 8:30 am, and Trent and Roland went through the boxes and posted the pictures and locations where the victims were last seen. The board was just big enough to accommodate all the pictures and info on each victim. Roland stood back from the board, looked at Trent, and said, "How can you live with yourself knowing some lunatic was killing these girls?"

"Damn it, Roland, that's not fair! My hands were tied. I was originally assigned the first three cases, and then my boss decided I was needed elsewhere. Not that I didn't keep a detailed record of the evidence and duplicated copies of additional cases with similar MO. The other cases were assigned to rookies, and I then knew someone upstairs was pulling strings. I have had to watch my ass for quite some time."

"Why are you here now?"

"You want the truth, or what I'm supposed to tell you?"

"Why, the truth, fool."

"Well it went like this: I was to get close to you to see what you knew and report directly to the state attorney's office. From there, I gathered the information, and was sent to a Washington senator of intelligence."

"Now that's a conflict of terms; senator of intelligence. Ha. Besides, you are being a leak, how many more do I have?"

"Well, don't trust the Major or anybody in the jail system. And I'm pretty sure the local police follow the chief's orders, and he is the worst. I have tracked down over $100,000.00 of payments to him, all non-traceable, in the Cayman Islands."

"Shit, who can we trust?"

"The assistant state attorney is a standup guy. He hasn't been in the system long enough to be tainted, but I would still be careful."

"Are you aware of all who are coming to the meeting this morning, or should I ask?"

"Trooper Jones, DEA agent Charlie, Assistant State Attorney Adams, a telephonic call from Montgomery, from the coroner, and informant information from George, who you have under protective custody. Have I missed anybody?"

"You missed one. My undercover officer, and I invited the sheriff from Homerville."

"You got to be kidding! He is a direct line to our enemy. Anything we say or do might as well be yelled from the rooftops. You fool!"

Roland walked over to within two inches of Trent's face and said, "That will be the last time you call me a fool. Got it! I hate to resort to violence. I'd hate to disfigure your face." Trent's face turned white as a sheet. Timidly, he asked, "Why the sheriff from Homerville?"

"Well, you see, we are going to need someone to feed false information to our adversaries, and the sheriff has won that job. He also thinks he has an insurance policy on the third victim and information on where she is located. He is wrong there also. The body has been moved. He is perfect for what we will need him for."

"Brilliant."

"I'd have to agree." Mildred came over the phone, and said, "Sheriff, you had better pick up line two." Roland was not used to Mildred using that tone of voice, and it scared him as he picked up the line. "Roland here…What!!! Anderson, was there any tampering? You mean to tell me it was buried that way? Fuck!! Fuck!! I want those bags of sand impounded and taken to Auburn to be analyzed. After all these years it was empty. Who handled the burial? Ed, of course. Thanks, come on back. Tag it and bag it. Bye." Trent looked at Roland, and said nothing, for he knew from the conversation the coffin was empty. It was 9:00 am, and Roland's other guests had arrived. Trent and Roland put up the pictures from the boxes Trent had brought. They put them in chronological order as to the year of the disappearances. The board filled up quickly. The next people that walked into the office were Assistant Attorney Adams and Trooper Jones. They both took a long look at the evidence board with open mouths. Adams was the first to speak, "What's all this?"

Roland gave him time to absorb all the pictures on the board, and then said, "Well, Mr. Adams, my friend here from the FBI has had these open cases since 1989, and these people were missing from our state and surrounding areas." Jones spoke up, "Holy shit." They all took a seat and Agent Trent explained how he inherited the case and how he kept all evidence, even when he was told to dispose of it. He also explained how orders from DC came down to make this all disappear. Jones spoke up, "That make sense. We would get missing person bulletins, and then after a while, they were no longer a priority. I always wondered if they were found, or what?"

"'Or what?' That's what we are now considering. Just before you got here, Deputy Anderson informed me the body we were exhuming was an empty casket. There were two 50lb bags of sand in the coffin." Both Adams and Jones gasped. Jones fumbled around in his pocket and pulled out his phone. After a minute or two, he pulled up a picture. He showed it to Roland, and asked, "Is this your mechanic?"

"Don't know. Never saw him. Send that to my phone and we will have an answer fast. Where did you get that?"

"A couple of my troopers found one mechanic to be suspicious, and captured him on his body cam. Thought it might be of use." Jones sent the picture to Roland's phone. Then Roland dialed Doc's burner phone with the picture for a positive ID. It took a little too long, so Roland dialed direct. When the person on the other end of the phone answered, it was a female. Roland was a bit heated, "Who the hell is this?"

"Well, just who the hell is this?"

"I'm Roland, the sheriff, and I need to talk to Doc now!"

"Well, I'm CoCo, and there is no need to be rude. He is in the shower. I will tell him you called when he gets out." "No...No... No, I'm here." Doc overheard the conversation. "Roland, what can I do for you?"

"It appears you are taking your undercover seriously. There is a picture I sent you on the phone. Is that the mechanic you met at Fred's?"

"Just a sec. Whoops! Oh shit!"

"What's wrong?"

"I dropped my towel." One could hear CoCo in the background. "Damn, boy, you ready to go again,"

"Doc, damn it, can you see the picture?"

"Yes, Roland, that's the same guy except for the red hair. Looks like he forgot to dye his eyebrows. It is him. No doubt. Hey, also, before that fire, a man went by the mausoleum and asked questions about the cremation of our third girl. Don't worry; old man Wilson played it perfect. He said he gave the ashes to Ed and that's all he knew."

"Doc, you need to play it cool around Sheriff Bradley. He might be a leak. Ok?"

"Sure."

"And don't spend all that money I gave you."

"Don't worry, Sheriff, it was a freebie."

"Doc, nothing is free in life! All right, Jones, that was our killer. Where was he heading?"

"My trooper said Mississippi, but he believed he was headed to New Orleans."

"Why?"

"Gut instinct."

"Sounds good to me." As if right on time, the DEA agent and Sheriff Bradley walked into the office. They, too, looked at the crime board and were amazed to see so many girls' pictures. Bradley looked at Roland and said, "I thought there was only one or two?"

"Bradley, the FBI is now involved." Bradley looked nervous. DEA Charlie introduced himself to everybody except Trent. They shared the same federal building. Adams began to question where his jurisdiction began and the federal began. He picked a corner and listened intently.

Roland opened the conversation by stating everything that had happened, all the way to the mechanic who escaped out of their jurisdiction. Here he had hoped for help from Trent and Charlie. It was obvious to everyone in the room the man was a professional and possible ex-CIA. Trent looked over at Charlie and asked, "What's your clearance?" Charlie took a little offense and said, "More than yours." Roland felt it necessary to jump in. "No time for a pissing match. Do you two think you can hop on your secure laptops and run his aliases? They are Joey Michaels and something McSweeney."

"You got a hard wire hookup we can use? We can put a filter on it. Think you can handle that, Trent?"

"Always a comic?" Bradley just stared at the crime board in total amazement. He never even thought that there had been so many missing from this area. He thought about the body that was hidden and had kept quiet for insurance purposes. He also thought it was time to cash in. The only problem with all this law enforcement here was how to do it. Then he thought about Doc at the boarding house. He would be the perfect stool pigeon. It had been bad enough they had killed his income from the meth production. Now all he needed was one big score. He had a number to call in case of emergency. It was time to make that call outside of the sheriff's office. The only flaw with the sheriff's plan was that Nelson didn't trust him and had given him the wrong site where the body was. The only people that knew were Doc and Nelson. This proved to be a wise move on Nelson's part.

Before Bradley had gone outside, Roland walked over to Charlie and asked him, "You still got that telephone surveillance system for wireless. If I give you one number, can you tap the GPS location and record conversation?"

"Of course, that's standard equipment."

"How fast can you set it up?"

"You'll have to give me fifteen minutes. Also, I'll need the radius of where the call is originating from."

"From here, probably outside. Need you to do it now. Here's the number. Get started. I'll stall as long as I can."

"But..."

"No buts. Can you do it?"

"Yes."

"Then do it." Roland walked over to Bradley, who had been making his way outside. Roland yelled, "Hey, Bradley, could you come here for a moment?" Bradley, who had been taken off guard, obliged. He walked over to Roland's desk, and Roland took out a calendar. Bradley looked at the calendar confused, and waited for Roland to speak. "Doc told me you and Wilson wanted to go hunting. He said y'all thought you could whoop me at the draw."

Relieved, Bradley answered, "Now we didn't say we could beat you at the draw. However, in the long rifle, we could do better."

"Well, now, that's why I got the calendar out. Let's pick a day and a no-show automatically loses. No take backs." Bradley turned the calendar toward him to get a good look. While he looked, Roland looked over at Charlie and raised 5 fingers. "Here we go. The 25th."

"Now, when you say long rifle, you mean like this one?" Roland opened up his gun cabinet, where he had six long rifles and a 30 opt 6 with a scope. Bradley was truly impressed. He picked up the one with the scope and looked down the barrel. "Nice." Charlie was signaling, thumbs up.

"It's a date then." Bradley walked away and turned to Roland. "Got to smoke one."

"Go ahead."

Roland walked over to Charlie and they split a headphone. Everyone else in the office had been busy doing other work, and

Trent had been working on a secure connection. Everyone had been oblivious to what Roland and Charlie were doing. Over the headphones, they both heard two clicks. Then Bradley said, "Source 246 emergency, body found. I can provide location. Price: 1 million. Roger." A voice on the other side answered. "One million approved. Meet in Homerville at boarding house, 2pm tomorrow."

"I expect cash on hand. No double cross or tape records, and real estate deals will be revealed."

"No need for threats. All good. Out."

Roland had been beside himself. "I love it when a plan comes together. Please tell me you taped that."

"Roland, you know I did. However, there is no court that will allow it. You had no warrant."

"What about extremes circumstances of ultimate harm."

"What harm?"

"My foot up his ass."

"You are going to need Adams and some creative law. Shut up, here he comes. "Mums the word."

Roland had another one of his brainstorms. "Bradley, why don't you go and keep guard over where that other body is and make sure it remains secure. If you have any problems, call us. I'll feel better if you were there. I think Doc is enjoying the boarding house a little too much."

"Sure, I can do that for you, Roland."

As he drove down the road, Roland looked at the car with all the hatred he could muster up in his eye, and said, "Bastard!" As he walked back into his office, he mentioned to Mildred, "Anything on the property?"

"Roland, it's more confusing than Father's Day at a dog kennel."

"Keep at it. I have faith in you." He walked back to his office to see how everyone else had been doing. Adams had been on the phone, and from the looks of it, he had not had a pleasant conversation. Trooper Jones had been talking to the other troopers to get a lead on the hit man who had been released. Charlie had been tracking down the last meth purchase, and it was out of the county. Dead ends had prevailed. One thing Roland had known was that the last victim had been hidden, and if he could get a legal exhumation, he would be on the winning side. The problem was, there were no witnesses.

Roland went over to Charlie. "Can you get a location on the other caller?"

"No way. He was using a scrambler phone. It sent his signal a million places before I could tag it. What the other person was using is government grade stuff. I do not know who we are dealing with here, but they are ghosts."

"Ghosts? As in?"

"Yes."

"Well, I don't give a damn! The people who died are ghosts too. Charlie, I do not want to get you into trouble, but can you help me?"

"Of course. You know I hate my bosses." Adams had gotten off the phone, and he had been mad. He looked at Roland and said, "Well, I just got fired. It seems the Honorable Jackson told my boss that I did not do a single thing that was asked of me."

Roland looked rather surprised and asked why. "Well, Roland, I was supposed to get dirt on you and pressure you to drop this case or use said dirt to smear you."

"Well, I'll be a monkey's uncle. Who did I piss off?"

"No one. They just don't want the person convicted of the crime to leave death row. You know, the first girl who was killed, and they railroaded him to prison."

"Do they even care if he is innocent?"

"NO." Roland called Mildred and told her to bring the safe box. He looked at Adams and asked him if he needed a job. Adams was surprised, to say the least. "I guess you could say I need a job." Mildred entered the office with a large lockbox and put it on Roland's desk. She then handed him the key. "Do you want me to witness this?" Roland mentioned she had better not know, and she left the office. Roland then called Charlie, Jones, and Adams to his desk. He opened the box and pulled out $2000.00, which he handed to Adams. "Will this be a large enough retainer to take over the appeals of our wrongfully convicted man sitting at Atmore Prison?" All three were shocked. Jones spoke first, "Where did that money come from?"

Roland took his time and explained. "You see, my deputies ran across this money in a drug deal gone bad. We tagged it and marked it as evidence in 1999. Nobody has claimed it. Therefore, under the law, it falls to the jurisdiction of the sheriff's department to be used for legal services and supplies. We have been sitting on this for just the right occasion. Wouldn't you guys say this is the right occasion?"

Adams and Charlie both asked at the same time, "How much is there?"

Roland smiled one of his big smiles, "$350,000.00, give or take."

"Holy shit," Adams had been the first to exclaim, while the others remained speechless. Then Adams said, "I'll file a notice to appear on his behalf. You hired yourself a lawyer. I'm going to love this."

"Now, you can't mention where the funds are coming from. Consider it a gift from a benefactor. That will get the hornets stirring." Mildred knocked and then entered Roland's office. She had the look of the cat that just ate the possum. Roland knew that look and said, "Ok, Mildred, it would appear you have something to say?"

"You bet I do. You know I would never do anything illegal, right? Well, it seems all that land where everything seems to be blowing up or not belongs to the one and only Alex B. Jackson."

Roland was astonished. "How did you find that out?"

"I'd rather not say, and I doubt it will hold up in court."

"Your cousin, wasn't it?"

"As I said, Roland, I'd rather not say."

"Thanks, you can go." As Mildred left the office, everybody looked at each other, and waited for someone to state the obvious. Roland finally spoke up. "I'm going to take a trip to Homerville with a hearse. I will personally escort the remains to Montgomery, and I will take Cobb with me in case there is any trouble. I'm just waiting for an exhumation order from Spurlin. Charlie, I will need your help in Homerville since tomorrow will be a day some people will be meeting. Remember, DOC is on our side, as well as Nelson. And my FBI friend, you have been working on this the longest. I will need you to find out about that old plantation house Jackson owns. I got a feeling there is more on that property than what meets the eye. Get your bosses to help you preserve it for historical reasons. Say I want to dig it up. And my friend, Trooper Jones, we need to follow up on our assassin. You have the picture, and it's confirmed. We need to find him. Coordinate with Mississippi and Louisiana. Oh, I almost forgot. Adams, did you get immunity for George before your termination?"

"Sure did. Last night."

"Then get that to Deputy Cobb right away, and let's see what else we can add to the pot. Also, tell Cobb I need him, and to replace himself with Ann. Well, guys, we are on a crusade, and I pray we prevail. It would seem the powers that be find the poor and helpless a liability. Well, I beg to differ. I believe all life matters and all life deserves protection under the law. Are we in accordance?"

Everybody in the office nodded, and over the telephone speaker, Mildred said, "You damn straight, whoops."

"Mildred."

"Sorry, forgot the speaker was on."

"Yea, right."

Chapter 25

Joey Michaels, McSweeney, or whatever the mechanic had been calling himself, lived in New Orleans on the money he had made doing what he thought was black ops. He had bought a very old building near the French Quarter. It was a two-story brick structure, which he had remodeled under the name Robert Mathews, another alias. During the Prohibition, this structure had been a speakeasy. It had secret corridors and an elaborate basement not shown in the city blueprints. Robert converted the downstairs into two apartments, which he had rented for $2000.00 a month each. Robert had the entire upstairs. One could say this was Robert's lair. The apartments were both 2700 sq. feet and his was 4500 sq. feet. The remaining space he had incorporated into a panic room, reinforced with steel and a passage down to the basement. In the basement, there were three different tunnels through which one could escape to the city. He also kept all his weapons, passports, makeup, and identities he had ever used. He had installed a demolition explosive to wipe out only his place upstairs and collapse the basement without damaging the apartments. He was prepared for an eventual retaliation against him. To get through the front door, there was a video buzz-in panel. If one wished to visit a tenant, he had to buzz the apartment. Each apartment had a video monitor of the front door so the person at the front could be seen. The door was operated on a magnetic lock system, and only the apartment tenants or Robert could release the lock. The security was top notch, a strong selling point to the tenants. The front door was a bulletproof glass door with a steel reinforced frame. One could say it was overkill, but not Robert. To get through, one would have to blow up the lock.

In Robert's business, it paid to be prepared. It had all started simple enough. He had enlisted in the Marines, and at basic training, it had been discovered he was an excellent shot at long and short distances. Weapons came naturally to Robert. He was soon promoted to Special Forces. While in Special Forces, he received numerous medals and recognition. Then one day, the CIA had approached Robert to go dark and work for them. He had agreed. He believed he had been promoting democracy. He had worked for the CIA two years when the NIA (National Intelligence Agency) wanted him to serve. Before he could serve, they had to erase his original name of Joseph Winters. They did this by faking his death in a helicopter accident. That, in a nutshell, was what created the mechanic, except now Robert had questioned his missions. They were supposed to be around domestic terrorism, and he had felt it was way off course. His direct boss, Alex B. Jackson, had asked him to do some very questionable things lately. He saw the innocent face of Ronnie. The kid's only crime had been to be recruited by Jackson. He had followed orders, but Jackson had gone too far, and something had to be done about it. Robert knew it would not be long before he would be getting a call from Jackson, and he had been ready. He now knew that it was Jackson who had killed those girls, and he had been doing Jackson's dirty work, and had covered it up. And he also realized he would take the fall for Ronnie's death. It had been his reason for his quick departure from Alabama. Robert would now turn the tables. He had the resources and several others Mr. Alex had not known about. No more. Not today, tomorrow, not ever. The line in the sand had been drawn. He favored Sheriff Roland, for he had seen him as equal and honest. He knew he would have to contact him, for his life had surely been in danger. The only way Robert could stay safe would be to go deep undercover again and eliminate his threats. It would be ghost time once again, and time to use aliases he had hidden from the agency. The number one threat had been Alex B. Jackson.

Robert had been fixing himself a well-deserved frozen pizza when the phone rang. Robert had three phones, and this had been the secured phone. This meant that Alex had been calling. Before he answered the phone, Robert mumbled, "Let the games begin." Then answered, "Yes." On the other end of the phone, there had been a long pause, and then, "Well, it appears someone has fallen off the reservation. Why did you leave Alabama?"

"I knew I would be hearing from you. Let's just start by asking why you wanted me to be caught!"

"Don't be silly, Joe, or whoever you are now. It was set up clean."

"You and I both know that's a lie."

"You need to go back. Your job is not finished."

"Oh, I'm going back to finish all right."

"And what the hell is that supposed to mean?"

"I think you know. It's really stupid for you to think that I do not really know what's going on here. But, I'll humor you. What do you want?"

"I want the damn job finished. They've got a witness they are protecting. The guard you handsomely paid, and there seems to be question about another body hidden somewhere. This all must go away, and you are going to do it. Do you understand me?"

"The only thing that is going away is going to be you, you sick fuck. I know it was you who killed those girls, and Ed was your cleanup man."

There had been a long pause on the other end of the line. Then, finally, in a casual tone, Alex said, "Why don't you look out your window? See the two black sedans parked across the street?"

Robert, wary, had edged toward the fortified window he had installed to look down at the street in front of his building. Sure enough, there were two black sedans parked across his building. As he looked, a loud splat hit the window where he had been standing. There was a sniper's bullet lodged in the window near where his head had been. He laughed over the phone, and said, "Alex, did you really think it would be that easy? I'm afraid you lose. Watch your back, I'm coming for you. How did you get off on those girls? Did they just laugh at your lack of manhood? Doesn't matter. Your time is now up." He hung up the phone. Two more shots hit the window. Robert had stepped back and had noticed four men in black suits get out of the cars and head for his front door. He went over to the video monitoring system and watched them attempt to break in the front door. They had a time of it when he had seen one pull out some C-4 to blow the lock. He had pushed a button on his console to release a sliding steel door above the glass door, and it had encased the door completely. This did not stop them. They added additional C-4. This had signaled Robert it had been time to get his pizza and go to his panic room. The door to his apartment had reinforced steel, so he knew he had some time. He took one more look to see where the sniper position had been. He raised his arm and made his hand look like a pistol pointed in the direction of the sniper. He pretended to fire twice, then blew off the tip of his finger. The sniper cussed and saw all of this through his scope. Everybody knew Robert's reputation, and this had worried the sniper as he had pulled up his position. Robert went to his hidden switch for the panic room door and opened it. Once through the door, he hit the panic button on the inside and sealed the room, yet another solid steel door slid down into place. He proceeded to the basement. After he went past the first floor, he pushed another button and a steel door slid across the stairs. Once again in the basement, he pushed one more button and another steel door sealed the basement, he now had plenty of time to make his preparations for departure. First, he turned on his surveillance system. There were six monitors. They covered the back, front, entryway, and his living space. He noticed immediately that there had been no one at the front door anymore. He pushed a button to retract the steel door from the front. As the door lifted, he noticed the black SUVs were still out front. Once the steel door had fully retracted, he heard an explosion and had seen that they had blown the front door open. He thought to himself that they were quite persistent. He checked all cameras. The back was clear close to his exit. It was then that he started to put on his disguise. He had decided on the long black hair and a scar prosthetic over his nose to his cheek. This disguise he had not used, therefore, he would be safe from Alex. While he worked on his face, he closely watched the monitors. He saw four men in dark suits enter and work their way to the upstairs. He laughed to himself, as he knew they would have difficulty with his door. He wondered why the tenants had not left their apartments to see what was going on. Must not be home, he had surmised. Almost finished with his disguise, he went over to a rather large wooden cabinet and opened it. Inside were any type of a gun or explosive one would need for a small invasion. He took a duffle bag down and started packing the ordnance he would need. He once again checked the monitor for his apartment and had been pleased to see no one had breached his door yet. Robert worked quickly, gathering everything he felt he would need. To secure the basement, he switched on all the magnetic locks. He then looked around to see if everything had been secure. After finishing his checklist, he looked in the mirror to check his disguise. The mirror reflected an old man hippie with black hair to the shoulders and a face that was scarred on the right side. Robert went to his desk and found the corresponding IDs. Once everything was in hand, he checked the monitors. The back still clear, the front door of his apartment still not breached, and only one person in front, standing by the SUVs. He screwed in the silencer on his 9mm and stuffed it into his pants. He turned off the video system and flicked the switch to allow remote access, and he went to a heavy wooden door to escape.

The door led to a brick incased catacomb. The catacomb led to three different directions. He locked the door and went to the exit where it showed clear. There had been one more door to open. It had steel bars with a heavy padlock keeping it in place. Once through it, he proceeded to the exit. The exit brought him out into an alleyway one half block from his place. He stood in the alley and called the New Orleans Police Department and reported a break-in with the culprits carrying heavy arms. He then made a call to his contractor to let him know someone tried to break in his place and to start repairs as soon as possible. The contractor had been in disbelief, for he had helped construct the re-model. He said, "Somebody had to have a bulldozer?"

"No, explosives. Can you take care of this without question?"

"Be on it in the morning."

He had only one block to go where he had a car stashed in a storage unit. Once in the car, he took off for Alabama.

Chapter 26

R oland awoke with a heavy burden on his mind. Today he would gather the remains of the hidden victim and try to get an exhumation order from the judge. He had to get an autopsy performed that would hold up in court. Also, there had been many players involved: the state trooper, former assistant state attorney, FBI, and the DEA. In his mind, there had been so many possibilities of what could go wrong. Regardless, he would go and remain positive and get it done, hell or high water.

First, he would head toward his office to make sure everyone would be on the same page. Once at the office, Mildred said her regular hello and asked how he was doing. He acknowledged her and went to his office. He looked at his crime board and noticed the spot for the main suspect had been blank. Most of the underlying suspects had been dead. This had bothered him. Then his burner phone rang. Doc would only use this, and he noticed a different number on it. He answered, "Hello."

"You don't know me, or should I say you don't know who I am. I want you to know I am here to help you. I was the one who killed Ronnie, and I have been the one who has hindered your investigation."

"Well, then, why are you calling me now?"

"Let's say my boss has fallen off the reservation and I consider him a very sick and twisted man. He needs to be stopped."

"You have no argument from me. Who is he?"

157

"All in good time. You do not realize how deep you are into a government-sanctioned operation. They will do anything to cover up what they have done. Your life and some of your deputies' lives are in danger. I'm going to make sure no more killing occurs. You see, we have parted ways, and I am now considered expendable and a liability. I must insist that you keep me a private source of information. It is imperative. If they found out I said anything to you, we both would be dead within twenty-four hours. Now look in your upper left-hand drawer. There is a phone there we will talk on from now on. I do not trust the one you use for DOC."

Roland opened the left-handed drawer, and sure enough, there had been a phone. He put it in his pocket. "I guess it would be a stupid question to ask how you got into my office?"

"Yes, it would. Now, it is my understanding you are waiting for Judge Spurlin to give you a warrant for the missing body that was supposed to be cremated and was not. My suggestion is not to wait for the warrant. Go ahead and retrieve the body and take it to Montgomery, and wait for a telephonic warrant. I will call Judge Spurlin and express the urgency. This will be a matter of national security."

"Listen, I don't know who you are except a cold-blooded murderer. Why should I do anything you say?"

"You're right. I am a cold-blooded murderer, but I did it for my country. At least, I thought I was making a difference. I was supposed to be fighting domestic terrorism. Let's just say, in the process, something got exceptionally twisted and I could no longer be a part of senseless killing."

"OK, let's say you're telling the truth. Why not just tell me who is responsible so I can arrest him and be done with it?"

"Because you would be dead and I would be on the run. Although, I am on the run already. Let me tell you this, your sheriff from Homerville is already missing. Check it out. He should not have tried to extort money for the location of the girl's remains. And if he knew, your time is short. They would have most definitely gone to the site to remove what was there. You need to get moving and stay well armed. These guys do not play."

"Wait, what do I call you?"

"You once called me Michael McSweeney, but the troopers are all over that. Can I trust you?"

"Yes, you have my word. And my word is golden. Ask anyone."

"Your reputation is intact. Call me Cody. Now get moving with Cobb to Homerville and get that body out of there. I will be in touch on the phone I gave you. By the way, your office is bugged." Roland plopped in his chair, "Well, I'll be damned." He got on the phone and called for Mildred to come to his office. Once she had entered, he made gestures so she would realize the office had been bugged. She then spoke up, "Coffee? You know I should make you get your own coffee."

"No, I already had my coffee. I was wondering if you could get your cousin down here to my office to revamp the phone and intercom system he promised to work on a month ago?"

"Now, Roland, you know all well and good, he prom…oh, that's right. I forgot. I'll have him on it tomorrow."

"What's wrong with now?"

"Oh, well, I guess I will just have to give him a call. You know how busy he is."

"Sure, that ankle bracelet he's wearing really ties him down. Tell him I will have it turned off for the duration. No need to call him. Why don't you just go over and get him?"

"No need to be testy. Oh, I see. I'm not punching out for the trip."

"Of course not. I will be going over to the judge's office to get that warrant." Mildred left the office, and Roland had to come up with a whole new strategy. He would take the advice of this McSweeney character. Oddly enough, it made a whole lot of sense and explained a whole lot more. First, he would make a call to Trooper Jones, bugs, or not.

"Hey, Jones, my buddy. Got a favor to ask you. Need you to drop the APB on Michael McSweeney. For one thing, his name has changed, and another, I believe he is a ghost. We would be chasing our tails. I need, however, many cars you can spare over to Homerville. The sheriff there has met an untimely end. We need to make ourselves known in the area. I will be there as fast as my jeep will get me there. Cobb, poor guy, will be driving a hearse."

"Damn, Roland, what's up with the change? I am going to have to move a lot of people around."

"That's true, and I would like to see a lot of them on 231, the route to Montgomery."

"Is there something you are not telling me?"

"Yep, sure enough. I will talk to you face-to-face in Homerville, and DOC, if we can get him out of the boarding house."

Trooper Jones began to laugh, "I'll be there."

Meanwhile, Adams would begin to meet with his client on death row in Atmore prison. Atmore was a rather large prison. It housed about 5000 inmates, not including the ones on death row. Death row was a private area there for condemned inmates with a private exercise yard. Once the inmate had been escorted to a secluded room, shackled from hands to ankles, he had been seated at a table across from Adams. After the inmate had been chained to the table, the guards left the room.

Adams opened up and said, "I'm Adams, former assistant state attorney, and I know you are innocent of the crime you were convicted of."

The inmate just looked at him for a moment and spoke with a lisp through the three teeth he had left in his mouth. "Well, I'll be damned! You mean I didn't kill that little girl?"

"No, sir, you didn't. Did you think you did?"

"Back in those days, I was a dedicated alcoholic. I couldn't tell you what I did from one day to the next. Mostly, I panhandled for alcohol. And when they told me I killed that poor little girl, I assumed I did it. Hell, her blood was all over me."

Adams replied, "I believe in a drunken stupor, you fell over the girl, and in an awkward attempt to get up, you just smeared her blood on your body. There was no murder weapon, and I must say, you were in no condition to make the precise blow that caused her death. No, sir, you are innocent, and I want to appear on your behalf on an appeal for a re-trial. I believe you were railroaded into this conviction. Will you sign these papers to allow me to represent you?"

"What these thangs say? You know I can't read nor write."

"Did they read you your confession when they had you sign it?"

"No, sir, they just said sign here and here and here. It seemed to go on forever. Next thing the judge said I was to be electrocuted till dead, and may God have mercy on my soul."

"I know this is hard for you, but please sign here and here. I am going to get you out of jail for good."

"Not trying to be rude, but sir, where will I live? Before, I lived on the streets."

"I promise I will find you a place and a job. You are all cleaned up now. Right?"

"Yes, but who's to say I won't go back to the way I was."

"I will."

"What makes you say all that?"

"I care for justice, and you have been done wrong in the worst sense of wrong. I want to make the real murderer pay for the crime to that little girl." The inmate had been bewildered by this man and responded. "I have been on the streets all my life, and this is the first time I have had three squares a day and a bed. Can you promise me that?"

"I can promise you I will not kill you in a month. Have you forgotten that? You are to be sentenced to death in one month. Is that what you want?"

"I forgot about that. Well, you seem to care. I signed the papers. Do what you may. I have been Black all my life, and if you think those White people who put me here are going to just roll over, you got another thing coming. I'm used to being beaten and starved. That has been my life. White people just don't care for Black people, and you are White."

"We are not all the same. And this White person is going to set you free. Will that be ok for you?"

"Just don't lie to me."

"I won't. I will be filing the papers you signed today and get a stay of execution and petition for a re-trial. Also, there might not be a need for a re-trial if Roland gets his way."

"You said Roland, the sheriff. Now I know I will get a fair shake. He has been nothing but kind to me. Roland is a stand-up man. And I mean a real man. You just gave me something I can hold on to. Thanks, Mr. Adams." Inmate Thaddeus sat for a moment and looked straight in the eyes and asked Adams, "Why do you want to help this Black man?"

Adams had not been prepared for a question like this, but responded, "I don't care that you're Black. I care for what's right, and what's happening here is not at all right."

The inmate was escorted to his cell, while Mr. Adams sat there and contemplated on how twisted the justice system was and how he would get it back into balance. This would be a long journey, and he would be prepared. First, he needed to file the papers at the county court and the appeals court. He immediately stood up and headed for the exit when two guards greeted him.

One guard stood in his way and said, "What you think you goin' to do with that nigger? We lookin' forward to his BBQ next month. You ain't trying to prevent that, are ya?"

Then the other guard said, "You know, it ain't healthy for one to meddle into other affairs. One could get hurt or even have an accident on the road. Long way to the courthouse."

"Gentlemen, I'm sure you want to see justice here. You know this man is innocent."

The first guard said, "Innocent, hell. That boy is guilty as sin. He is going to fry like a chicken in a vat of grease."

"Well, I see your point. If you would please let me pass. I will discuss your sentiments to the people who care."

"Damn straight you will. Be careful driving. Hate to see anything happen to you." They both laughed, with no smile in their eyes.

Chapter 27

R oland had been on his way to Homerville at a rapid clip when he got pulled over by state trooper. Roland cussed under his breath, pulled over, and waited for the officer to come to his car. Once the officer came to his window, Roland handed him his badge and asked him if he cared to escort him at a quicker pace. The officer looked at the badge and remembered what his boss, Jones, had announced. He quickly apologized, returned the badge, and said, "Follow me."

He ran to his car, flipped on the sirens, and hit the road. He radioed Roland, "Where to?" Roland said the mausoleum.

Doc had been at the boarding house when he had heard all the sirens. He figured something had been up, but he had been indisposed with CoCo. He quickly put on his clothes and ran two doors where Nelson had been and banged on the door. A faint voice on the other side said, "Nobody's home." Doc got pissed off and yelled, "Nelson, hurry, we have an emergency!" Then immediately, there had been a ruckus and things being shoved about. Finally, Nelson said, "On my way," then a loud noise like someone had fallen. Doc busted the door down to see Nelson on the floor with his pants down to his ankles; he had tried desper- ately to pull them up. His lady companion had attempted to help him along. Once all the clothes were on, Doc and Nelson had run down to Doc's car to go to the mausoleum. That was until Nelson said, "Let's take my truck. Your car is shit." With no room to argue,

Doc agreed. They got into Nelson's truck and sped off with the two girls having waved bye from the boarding house door.

When they arrived at the mausoleum, Roland and two state trooper cars were parked there, along with two unmarked vehicles. Nelson and Doc ran to the place where only they knew where the body had been stashed, and it was untouched. They then went where they confided to the sheriff where Nelson had put the body. Jones, DEA, FBI, and Johnny the radio station owner-apparently, Johnny had been monitoring the radio traffic and had the jump on everybody. He would get his story, do or die. They all looked at a smashed-in tombstone marker and a coffin within the tomb. It appeared it had been taken out and then shoved in haphazardly. The grave robbers had not found what they had been looking for. Roland turned to Doc, "I thought I told you to keep a close eye here!"

Nelson interjected, "Good God, Roland, short of putting a sleeping bag out here, I could not have been any closer. We both knew the body in question was safe."

"And how did you know that?"

"Well, Mr. Smarty Pants, when would you like it loaded?" At that time, Cobb pulled up in a hearse. Roland cooled down and looked at Doc. "Well, Doc, I guess you did a good job." Nelson got upset and spoke up, "What the hell am I, chopped liver? You arrogant ass. I was the one who kept this under wraps and didn't trust the sheriff. If it weren't for me, that body would be gone. What do you think about that?"

"Nelson, I must admit I underestimated you. I'm positive you and Doc had matters under control. I apologize."

"That's better. Now we best get that body loaded before any more of these assholes tear up my property." Roland looked around the surrounding area and thought he saw the reflection of some binocular glasses, or worse yet, the scope of a rifle. "Everybody move quickly into the mausoleum. Now! Run! As soon as he said it, a bullet shot sounded, and it tore at Roland's sleeve. Had he not moved when he did, he would have surely had a fatal wound. Another shot had sounded, and there was a scream in the direction of the first shot. A body tumbled down the hill. FBI

Agent Trent Mathews looked at Roland, "What you got, a guardian angel?" Right then, Cody had called on the burner phone. Before Roland answered it, he barked orders to see who that was up there. Roland answered with a quickness, "I supposed that was you covering my ass?"

"You only got one hour. I would suggest getting that body now and head down the road. It's not going to be an easy trip. Use the trooper escort. Stay low with the FBI. And use the hearse as a decoy. What I mean is, put the body in your friend's trunk. You know, the DEA dude. Throw the coffin they already dug up into the hearse and sneak the real body into his trunk. You follow him and let the hearse lead with two trooper cars while y'all drag. Got it?"

"Like it. Just have to get my buddy on the same page."

"Tell him it came from the mechanic. He'll agree."

"So, you are a popular guy."

"I'll be watching your back."

"Cobb, load the coffin into the hearse now. We might get fibers."

Cobb looked at him closely. "Is there something I need to know?"

"Yes, I want you in full riot gear. That includes a bulletproof vest and helmet. You are going to be my sitting duck. I need you to be especially observant." Cobb had never seen Roland so serious and followed his orders to the tee.

"Doc, Nelson, and Mr. DEA, with me." Roland eased away from everyone and instructed Doc and Nelson to sneak the body to Charlie's trunk. No objections were made. All had been done and nobody was the wiser.

Roland called over to Doc. "Ok, Doc, how much money you got left?"

"How much you give me?"

"Now, you know it was five hundred plus expenses. I understand it's $25 a night, plus meals." Doc interrupted, "I had to put up a $300.00 deposit for damages, refundable of course."

"So, I guess I owe you some more money? I need you to stay a little longer."

"But, Roland, this is a hard job. I'm going to need a $35.00 per diem."

"Ok." Roland dug in his pocket and handed him $700.00 more in cash. Don't think I'm completely stupid. I know you are partaking of some companionship."

"Not me Roland. Now Nelson is another story. I get mine free. CoCo and I kind of hit it off in a good way."

"Holy shit, who would have thunk it?" Roland had gathered everybody together to go over the game plan. "Jones, I want two trooper cars leading the hearse and one tailing. I will be towards the back for support. Charles will be riding with me and we will have heavy ordnance, like grenade launchers, MI6s, three AR15s with bump stocks, and a case of tear gas and stun grenades. Jones, I want you in front of me. FBI Trent, I need you and your two men to scout ahead and clear the way. Once we hit Montgomery, I will need you to pull your influence on the city cops to stop traffic so we have a clear shot to the morgue. And have your other agent run drag behind the hearse. Any questions?"

Trent, not used to being bossed by a sheriff, said, "Who got shot up on that hill?"

"The bullet was meant for me. Someone doesn't want this body to make it to the morgue. It just so happens I do have a guardian angel, and I will disclose him later. Right now, we need to buckle up and roll. I'm not sugarcoating it when I say there are some strong forces stacked up against us. And I must admit they are just following orders. They think this is a national security issue. And we all know it's a pervert in the highest degree. Let's not let whoever it is get away with the killing and molesting of our youth. Let's rock and roll!"

Trent had looked at Jones and Jones had looked at Cobb. "Rock and roll? What the fuck?" They all had shaken their heads and went to their vehicles. Doc ran over to Roland to look at where he had been struck with the bullet. There had been a scant amount of blood flow from the wound and his shirt had been ripped. Doc grabbed Roland by the other arm and said, "You are not going anywhere until I dress that wound." Roland had begun to object, but he saw Nelson had walked over with some gauze in his hand. "OK, damn it, make it quick. I don't need to see all this fuss over a scratch." When Doc had removed the shirt covering the wound, he had noticed that the bullet had made a deep furrow through the top layer of the skin. Knowing Roland wouldn't get stitches, he applied Steri-Strips and some super glue to hold the skin together. He cleaned the wound with peroxide and wrapped it extensively with the gauze. He asked Roland if he had another shirt, to which he had said no. "Here, wear mine and I'll wear yours. Might get some sympathy at the house." They switched shirts and now everybody began to take off. Jones yelled out, "Will he live, Doc?" to which Doc replied, "He's too ornery to die." They all had a good belly laugh on that one, and began their trip to Montgomery. There would be a total of six cars making the trip to Montgomery. Roland's jeep carried the original body covered up with a hunter's blanket. Cobb drove the hearse with one of Jones' troopers. Then there were two trooper cars and two unmarked FBI cars. All appeared to be safe, and if anybody tried to intervene, there would be a substantial firefight.

Doc had been at the boarding house, relaxing with an ice-cold Budweiser. He truly loved his role in this covert operation till now. CoCo ran up to him and told him to follow her quickly. Doc got up immediately and followed CoCo out the back door. She pointed out two black SUVs with four people in each, all wore suits, and packed up what appeared to be small arms and a grenade launcher. There was a clothesline where they were, so their presence had not been easily detected. Without drawing attention to themselves, they had started taking down some sheets and brought them into the house. Doc turned to CoCo and said, "When did you notice them?"

"Right after everybody left for Montgomery."

"Well, we got a shitstorm now. My car won't make it in time. I need to call Roland now. Going to need to have some privacy, baby." CoCo left the room, and Doc called Roland. There had been no answer. He tried again and again. By this time, the black cars were well gone. Doc became worried as to what to do.

Doc couldn't get through because Roland had been talking to Cody. Cody had informed him he had a leak in the caravan. So, Roland and his rider Nelson had concocted an idea that just might work. At the Greenville Junction, Roland would veer off on the old moonshine roads. Charlie now spoke up, "Now I see why we loaded the jeep instead of my squad car. You know, Roland, you have a half-size brain sometimes."

"We can't let the others know. At the fork in the road, we will make a sharp left and punch it down the ravine. There we'll hide behind those logger trucks that have been there forever. I'll radio Jones and we will meet him there to tell him we are going a different route. In the meantime, I'll get with Cody to kidnap the coroner so he can do an autopsy where no one will suspect. Right then, Roland got on the phone to Cody. "I need you to kidnap the coroner and secure a lab where we can conclusively prove it was a certain person who perpetrated these crimes."

"Oh, is that all?"

"Well, I didn't say it was going to be easy,"

"Just do your part. I have already got it handled. And don't fuck up."

Chapter 28

S enator Jackson had been in his private office, adjacent to his main office, going over reports of the happenings in Hope. Nothing had gone as planned. In fact, what could go wrong did go wrong, and now he had lost one of his best agents to the other side. His attempt to kill Robert in New Orleans had been a debacle, to say the least. Hell, his agents could not even breach his apartment before the New Orleans PD had arrived. He used the National Security Investigation as an excuse. But since he had no warrants, the NOPD had escorted them off the premises. The icing on the cake was there was a body intact that Ed Dixon had not disposed of. As he had read each of these reports, he put them through a paper shredder. A secure phone rang. "Yes?"

"This is Agent Williams, and they are moving the body to Montgomery. It's going to be a caravan of cars. FBI, DEA, state troopers, and Roland himself, is accompanying them."

"I thought Roland was supposed to be dead."

"He was hit, but non-life threating. The shooter was killed with a single shot through the head."

"It looks like Roland is getting some help. We got our boys following?"

"Yes, sir, eight agents in two cars about four miles back."

"Ok, let's close the gap. Do they have the papers from Judge Spurlin?"

"Yes, sir, but not signed."

"Hell, you sign them. Go ahead and pursue and close the distance, and when you get to a sparsely populated area, pull them over and show them the papers. Tell them they need to turn around; that what they are doing is illegal, and if they fail to comply, deadly force will be the only option. Also, get somebody to track the GPS on Roland's phone. I want no surprises."

"Yes, sir."

Roland had received a call on his regular phone and it had been Judge Spurlin. "Roland, what have you got yourself into? Senator Jackson called my office to squash the order to exhume the body in question."

Roland, nervous about his phone, had asked the judge to call back on the phone Cody gave him. The judge had complied. "I must say, there is a lot of cloak and dagger going on here."

"Judge, if you only knew. Do I have my telephonic exhumation order for this Jane Doe? Judge, you do not realize how important it is we find out if this girl correlates with the previous killings. We have a serial killer that dates to the 1970s. Please say yes, Judge."

"Roland, Senator Jackson has considerable influence in this area and elsewhere. He almost threatened me if I issue the order. Son, you need to realize your evidence is slim and none. I have to be a fool to issue you the order. And a fool I am. I'm texting it to this number, I guess?"

"Oh, thank you, God!"

"I'm not God. Good luck, you are going to need it."

It could not have been more perfect timing. The fork in the road was just around the bend. Roland, being the last car, had swerved off the road and took the dirt road in the fork. It had been a perfect departure, for the car ahead of Roland had not noticed he had left the road. Charles spoke up to Roland, "Hey I think it's wise to turn off your phone. They can track your GPS, and we will be found."

"Charles, I'm so glad you are with us." Roland turned off his phone. In the passenger seat, Nelson loaded his shotgun. Charles checked his loads in his 9mm. Then he peeked under the blanket covering the body. It had been spooky how well-preserved the body had been. He mentioned that fact to Nelson. Nelson told

Charles how he had been a taxidermist also. The road they had been traveling was exceptionally bumpy. Charles spoke up, "Damn, Roland, are you trying to hit every hole?"

"You city boys need to get out in the country more often. How about you, Nelson?"

"Hell, this is smooth as a baby's ass."

"Y'all are crazy."

They all laughed.

Adams had been at the appeals court, filing his notice to represent Jacob Thaddeus Jackson for the charge of murder. When the clerk noticed the name on the appeal, he had told Adams to wait just a moment. Within a minute, his old boss had come around the counter. "Why don't you come to my office?"

"Why don't you go to hell?" The clerk watched this with a hint of satisfaction. He disliked the state attorney.

"I don't see why we can't be civil here."

"You mean when you wanted me to smear a good man upholding the law? And when I refused to do such an unethical act, you fired me? Now, if you will get your ugly ass out of my way, I have some papers to file legally. You understand doing things legally?"

"Do what you got to do. I must say, you are out of your league here. I hope you are prepared."

"If you mean I'm paid off by illegal means and breaking my oath to the bar association, then yes, I'm prepared. Because I've done none of those things like you. Now if you will please move your crooked ass out of my way." The clerk couldn't hide the grin on his face when his boss had retreated back to his office. Adams handed the papers to the clerk to get stamped. "Could I get three copies of the notices? I would hate for them to get lost in a paper shuffle."

"I understand completely, Mr. Adams. I will personally deliver to Judge Macalister your notice to represent and the appeal for a new trial. I must say, this is exciting. I have never heard anybody talk to the boss that way. Thank you for making my day."

"I aim to please. Be sure those papers go on top of the pile. They plan to kill my client in a month."

"You should have said so." He got another stamp along with the date stamp, which printed out "URGENT" in red. "There, that should do it."

"Thank you. What's your name?"

"James Rowell, and I'm glad to be of service."

Roland had finally reached the end of the dirt road. Before him was the paved road to take him to Selma. Charles had been a hot mess. On the dirt road, Roland appeared to have hit every mud hole and bump, tossing Charles all over the back seat. Nelson loved the ride and had been ready to go again. Roland had a wide smile on his face when he checked on Charles. Doc's phone began to ring. Roland answered it quickly. "Hello."

"Roland, Doc. I have been trying to reach you for thirty minutes."

"You got me. What's up?"

"Right after y'all left, eight guys in two black cars followed you."

"It's ok, Doc, I was expecting that. Has anyone found the sheriff? And did y'all get an identity on the shooter?"

"The sheriff's deputies were on the scene right after you left. The body had no ID, and his fingerprints were burnt off. They are still out there trying to figure out the path of the other shot. Whoever shot him was good. He popped him right between the eyes. Oh, nobody has seen the sheriff."

"You did good, Doc. Hang in there till you hear from me again. Ok?"

"Sure thing, Roland. I kind of like this place."

"Bet you do. Bye."

Charles had finally gained his composure and said, "Roland, we need to pull over and let me get rid of my DEA phone. It can be traced through GPS. Even if I have the phone off, it can be accessed remotely for location."

"All right, Charles. Just up the road is a gas station where I'm going to fuel up. May I suggest you stash it in somebody's car going South."

"Cool. Well, let's get going."

Roland jumped out of the woods and hit the paved road with a quickness. It was just a mile up, and they pulled over for gas. Roland went in to pay while Charles pumped the gas. Nelson stepped out of the jeep and held his shotgun under his right arm. They looked like what one would see if an armored car had been present. As he finished up the gas, Charles checked out tags. He wanted to find one with the Mobile prefix. He found one, and he proceeded to it to place his phone on it. The phone had a magnetic back, so it easily stuck under the back bumper. Just as he had finished, a man came toward him. He spoke up, "Hey, what are you doing to my car?"

Charles flashed him his badge and asked, "Where are you heading?"

"Mobile, what's going on?"

"Your car looked like one that was stolen. I checked further and this is not the stolen car. My apologies."

"Ok. No problem. May I go?"

"Sure, sorry for the mix-up."

That having been said, the man got in his car and headed south to Mobile. Charles wiped a little sweat off and told Roland what he did. Nelson just observed with the shotgun securely at his side. "Alright, guys, let's hit it." Soon they were all in the jeep and headed north to Selma.

Chapter 29

T he two black SUVs finally caught up with Trent and Cobb, and drove patiently till the highway split into four lanes. Once the four-lane appeared, they popped on their lights and sirens and proceeded to pull over the caravan of the hearse, trooper car, FBI Trent's car, and Jones. Once everyone was on the shoulder of the road, one black SUV was at the front and the other at the rear. The first out of his car was FBI Trent. The second was Trooper Jones. The four men in the front SUV all exited at the same time in a tactical position and carried machine guns around their shoulders. Trent's passenger was a fellow agent he had brought along for backup. They would find out later he was the leak to opposition. The men from the SUVs spread out to cover all vehicles, and one of them had approached Trent. "I have a court order here in my hand for this party to end forthwith." He handed the paper to Trent, who immediately looked at it very carefully. Meanwhile, Cobb had signaled Roland on his police radio while they had been stopped. Cobb and Roland had secretly used Morse code, and he had been tapping away. Roland had been on the road when he heard the code coming through. He immediately pulled off and started to decipher what had been said while Nelson and Charles remained silent, not understanding what had been transmitted. The passenger with Cobb looked at him queerly, a perplexed look to his face. Trent finally looked up to the man who had detained them and said, "Well, I guess this is all in order. Are you going to take the hearse?" The man in the suit replied that was exactly what he would do. Trent looked to his fellow FBI agent and asked, "I wonder how they knew where we were and what we were doing? You wouldn't happen to know, Joe?

Joe looked at Trent with a little indignation and said, "These guys are with Homeland Security, and I felt it my obligation, sir."

"Well, Joe, I feel it's now my obligation to tell you that you are now assigned to the desk at Montgomery. And I promise you, that's where you will stay."

Joe, confused, thought he had done the right thing. Boy, would he be sorely mistaken. Doug Jones exited his trooper car and walked up to Trent. "What the fuck is going on here?"

Trent tried to remain composed and said, "It seems I had a snitch, and now we have to head back to Hope."

The man in the suit suddenly asked, "Where is Sheriff Roland? And I do believe DEA agent Charles is with him also?" Everybody had been tightlipped and volunteered no information. Cobb exited the hearse and overheard the question; he said, "Oh, he decided to go fishing for corrupt officials who are guilty of obstructing justice. I believe that would mean nothing you know about."

The man in the suit ordered one of his men to get in the hearse, and told the rest of the people they could proceed back to Hope. After that comment, Trent interjected emphatically, "Don't forget to take Joe here. He no longer has a ride with me, nor is he to be around me. Thanks." With that last comment, the two black SUVs and the hearse drove off up the road to Montgomery with Joe. The lead man in a suit pulled out his secured cell to inform the senator of a successful capture of the body without complications. It only took a moment, and the senator was on the other end. "So, you got the body? Was Roland with them, and did you check the body?"

"Well, sir, not yet. We just separated from them. And neither Roland nor DEA Charles was with them."

"Damn it! Pull over and check the body now! I will stay on the line."

Immediately they all pulled over, and some agents approached the hearse to satisfy their curiosity. One of the agents asked, "Why are we stopping?"

"The lead man responded quickly, "We have to check the body."

That being said, they opened the back of the hearse and rolled the casket back so they could raise the lid. Once opened, the contents revealed the body of an old man. The lead man had been noticeably upset. He immediately went back to the phone to respond to the senator. "Sir, it looks like there is an old man in the casket." The senator was outraged. "Damn it, man! Roland has the body. This was a decoy. You say Charles was traveling with him?"

"Yes, sir."

"Well, they might not be that smart. You got that cell GPS tracker in your car?"

"Yes, sir."

"Hold on for a sec." The senator fumbled through some of his classified correspondences and finally came across what he had been looking for. "Here we go. Write down this numerical code: 1425697. Key that in your GPS tracker. It will pinpoint where Charles is. All DEA agents have an emergency tracker in their phones so they can be found. I'll wait."

He followed the instructions and the agent went to his car and engaged the tracker. He entered the code given, and within moments, it showed the phone moving south to Mobile. He related the information to the senator. The senator, feeling pleased with himself for being smarter than the sheriff, said, "Well, I guess you know now where you are going. Dump the hearse back where it came from. Now posthaste, you and four agents hit your way after that signal. Use all discretionary measures at your disposal. They must not reach Mobile, but if they get there, I will activate our assets in Mobile. Keep me informed. We cannot allow this exposure to happen. I hope you understand?"

"Yes, sir. We are on it now." He hung up and relayed the new orders. Everyone proceeded to their destination.

It took a moment for Roland to explain what the message was from Cobb. "Well, guys, it seems we have played our cards right. Heavily armed men intercepted the caravan to Montgomery, and they took the hearse. One nice note is they didn't bother to see who was in the casket. That will give us some extra time. Also, the informant was the one of Trent's agents. Charles, they also know you are with me. Good thinking on moving the phone. Maybe they will take the bait and head South."

Charles thought about it for a moment and said, "Not until they realize they are traveling with the wrong body. Oh, I wish I could be there to see the looks on their faces." Nelson showed concern on his face and said, "Roland, these boys have some serious intel. I suggest we haul ass to Selma. This can turn sour quickly. I want what I protected so long to point out the culprit. By God, we have to make this happen and happen now. It appears we are working against a stacked deck. Time to git it done." Everyone agreed. Roland was amazed at Nelson's foresight. He then popped lights on and hit the road with burning rubber.

Thirty minutes later, Roland and company arrived at the Selma mortuary. Outside, three men with lab coats stood next to a gurney. Roland first exited the Jeep and introduced himself while Nelson and Charles got out. "Roland Smith, here with Charles from the DEA and Nelson, who we have to thank for the preservation of the body." Dr. Wilkins replied, "I'm Dr. Wilkins, and these young men are my trusted assistants, Joseph and William. I received a rather detailed phone call about the importance of this autopsy. I realize that it is highly classified. I want you to know there will be no leak from this end. Now, can we get the remains on the gurney?"

Roland opened the back of the jeep, along with Charles and Nelson, and revealed the body of the young girl tightly sealed in her plastic wrap. They transferred the body to the gurney. All eyes stared at the body in amazement. The body had been well preserved, and Dr. Wilkins had to ask, "Who prepared the remains in such a fashion? I'm not complaining. I'm just amazed since it is over 7 years old."

Nelson felt proud and responded, "That would be me. At the time, I found the situation of this girl's poor death to be of a fishy nature. I preserved the body as best as I know how, and hid the remains until some honest people came along to find the sick bastard who did this." The doctor had taken two steps back and went around the body. He looked at every aspect of the encasing. He instructed his assistant to get the body inside. He responded quickly. He turned to Roland and Charles and stated, "I believe there is a lot of heat following y'all. The only thing I can promise you is that we can document as much evidence as we can here. This facility has some very impressive equipment to allow us toxic screening and DNA. I feel that it will be important to get these results ASAP. The caller, who I know is a consummate professional and has the highest clearance of any of my contacts; I do not want to know y'all's relationship, for it will not help me. The one thing I do know is that I will have to get back to Montgomery rather quickly, as to not raise any suspicion."

Roland knew who he thought the caller was and asked, "Was it Robert, then, who called you?"

"No, it was Joey Michaels. I have known him for over twenty years, and I know he ranks high with the NSA." Roland acknowledged the statement, and all went inside. The answer given to Roland had been as confusing as the help he had been getting from Robert. Perhaps these were all the same person? Charles looked just as confused, and Nelson didn't give a shit. He just wanted to know if what he did to preserve the body worked. The body had been taken into an examining room and Roland, Nelson, and Charles were not let in. Roland had asked Nelson to keep an eye outside for anything peculiar. Now it was time to hurry up and wait.

Meanwhile, the driver with Charles' stashed phone on his car headed for Mobile. He had decided to pull off at an Indian casino at the Atmore exit. The driver, Willy, loved to gamble, and had seen this as a great opportunity. He had also been paranoid about his car and where he parked. He had always thought someone would steal his car. He had equipped it with a cell and lock jammer so no one could remotely access his car. When he had exited the car, he turned on the jammer and was ready to gamble. With the car locked up tightly and the jammer working, he thought this was going to be his lucky day. As soon as he turned on the jammer, the suits in the black SUVs lost the signal. They had been some seventy miles behind. The lead suit had cussed, and the others all had been in consensus. *Well, what now?* The lead suit had thought for a moment and then explained to the others. "Guys, they have been one step ahead of us all the way. I believe Roland is getting help. Hell, he should have been dead at Homerville; instead, one of ours is. It seems at every turn, we are behind. Well, not anymore. The senator said he was going to alert the Mobile assets. Charles must have remembered he could be tracked. Now we will just pick up the pace to Mobile. Oh, where was it we lost the signal?"

"Sir, it was at Atmore."

"Shit, no one in their right mind would stop there, especially with a body. Hell, no. That's when they noticed they were being tracked. We got them now. They're not so smart. Gentlemen, I do believe we've got them now."

Dr. Wilkins walked out of the examining room to speak to Roland and Charles. He looked at them both, and had an odd smile on his face. "I do not know where you guys got this Nelson fellow, but he was a Godsend. No evidence we were able to retrieve was contaminated. In fact, it was in pristine condition. This guy has a career in forensic science."

Roland, rather anxious, had stated, "We will tell him you said so. Well, Doctor, in comparing the files I gave you and what you have on the table, tell me, are they the same?"

"Roland, they were done by the same person. I would not hesitate to say this is part of a serial killing. DNA is processing now. We found several places the DNA samples were deposited, one of which was the anus. Due to the age of the remains, it's hard to determine if it was deposited post mortem or not. We do know this body is a treasure trove of evidence. We have yet to scratch the surface. And don't tell me our time is limited. I thought I would give you a preliminary. Now, you will have to excuse me. I need to dictate the additional findings, and I will give you a copy of the tape as well as the paperwork that is required. One last thing, whoever did this has done it more than three times. It's obvious because of his brazen nature of attack. Y'all, catch this guy. He will not stop until he is caught. And he is one sick son of a bitch." With that said, the doctor walked back into the exam area. Roland looked at Charles. They both were sickened, but they seemed to raise to high-five each other because they knew they would catch the guy.

Willy walked out of the casino as one happy person. He was richer by $3500.00 he had won at the blackjack table. He headed for his car. He switched off the jamming device and entered the car. He would now be on his way to Mobile with a rather large and satisfying smile on his face. This was the first time he had won so big. He peeled out of the parking area and headed toward the interstate to go South.

The suits, already in Mobile, had been disgusted they could not pick up any signal until the tracking device started pinging again. The one monitoring the device had yelled, "We got him!"

The lead suit said, "What the hell do you mean?"

"I'm not sure, but the signature ping just reappeared, and it's at Atmore, heading South."

"Alright, guys, we need to backtrack to the exits entering Mobile. What's his rate of speed?"

"Looks like he's taking the limit, around 75mph."

"Good, that give us an hour to get in place. We will use the Pritchard exit. I cannot stress enough, Roland cannot get past us." The suits proceeded to their lookout positions. Willy, oblivious, had his radio blaring and was the happiest man on earth, not knowing what would be waiting ahead for him.

Chapter 30

W illy had only been ten miles out from Mobile, and his happiness had not diminished. He calculated how he would
spend the money or just save it for his next trip to the casino. He
had gone under the overpass to the Pritchard exit when he had
noticed in his rearview mirror a dark black SUV tailing him very
closely. His happiness turned to worry. Was somebody going to
rob him? Had they seen him leaving the casino? Why were they
so close? Then he saw blue lights coming from inside the vehicle's window and heard a siren. He eventually pulled over to the
side of the interstate. Through his rearview mirror, he saw four
men in black suits exit the car behind him. This made him very
nervous. One of the suits tapped his window, which he quickly
rolled down. Willy noticed the man in the suit was heavily armed.
He could see the guns under the suit. Silence was broken when
the man in the suit told Willy to exit the vehicle. He didn't want
to disobey, so he immediately got out of the car. He had been
instructed to go to the back of the car, where he was handcuffed,
and told to lie face down on the hood. The man with the tracker
went throughout the vehicle. The signal was strong. Finally, the
lead suit asked Willy, "Do you know a sheriff named Roland, or
a DEA agent named Charles?"

"No, sir. But there was a man looking over my car at Greenville.
He said he thought it was stolen."

"What did he look like, and was there anybody else with him?"

"Why yes, now that you mentioned it. There was a rather lanky man carrying a shotgun and another fellow in a sheriff's outfit. The guy I talked to was casually dressed and flashed a badge at me. I thought nothing about it since I knew it was my car."

The lead suit looked at another suit and told him to pop the trunk. The opened trunk revealed an extreme amount of women's lingerie. Willy looked embarrassed and scrambled to explain the clothing. "I'm a salesman, you see. Perhaps you would like to take something home to the missus?"

The lead suit was not amused. The tracker started to make repeated noise at the rear bumper. The man with the tracker reached under the bumper to remove the phone, which had been lodged there by Charles. Willy immediately sounded off, "What the fuck. That's not mine. Who would do such a thing? This is not right. I want a lawyer. Somebody is going to pay!" The lead suit pulled his gun from under his jacket and stuck the barrel under Willy's chin.

"There are a couple of things you need to know and remember if you care to live. Nod if you understand." As Willy nodded, he lost control of his water and peed down his leg. He was completely petrified. The lead suit continued, "You have not seen us, nor you do not remember the event in Greenville, nor do you even have any idea what any of us looks like. If I hear anything about this coming from your mouth, it will be sealed permanently. Do you understand me?"

"Yes."

"You might want to change your pants and get in your car. Remember, nothing or you're dead." Right then, the suits got in their car with Charles' cell and peeled out across the median, heading north to Greenville. All had been cussing in the car for being taken as fools. Willy just stood by his car, unable to move, until a passing car honked at him. The honk brought him back from what he had felt was his worst nightmare ever. He immediately changed his pants from a suitcase he had in the backseat, and resumed his course to Mobile, visibly shaken.

Roland and Charles sat patiently when the burner phone from Doc rang. Roland answered, "Talk to me."

Doc, on the other end, gave his update, "The hearse is back, along with everybody who went to escort. Trent is fit to be tied. One of his agents was a leak for the other side, and they were ambushed some twenty miles from Montgomery. Trooper Jones is not happy either. I would say the plan failed."

"Doc, quite the contrary. I need you to tell Jones to gas up the hearse and pick up the body at the Selma coroner's office now. We have gotten all the evidence to vindicate our man at Atmore prison. I will get with Adams. Now, I need you to go back to your ordinary routines. You might want to drop by Fred's with your ears open and see if any crazy gossip might be happening."

"I could use a couple of beers after all this shit. You know they still haven't found the body of the sheriff."

"They probably never will. Let me know what they say at Fred's."

"Just a quick question. Do I still have an expense account?"

"Doc, you are a mystery. I guess I owe it to you. Sure. We will tally up in a few days."

"Wait, don't hang up. There's one more thing. I have been told there has been a lot of activity around the old Jackson plantation. Not quite sure what to make of it. Just thought it was worth mentioning."

"Thanks, go have a beer."

After Roland got off the phone, the CSI/coroner, Dr. Wilkins, walked to Roland and handed him three USB ports. "What you got there is toxicology, DNA, and cause of death. I also put in my opinion that this murder is consistent with all previous murders that have occurred over the 15 years. They bear the same etiology and have the signature of the same person. All evidence I could gather from the remains has been categorized and documented. There should be enough evidence to release the man at Atmore for wrongful conviction. It is my understanding you had a potential weapon."

"Yes, it was a Civil War saw used for amputation. I have it under lockup at my office, after it was tested by an associate of yours in Montgomery."

"Who?"

"Tom McGruder. Please say he is not compromised."
"Actually, you did well, even if by luck. He is a standup guy.
I just pray he is safe. We might need to put a detail on him. His
testimony could be damaging to whoever is involved." Charlie
chimed in, "I have some new and eager cadets. I'll put them on
him as soon as I get a phone."

Roland was suddenly concerned. "Damn it, we have been
here too long. Nelson, look out around the building and especially
around my jeep. Doctor, there will be a hearse here in an hour to
pick up the body. I suggest you and your associates take off now.
We cannot have any more people in danger."

"Roland, calm down. My man Michaels has taken care of our
exit. As a matter of fact, you hear the sirens?" In the background,
sirens had approached quickly. They ran to the loading dock to
see one ambulance had backed in, and two heavily armed men had
exited. "Dr. Wilkins, Joseph, and William, your Uber has arrived."

Dr. Wilkins turned to Roland, "Uber is the code word. We
will be safe, and no one will know we were even here. It was a
pleasure to be of assistance. Oh, the DNA profile is on the disks I
gave you. You can run them through your database to get a match.
If you do get a match, that's your killer. Well, I hate long good-
byes. So long. You got my private number, and if you can't reach
me, go through Michaels." Once loaded, they were off, back to
Montgomery, where hopefully no one was the wiser.

Nelson walked around the corner of the building. "Nobody has
gotten here yet. Shall we leave and not press our luck?"

With no argument given, they entered Roland's jeep and
headed back to Hope. Just as they had left town, two black SUVs
pulled into the coroner's office. All men exited to find the doors
locked. At the main entrance, they located a security guard. The
lead suit confronted the guard. "Has there been any activity here
in the past couple of hours?"

The guard had been aware of everything, and was loyal to
Michaels, so his response had already been measured. "It's been
slower here than a sloth climbing a tree."

Not satisfied with the answer, the lead suit said, "Then you
won't mind if we look around?"

The muscle-bound guard had always enjoyed a good fight and was ready for whatever this pest had wanted. "Why, sure, you can look at the whole place if you wish. Present me with the proper credentials, and I will give you a guided tour."

The lead suit pulled out his NSA badge. The security guard looked at it carefully and said, "Follow me." The morgue had been divided into two sections. The section Dr. Wilkins used was the old section, and the guard knew this. He took all the suits to the new section, which was all shiny and pristine. There was no evidence of it having been used. The suits had been getting angrier at each step, until they saw a doorway to the older section.

"What's behind that door?"

The guard reluctantly responded, "That area was condemned back in 1999. It has been locked off ever since. Hell, I don't even have keys to it. I couldn't get in there with a sledge hammer."

The lead suit walked over to the door, which had a window. What he saw was nothing but cobwebs and rusted equipment. "Guess you're right."

They walked away. They soon left the building, but something had bothered the lead suit. He walked around back to the loading dock and noticed fresh tire tracks. He decided he wanted another talk with that security guard. When he got around to the guard station, no one was in sight. The lead suit yelled at one of his counterparts to get the bolt cutters and to follow him. He went back to the loading dock. The doors had been chained shut. The bolt cutters snapped the chain off in seconds. Once through the door, he saw where a gurney had been used to transport a body to an examining room. He turned on the light switch, flooding the room with bright light. He also examined the autopsy table, and it was wet. He could smell the faint odor of chemicals. Across the way were the coolers where the bodies were kept. They checked all the drawers for a body, and the agents found nothing. This confused the lead suit. Then he realized the body had probably been moved to the new section. Backtracing their steps, they went to the new section and found the security guard watching TV.

The lead suit had been mad as hell. He confronted the security guard. "I thought you said there was nobody here? Well, it appears you are not very observant, for the old section was just used. And I would say someone was there for quite a while doing an autopsy. I find it very difficult you would not notice. What do you have to say for yourself?" The security guard realized he had been in a tight spot until the mayor and chief of police had walked through the door. Mayor Roger Pendergrass looked at the security guard and winked. He then turned around to the lead suit and said, "Wow, now who do we have here? Why hasn't my office, or my chief of police, been notified? Who the hell are you?" The lead suit finally spoke, "We are with the NSA. We are following up on a body illegally exhumed in an effort to undermine the national security of an ongoing operation. We would appreciate any cooperation you can give us to help expedite the apprehension of the people involved."

"Well, I'll be, ain't we all popular? Clint, call the newspaper reporter Al Goldstein over here. I'll bet he would love this story. You guys being NSA and all. This should make front page. Oh, where is your court order from Spurlin? You see, Judge Spurlin is my cousin, and he alerted me that some authority forged a signature on a legal document. He wants to know who. Now, you guys wouldn't know anything about that, would ya? I apologize. I didn't get your names."

The lead suit realized he was in a pickle, and it was time for a retreat. This was all a setup he had not been prepared to handle. The forged warrant in his pocket made him more nervous. In an attempt to pacify the group assembled, he ordered his men to get back to the cars. He tried to explain to the others why he was involved with this case. "Sorry, I'm Doug Fisher, and I have been with the NSA for five years. Prior to that, I was a SEAL commander for six years, and before that, I was assigned to special assignment. My duties were classified, just as what I'm doing now is classified for national security."

The mayor couldn't help but have fun with this guy since he had already gotten all the scoop from Joey Michaels (one of the many aliases of the so-called turncoat).

"You mean to tell me, this little town of Selma, the historical site for civil rights, has something to do with national security?

Maybe in the 60s, but not now. Son, you are yanking my chain. And frankly, I think you are full of shit. You know what I think? I think you are trying to cover something up for your boss, whoever that may be. I also feel that you are after one of the best sheriffs in this here state. If I were you, I would vigorously reexamine your moral compass because I believe you are going in the wrong direction."

"I see you have a strong opinion. I need to know if you are holding a body here delivered by Roland, Charles, and a man named Nelson?"

"Well, if you are not right to the point. I don't know. Our security guard's name is Clint Murdock. Why don't you ask him?"

"Ok, Clint, was a body transferred here by the people I mentioned, and was an autopsy performed?"

Clint looked intently into Doug's eyes with all the hate he could muster and responded, "If you had asked the correct questions to begin with, there never would have been a delay in my answer. But you came in here flashing all your heavily armed men, totally disregarding anybody who was in your way. That pissed me off."

"Can we talk now?"

"Sure. Roland, Charles, and my buddy Nelson were all here, and they brought a body that had been severely mutilated. A team of three pathologists conducted an autopsy as per the orders of Judge Spurling and Judge Macalister; orders that were proper and legal. The body is still here and will remain here till the hearse comes to lay that poor girl to rest. You know, it's a crying shame when one sides against the innocent."

"I hope you are not directing that at me!"

"Shoe fits, bitch, wear it." Right then, Doug threw a right cross at Clint and clipped him on the chin. That was all it took for a full-fledged fight to erupt. The suits got out of the vehicles, and Doug waved them off. He would take Clint alone. Clint feigned a left, then came around with a smashing right to the jaw and split the skin. They wrapped up like two animals fighting to the death. Chief Cody asked the mayor, "Should we break them apart?" The mayor looked at the chief seriously, and said, "No. But get back up here now. Get Trooper Jones and FBI Trent. They asked me to get answers. I think this fight might turn fruitful. Hurry." The fight went on for what seemed like hours, but it had been only thirty minutes. Both men were bloody from face to torso. It looked like Doug had gotten the worst of it. Clint walked over to shake Doug's hand. However, Doug slapped it away and said, "Next time, you won't have anybody around to protect you."

"Should have known you fight dirty. Your grandfather must have been a dry gulcher of men." With that statement, Doug jumped up, yelling, "You take that back or you're dead." Clint laughed at Doug. "I guess it runs in the family. Bet you were the one that took that shot at Robert in New Orleans. Good thing his windows were strong." Doug dismissed that statement, rinsed off his face, and joined his men. They all looked at him. It was obvious he had taken a beating. One of the suits spoke up, "What now, boss?"

"Well, I have to report our failure, and you all know how they feel about that. The body is a loss. We must wait for new instructions. All I know is this Roland guy has too many friends. This is no longer a simple matter. And I want another go at this Clint guy. Believe me, the lid is going to blow off, and I'm going to light the charge with Roland, Charles, Nelson, and Clint at the base."

Chapter 31

S enator Alex "Bodacious" Jackson sat alone in his private
office in DC, going over all the field reports. None of them
looked good. He had a major decision to make. He would have to
terminate the operation: "Home Security." He was halfway there.
All he had to do was eliminate the loose ends. As far as Roland and
the extra people who infiltrated the project, he had to determine
how much they knew and whether they were a threat. Though he
did not like Roland, Trent, and Charles, it would raise a considerable amount of unnecessary questions if they were terminated.
Then there would be the question of the bodies and a chance of
discovery of their location. If only Ed Nixon had done his job
and disposed of that Parrish girl properly. And then there was
Joey Michaels, who had betrayed the entire program. He would
be a clear and present danger to the entire operation. It would not
be easy to get rid of him. He had been an insider and knew too
much for his own good. Alex had decided to pull back all agents,
to surveil and report. He wanted no more intervention until he had
a clean shot at nothing coming back to him. All reports he had
studied he put through a paper shredder. He then issued orders
to all agents to stand down via encrypted text and to surveil and
report all activities. Alex would not lose this battle. He had the
power, or he thought he did.

Doc pulled into Fred's Pub and Package, and craved a well-deserved beer. In the back of his mind, he would take note of all

gossip milling around. When Doc entered the bar, all the regulars were present. Bartender Vicky was the first to talk to Doc. "Where the hell have you been? I figured you got captured at the boarding house and was humped to death." With that statement, everybody at the bar laughed. Doc turned slightly red and responded, "I must admit, I had a pleasant stay. Nice place." Sparky turned to him, "Did they at least change the sheets?"

"Why, Sparky, they run a top-notch boarding house there."

"I bet they do." Sparky motioned Doc to sit by him and whispered in his ear, "So, is it true? Do they have girls to give a man what he desires?" Doc was not sure how to respond, but, thankfully, Molly interrupted him. "You know, I worked there back in the 70s. And it was booming then." Johnny, the radioman, was on the other side of Doc and jumped right in with his questions. "I heard someone took a pot shot at Roland, and the guy who did the shooting was popped right between the eyes by someone else." Doc looked at Johnny very seriously and said, "Johnny, there is a lot more going on than what meets the eye. There are powerful sources at play here. You need to be careful with your questions. You're safe with me, but be careful. And to answer your question, yes, that is true. Also, the sheriff of that county is still missing. It is presumed he is dead."

"No loss there. Everybody knew he was crooked." Vicky overheard what Johnny said and jumped in, "No more crooked than anybody else." Doc defended Roland and said, "Roland does not fit that mold, Vicky." Vicky looked at Doc with an amused look on her face, and agreed with Doc's assessment. Johnny, still with a load of questions for Doc, continued, "What about that guy in prison for the murder some years back. Will he be released?"

"Mr. Adams is handling that, Johnny. You will need to get with him." Doc finished his first beer and ordered another one. As Vicky brought it over, Molly let loose the loudest fart ever. Sparky had been sitting next to her and yelped, "Good God, Molly, that sounded wet!"

Molly replied, "That was the chair." However, all realized it had not been the chair when the odorous fog permeated their nostrils. Sparky chimed in again, "Well, something died in that chair."

The door opened, and Trooper Jones walked in. His face made a repulsive look as if he had stepped in dog poo. He then asked Doc if they could speak outside. Doc said, "With pleasure, I need some fresh air." Once outside, Jones told Doc about the altercation that happened at the Selma morgue. "I was told everybody needed to be on their toes. By the way, what happened in there? It smelled like someone took a shit." Doc replied, "One of the regulars likes to bless us all with a little surprise now and again."

"I was going to have a beer, but I feel like I would be drinking ass."

"Forget about it. I'm sure Vicky has turned on the exhaust by now. It sucks it out quite fast. Besides, I'd love to introduce you to the regulars."

"Ok."

They walked back into Fred's, and the smell had dissipated. Doc introduced Trooper Jones to everyone, but not as a trooper, just as Doug Jones. Everybody shook hands, and Johnny was the first to jump in on Doug, "So, who the hell are you?"

"Wow, that's a blunt question. But I don't mind. Doc and I are acquaintances, and he told me here was the best place to get a cold beer."

"Well, Doc does have some common sense. Best place for a good beer and talk. So, what do you do?"

Doug knew the question would come up, so he had been prepared, "I'm an undertaker, and there seems to be an opening here, so I thought I'd grab the job."

Vicky handed Doug his beer and said, "That's bullshit. He's a state trooper, and a captain at that. Right, Doug?"

"Thanks, Vicky, I can't hide anywhere. She right, I'm afraid. I still like a cold beer."

Everybody gave Doug a second look so they would remember the face. Then Sparky spoke up, "I don't care if you are the President himself. Enjoy your beer, and if you want something stronger, we can kick ya a little moonshine." There was silence in the room for a second, then everybody laughed. Molly leaned over to Doug and said, "I've done a few officers in my time. You look like you could use a little lovin'." She licked her lips. Doug turned all shades of red and downed his beer in a single gulp. He got up and said, "A pleasure to meet all of you folks and Molly. Gotta go. Remember what I said, Doc." Then Doug couldn't hit the door fast enough.

Sparky spoke up, "What's up with him?" Johnny replied, "He's just not used to our Southern hospitality." Doc looked at everybody and said, "Well, I COULD USE ANOTHER BEER!" A voice from the back asked, "Are you buying?"

"Hell, no, I ain't got no money."

"Good enough for me. I'll have another one." Then everyone else started the landslide, and said they'd have another one. Vicky just looked at Doc like he was crazy.

Mildred had a concerned look on her face when Roland walked into the office. Roland noticed the way Mildred had been looking at him, and said, "Why such a gloomy face, Mildred?" Mildred looked Roland straight in the eyes with sincerity, "Roland, I heard someone tried to shoot you. I want you to know I will not work for anybody else, and if you go off and get killed, you will put me in the unemployment line. To be honest, I do not care to go there. So from now on, you will not put yourself in danger anymore. Do you understand me?"

"Well, Mildred, I didn't know you cared."

"Don't be a horse's ass. You heard me."

"Ok, ok, I will be careful. Any messages?"

"Yes, Mr. Adams would like to know if you got the evidence to vindicate his client?"

"Call him on the cell in your desk, and let him know I have it all, including a DNA profile. Tell him he can file for an immediate release. I need you to lock up this USB port in our safe and secure it with duct tape to the top compartment. That's in case someone tries to crack it."

"Well, it seems you had a productive trip."

"Come outside with me." Once they were outside, Roland mentioned that he figured that the office and phones had been bugged. He then told Mildred to put the USB port in their bookcase under the Bible. Mildred laughed, "You figure whoever wants this might not be too religious. Good thinking." They returned to the office, and Mildred discreetly did as Roland instructed. She called Adams and gave him the good news about the evidence to exonerate his client. Adams was fit to be tied, and stated he would set up a meeting with Judge Macalister.

Roland looked at his crime board in his office. He put up a new name: Alex Bodacious Jackson, and the location of his family plantation. He went to his chair and studied the board. This Joey Michaels was a mystery to him. Why was he helping? Why did he save his life? What was his connection to the people in Selma? Whatever the answers were, he was instrumental in solving this case. Mildred buzzed, "Trent from the FBI is here."

"Send him back."

When Trent walked into the office, he immediately apologized about the leak.

"I'm so sorry, had I known, I would have fed false information to him. The whole thing makes me sick. Now we have to start from the beginning."

"No, we don't."

"What?"

"I have a complete autopsy report, a DNA profile, and physical evidence, cataloged and legal, signed by two judges."

"The hell, you say. I mean, I'm not just ecstatic; I'm elated. I just don't know how."

"Well, Trent, I owe you an apology. You see, I used you as a decoy while Charles, Nelson, and I took a different route to get the autopsy done. And I might say, my confidential informant acquired the pathologist to conduct the autopsy." He pulled out one of the two remaining USB ports to illustrate his point. "On this, I have the DNA profile of the killer and the detailed findings of the pathologists." Trent sat down and sighed heavily. "After all these years, I will be able to rest at night." Roland plugged the USB port into his computer, switched it to the database for DNA profiles of known offenders, and ran the comparison. Roland asked Trent for the password to the FBI database for DNA profiles, which Trent gave to him without hesitation. As they waited, Trent said, "You know, if it weren't for you, I don't think I would have ever gotten a break in this case. You know, I can't even discipline my leak. He thought he was helping Homeland Security. What a joke."

Roland suddenly had a light go off in his head. "Wait a minute, Trent. What if this is Homeland Security-related? That would explain all the cloak and dagger operations. It would also explain why you were unable to make any progress. It could also explain why Adams lost his job for not discrediting me. And not least of all, it could explain all the people who were knifed in jail or simply disappeared. All were related to the Parrish murder."

"Holy shit, Roland, I hope this office is not bugged."

"Look here." Right by the light switch was another switch. "My friend Riley, with ATF, put in a jamming system that I can either turn on or off. Right now, it's on. Whoever is listening is hearing static. Take a peek here." Under a chair, he pointed out a bug; over by his desk was another bug. "It pays to know your enemy."

Trent was impressed with Roland at that moment.

Doc had been on his fourth beer when a loud Harley pulled up to the parking lot at Fred's. Everybody looked out the windows to see who it was, and nobody recognized the person. He got off his bike and walked in. Everyone pretended not to look at him. He walked straight up to Doc and said, "Excuse me, are you the one they call Doc?" Doc, quite surprised, looked at this person with a full beard and mustache, who wore a leather jacket, leather chaps, and a Confederate bandana. Doc responded, "Yep, they call me Doc. What can I do for you?"

The mysterious man stated, "Could we sit over here at a table? I have some news for you."

"Sure." They went over to a booth on the other side of the pool table with all eyes on them. The biker, in a low-keyed voice, said, "I'm Joey Michaels. I believe you know who I am."

"I sure do. You are wanted for killing Ronnie."

"Yes, that is true. I want you to know I was under orders to do that. It was that order that made me question who I was working for. I decided to help Sheriff Roland and all involved to expose what has been going on. You do not realize how deep this goes into the federal government, or how long the government has been doing operations of this nature. I have had enough. Ronnie was the straw that broke my back. He was just an innocent kid. He should never have been involved in this operation, let alone killed for his involvement. He was a part of a cleanup process. As far as that goes, my life is now a part of the same cleanup process."

"Are you the one who killed that guy who was shooting at Roland in Homerville?"

"Yes. I have been watching out for y'all ever since I turned."

"So, you are on our side now?"

"Yes. My time is limited. I need to move on elsewhere. You need to get to Roland and let him know there is another mole in his group. I'm currently trying to find out who it is. I also need you to tell him to get a sneak-and-peek warrant for Senator Jackson's plantation, especially the courtyard south of the gazebo. I'll be in touch. He then reached into his pocket and pulled out a cell phone, which he handed to Doc. "Keep this hidden. This will be our means of contact. Only you and Roland have one."

"Why do you trust me?"

"CoCo said you were a standup guy, and she is very insightful."

"CoCo. Well, I'll be damned."

"No, you won't. She is truly the only real person I could ever trust. She has been through a lot, and she is a patriot. Now to cover my exit, I'm going to hit you for screwing my girl at the boarding house."

"What?"

"That will be the cover for this conversation. Let me know when you're ready." But before Doc could respond, Joey got up quickly and slugged Doc across the face with quite a wallop. He then said, "Stay away from my woman at the boarding house. Got it? If not, there is more where that came from." He exited the bar, got on his hog, and peeled out, leaving a large dust cloud. Everyone, except Vicky, ran over to Doc to see if he was ok. Sparky mentioned, "Boy, that guy has a hell of a right cross."

Johnny perked up, "What the hell did you do, Doc?" Doc rubbed his jaw, and partially in shock, said, "I guess I screwed his girlfriend." Sparky retorted, "Well, shit, what did he expect with her working there and all? Damn, That's a hell of a note. What was his name?"

Doc responded, "We didn't get that far. Boy, he sure can hit! Well, I have had enough excitement for one day. I'm going home." Johnny and Sparky both spoke up. "Don't leave."

"Are you kidding me? I need to get ice on this, and I just want to lie down."

Sparky, feeling frisky, said "Thought you had been lying down a lot."

"Haha. See you guys later." Once in Doc's car, he called Roland who said, "Talk to me, Doc."

"You will never believe who just nearly knocked me out here at Fred's?"

Roland a little perplexed, answered, "Who?"

"Your buddy, Joey Michaels. He came in dressed as a biker. Had no idea who he was. I tell you, that guy can disguise himself very well."

"Why did he try to knock you out?"

"It was a cover. He wanted me to get you some information. Like getting a sneak-and-peek warrant for Senator Jackson's plantation, especially around the gazebo, and south of it. He believes you will find what you need there. He also gave me a burner phone. He says he can trust me, due to my relations with CoCo at the boarding house. It appears she is true blue. He also told me he was under orders to kill Ronnie. His guilt made him go turncoat to be able to help us."

"Well, it looks like he told you everything. I knew all this except for CoCo. And I had a suspicion about the plantation. Now that's confirmed, I will need to get to Judge Spurlin." Trent was still in his office, so Roland was mindful of what he had been saying. "So, did he have anything else of importance to say?"

"Yes, and it is scary. He said we have another mole in our ranks. He would not tell me who, and to be honest, I have no idea."

"Fuck, another one. Just remember we are the only ones who know about him. Nobody must know who he is, and I mean nobody. In fact, if anybody asks you if you might know, tell me who it is. That could be a clue."

"Makes sense, Sheriff. My jaw is a little sore, and I'm sure it will be black and blue before long, so I'm going home to check on the parents. Call me if anything comes up."

"Will do."

Trent had eavesdropped as usual, and asked the sheriff if there had been any new leads. Roland looked at Trent in a new light since the new information had come to light. From now on, everything would be played close to the vest. He turned to Trent and planted a false rumor. "We got a new informant other than the one that was helping us. That's two now. Looks like some people want whoever this sicko is to go down and go down hard." Trent looked at Roland and concurred. "Well, I got to get back to my office. FBI requires paperwork on what transpired with the movement of the body and subsequent replacement of the body." Roland stated, "You can mention that the real body is being transported back to Homerville for a proper burial."

"You forgot to mention that to me. Where from?"

"Selma. Thought you knew. That was where the autopsy was performed."

"Oh, hell, I'm losing it. You're right. What's next, beside the DNA search?"

"What do you suggest?"

"Suppose a search for a mass grave of about 22 bodies."

"Now that is where we need a lead. Let me know if you get anything."

"Will do." Trent vacated the building. As he exited, he nearly tripped over a biker dude walking up the steps. The biker dude said, "Excuse you." He looked in Trent's eyes and saw what he had not seen for a long time. It was his old Special Forces trainer from 15 years back. Luckily, he did not recognize him. Joey just turned and walked through the doors. He looked at Mildred and said, "Need to talk to the sheriff." Mildred looked at him and was not impressed. As she had done with many other vagrants, she would give him the shove-off. "Look, whoever you may be, the sheriff is a busy man and I think you should leave, now."

"Mildred, is it?"

"Yes."

"Look, I'm not going to get in a pissing match with you. Ok, just get me the damn sheriff now."

"Now, you hold your tongue. Nobody talks to me that way. You can just carry your nasty and nappy ass out of here, before I fry you with this taser." Mildred had spoken almost at the top of her lungs, and other officers began to circle the biker and pull out their cuffs. Roland could hear all this from his office and went to see what went on. First, he saw Mildred with a taser in her hand and four officers ready to pounce. Roland spoke up loudly, "Ok, what the hell is going on here?" The biker turned around, and locked eyes with Roland, the message was received. Roland exclaimed, "Roger, why you old coon dog. Where have you been? Hell, it's been over 20 years. It's ok, everybody. Roger was never one on social graces. Mildred, had I known he was coming I would have warned you. He doesn't like people. Mildred sat down and said, "Well, I don't like him and his nappy appearance." "Come on back to my office. Let's catch up." Roland immediately turned on the jamming switch. "Have a seat. You're not here to kill me, I hope? I see you have been making your rounds. Doc said you were at Fred's. Left quite an impression, and a sore jaw on Doc, I believe."

"It was necessary to make it believable. I made myself vulnerable to help you with your next step. From my intelligence, the agents have been ordered to stand down until your next move. Since they failed on the body recovery, they are regrouping at all cost to prevent the discovery of the other 21 bodies. You also have a mole who is close to you. I have been unable to discover his identity. I believe his purpose is to block any additional warrants or sneak-and-peeks you might attempt to get. Pretty sure he is in the judicial branch." Roland had to break in here, for there had been something nagging him for a while. "I know you're a spook or whatever they call you, but why Ronnie? He was such an innocent kid with prospects for a bright future. The death of this innocent was a crime against nature. Why?"

"Orders. I know that does not satisfy your question. Maybe this will. It's because of Ronnie's innocence I'm helping you now. It's because of the manipulation of Ronnie and the total disregard of his life that I'm helping you now. I have quit the black ops operations at my own peril because of Ronnie and people like Ronnie. I can no longer stand by and see the corrupt side of our government kill innocents for the sake of what they call patriotism. I now work for the oppressed and myself. I hope you understand. You have only witnessed one event. I have witnessed hundreds. I'm just grateful God has opened my eyes. I now ask for your forgiveness."

Roland leaned back in his chair and was silent. He took a long hard look at who he had guessed was Joey. Through those stern eyes, he could see heartbreak and years of suppressed emotion. Roland finally broke his silence, "I can't imagine what your life has been like, nor would I care to guess. I would never insult you by saying I know how you feel. I will never know how you feel. You ask me for forgiveness. I'm the wrong person. I can only show empathy for the experiences you have endured throughout your life. One thing I can tell you is that forgiveness comes from within. Maybe that's God's way of letting us know we are on the right course. For what you have done to help with this original case, I thank you, and for saving my life, I thank you. I will not be coming after you for Ronnie's death. I think you will have many others coming after you to hide all their murders of innocents. Now, if that is over, what's the next move?" Joey sat there and took in everything Roland had to say. There was a long pause. They both looked at each other like they'd known each other for years.

The silence was broken by Mildred, over the phone, "Roland, everything ok in there?"

"It's all good, Mildred. Thanks. Be sure we are not disturbed." Roland had a backdoor to his office and figured when he finished his conversation with Joey he would let him use it, instead of having to parade back out the front door.

Joey finally spoke up. "You are going to have to get some sort of sneak-and-peek warrant for Senator Jackson's plantation house, especially the courtyard by the gazebo, and south of it. Roland asked, "How do you know this?"

"I don't. That's the problem. It's a matter of deduction. You see, I didn't realize that Ed Nixon was Jackson's little perverted cleanup man. It wasn't until that Parrish girl was mishandled that

I realized Jackson's sickness. I correlated from Trent's FBI files, the locations of the missing girls, and they were all where the senator had visited, and Ed was always nearby. Then, when I got wind of Ed becoming the coroner of Hope, the pieces started to follow together. You see, the meth labs were government-funded though Homeland Security to infiltrate the drug cartels importing heroin and cocaine. What I didn't know was Jackson was transferring profits from the meth labs to offshore accounts. It's from these accounts he bribed prison officials, judges, and various law enforcement agencies, under the guise of busting them for taking bribes. Anyway, he held that over quite a few peoples' head. So, if you do not get a DNA match, you are sunk. I would suggest you get Adams to visit on a pretext of a possible suspect after he gets that guy released. This will peek Alex's interest. Then, while there, have him get something that will have his DNA on it. There is no other way."

"I like the way you think. Sounds like a plan."

"Mildred chimed in over the phone, "Sheriff, there is a man here in a suit with a NSA badge. He says he needs to talk to you now."

"Ok, be right there."

"Shit, that's one of Alex's men. Got to go, Roland. I'll be in touch. Back door?"

"Right here. Nobody knows of it. If they are watching outside, just go to the alley."

"Well, aren't you the smart one? I parked in the alley away from the station. I figure I might need a hasty getaway."

"Joey, be safe." With that, Roland left his office and went to Mildred's desk. The man in a black suit carried a gun. The man stood up and introduced himself, "Hi, I'm Doug Fisher. Here's my badge. I'm with the NSA."

Roland, acted unimpressed and responded, "Ok."

"Shall we go to your office?"

"No."

"Is there someone in there?" After he said that, he walked back to Roland's office to find no one. He came back and asked, "I thought you had a visitor?"

"What the hell do you want?"

"You see, we have a rogue agent going around starting trouble and spouting falsehoods. We are just trying to keep a lid on it. It is my understanding you just had an autopsy done on a cold case, or old murder, for which someone is serving time."

"Oh, that. You are right, and the person in jail has been vindicated due to the fact that the murder he was accused of was a part of a serial killing. There was no way he could have done it. We believe in justice around here."

"Really?"

"Oh, yes, really. And the best part is that we got the DNA of the real murderer. It's just a matter of time before we apprehend him."

"I'm afraid the evidence you obtained was illegal and a proper warrant was not issued at the time of the so-called autopsy. Hence, any evidence gathered is rendered inadmissible in a court of law."

"You are so wrong. I have proof positive. Would you like a taste?"

"Sure."

Roland pulled out his burner phone and pulled up the telephonic warrant issued by Judge Spurlin, dated and signed. He showed it to Doug, who fished in his pocket for something, but before he could pull it out, Roland jerked his phone back and threw it to Mildred. She caught it and put it in a metal box. Roland then grabbed Doug's hand and jerked it open. "Looks like you got a device there to delete cell phone data. Now, why in the hell would you want to do with that?"

"You don't know who you are messing with. I suggest you turn over that phone."

Roland looked him straight in the eye, and as serious as could be, said, "I suggest you kiss my ass, prick." With that statement, Doug attempted a right cross on Roland, but Mildred fired her taser right at Doug and dropped him like a stunned fish. Roland was amazed at Mildred. "Mildred, could you get the other deputies to help you throw out the trash." When they had escorted him outside, three other gentlemen in suits ran to the aid of their fallen comrade. One of the suits reached for his weapon while all three of Roland's deputies had their guns already drawn. Mildred bent down to Doug to pull out the taser cords. Everyone else was quite tense. Roland spoke up, "Why would the NSA come into my office, threatening me and my team, to hide or destroy evidence of a crime? Is this standard procedure for y'all?"

Doug was now able to speak. "We have our orders and it was noticed that a biker, resembling a turncoat agent of the force, was seen entering your office. This man is very dangerous, and it was for your safety we intervened."

"We were fine till you intervened to destroy evidence. I could charge you for that attempt, you know."

"It wouldn't stick, and you know it." Right then, Joey, on his hog, popped a willy in front of the station, shot the bird at the suits, and streaked off at a rapid rate of speed. All the suits ran to their SUV in an attempt to pursue, but by the time they had gotten into the vehicle, Joey was three blocks away. Roland looked at the spectacle and laughed, along with Mildred and the other deputies. Mildred spoke up, "I think I like your ole coon dog. Is he something more than you're letting on?"

"Mildred, this here is where you need to let sleeping dogs lie."

"Consider it done, Sheriff." The deputies were nearby and listened to what had been said, so Roland decided to address them also. "That man alone has helped us in so many ways I cannot mention. Just realize he's an asset for this office, and if anyone asks about him, get amnesia. Thanks for the backup, guys."

One of the deputies said, "Hell, we didn't do anything. We all better look out for Mildred." After that statement, they all chuckled, and Mildred turned red.

Adams had been in Judge Macalister's chambers, perusing a motion to vacate the murder conviction of the inmate called Thaddeus. He had no other name of record. Judge Macalister had the motion before him. He had been studying it carefully when the DA from Hope had come busting through the door, with the judge's clerk following him. The clerk spoke up quickly, "Judge, he just busted through. Said he was to be present."

"That's correct. He is to be present. Now, if you would get the court reporter in here with a little more decorum, I would appreciate it."

"Sorry for the tardiness, Your Honor. DA Barnes here for the state or City of Hope."

The judge looked at him like a wounded animal. "This here is former Assistant State Attorney Mr. Adams. We will make a ruling on this as soon as the court reporter arrives to document my order. I have just one question for you, Barnes. Did you convict just because he was Black and drunk or you just didn't want to investigate the crime?"

Barnes got rather upset and responded quickly, "Judge, he had the girl's blood all over him. He confessed and signed said confession. It was open and shut."

"Mr. Barnes, did you know that Thaddeus couldn't read nor write? And he was a chronic alcoholic, and that spot was his sleeping area? It just so happened he tripped over the body placed there and rolled all through the remains-hence your blood proof. Did anybody in your office even bother to investigate this at all?"

"Why, sir, there was no need to. It was open and shut."

"Holy shit, and the police wonder why they get a bad name." The court reporter entered the office. She set up and signaled to the judge she was ready. The judge looked at both lawyers and shook his head. "Ok, let's get started. Before me is a petition for the release of a Thaddeus, who is incarcerated at Atmore prison on death row. The crime of which he was convicted in the city court of Hope has numerous procedural errors, not limited to a forced confession. Also, the crime for which the defendant was convicted was replicated in the same manner, while he was incarcerated. This indicated a serial rapist was perpetuating these acts of aggression. The City of Hope wanted blood and hurriedly convicted the wrong person. I am hereby obligated to vacate all charges against the defendant and order his immediate release. I pray in the future that a tragedy such as this one never occurs again. I am also awarding Thaddeus the amount of $100,000.00 in restitution to be paid by the City of Hope so that he might be able to begin again with the life he was robbed. Mr. Adams, I take it you'll get transportation for the defendant to take him home. Mr. Adams, it is my understanding that you were terminated by the state attorney's office for this type of moral prudence. I am also ordering an investigation into the office of the state attorney's office concerning the reason for your dismissal."

"Yes, Your Honor, we have Deputy Cobb waiting at the prison for him to be processed out."

"So be it. And so, ordered as of this date in the year of our Lord, 2018."

As soon as Adams had gotten out of the courthouse, he called Cobb, who had been waiting for his call. "It's done! Roland said bring to him to the station, and we will work with him from there."

"You know, this is cool as hell. I'll be there as soon as they hand him over. Wait, oh shit, hold on." There was a long pause, then Cobb came back on the phone. "Adams, they beat the shit out of him. Bastards, they all just looked at me with grins on their faces. I'd like to shoot them all."

"Cobb, chill out. Take him to a medical center in Brewton and get pictures and X-rays. Then bring him here."

"They are all pigs."

"No doubt."

Chapter 32

S enator Jackson sat in his office and sipped on some scotch, and pondered where he was at in all this mess happening in Hope, Alabama. His family name used to mean a lot down there, and maybe it still did. At least in his mind, the name meant a lot and deserved respect. His anger was visibly present ever since the Parrish girl incident was not handled properly. Ed Nixon had gotten sloppy, and it was his own fault for not noticing. All he thought about were his deep dark secrets and how they could never come to light, or it would all be over for him. The phone buzzed, and his AA came over it. "Senator, the director of the CIA is here to see you."

"Send him in."

As the director shut the door, the senator asked, "How about a scotch, Arthur?"

"Hell, it's 10 am. Of course, I'll have a scotch." They both laughed. Alex poured up him a glass half-full. "Damn, Alex, that's a bit heavy."

"You'll need it. Let's go back to my private and secure room." Once they entered the adjoining office, they both took a seat. Arthur took the lead in starting the conversation. "Alex, you got a mess down there in Hope. Bodies being dug up, and your men flashing NSA badges. You know they were not to flash those unless it was an emergency. Anyway, what's this about, Robert or Joey, or whatever name he is using, gone rogue?"

"Just that, Arthur. He up and disappeared. He is now a ghost."

"Why? He was one of our best, and besides, he is a treasure trove of intelligence. We cannot afford to have him turn."

"I've got all assets in the area alerted, and we are actively seeking him out."

"Alex, I do not want him terminated. We need to understand what motivated the change of heart. Could it have anything to do with this domestic terrorism you are heading up?"

"There could be a link. We had to shut down two meth labs and lost three cartel suspects in the process. All of which had ISIS ties."

"Wait a minute. You told me you weren't running those meth labs. Were you?"

"Arthur, you didn't want to know details for plausible deniability. I only did what was necessary to produce results. And results we got. There are four more heads of terrorism in Cuba, as we speak."

"At what cost of innocent lives? I heard we lost Marcus, Ronnie, Amber, and some guy, Ed Nixon. Who was this Ed guy?"

"Ed was cleanup only. He had no intel."

"And what's the deal with this Parrish girl? They say it was some sort of serial rapist murder?"

"Want another drink?"

"Damn straight."

Alex poured two more stiff drinks and began, "Somehow, this girl's body was dumped very close to one of our meth labs. It was out of the city limits, so the county took over the investigation. They have a sheriff down there named Roland Smith. He is very popular and solved the case within 24 hours, or thought he did. You see, he caught Ed Nixon at the meth lab, and he was the prime suspect. Well, Ed came out with a shotgun, and Roland asked him to put it down. When he raised it, Roland shot him dead center with one shot and killed him."

"One shot? Hell, we need him on our team. So, what's the deal with this girl they dug up?"

"Well, apparently, she was killed in the same fashion as the Parrish girl, and another one some years back. This establishes a serial rapist. Hence, Judge Macalister vacated the conviction of the one they charged for the earlier rape since he could not have done it because he was in prison." They both took a long, deep drink. Arthur was off in his head somewhere, and Alex was nervous as a tick underneath some bug spray. After about ten minutes of silence, Arthur spoke. "Well, I hope you had the common sense to order everybody to stand down."

"Yes, except Doug thought he would erase the telephonic warrant on Roland's phone. The warrant concerned the exhumation of the body and DNA of the killer."

"Why? Don't we want to catch this guy? It sure would make our job easier."

"Of course, but he ended up getting tased by Roland's secretary."

"Secretary?"

"She's tougher than she looks. Anyway, they threw him out of the office, and when his partners looked up, they all saw Robert flipping them off while doing a willy on a hog, rolling out of town. They all got in their vehicle and pursued him, but they lost him on some dirt roads."

"Alex, you know he shared some information with the sheriff. This Roland is a liability. He needs to have an accident. Put James on it. We cannot have all this blow up in our face. You know it's your face that is exposed, not mine. Did they get some DNA, so they can catch this rapist?"

"They are running it through the databases, as we speak."

"Well, this is good news. We catch the rapist, generate positive press, and we can go back to business, as usual. Except, I don't like your idea of the meth labs. Let's stay away from that end. Sure, we will bust them, but no longer run them."

"But, sir, we got really good and tangible intel."

"And if someone finds out, you have a shit storm. No. And don't make me say it again. We were lucky this time. Lend them a helping hand to catch the rapist. Maybe invite Roland up here to DC. A lot of accidents happen here. As a matter of fact, do that. It's an order." Arthur left the office. Alex picked up a secure line and called James. "Hello."

"Code X-ray, Delta, Tango expedite."

"Howdy James, long time no hear. A man from Hope will be visiting me here in DC within a week. You should get the file this afternoon. You know how DC is. Sure, would hate for him to have an accident."

"Oh, an accident it is then. Tata."

Roland was still in his office with Cobb and the other two deputies who threw out the supposed NSA officer. Cobb, one of the better deputies, asked Roland, "Who was that on the Harley? If I wasn't mistaken, it was that Joey guy we were looking for."

"No, it wasn't Joey, but it was his brother. He is helping us."

"Well, that is good to know. What's up with all these suits in Hope, anyway?"

"Cobb, it appears we have stepped in a big pile of poop. And some higher ups want it kept secret. I am not sure how high it goes, but I think it goes all the way to DC." Everyone looked at each other and were all in agreement when Cobb said, "I think it's time we just get us a can opener, spill the beans, and see where they may fall." Everyone agreed. Roland was the first to say, "You damn straight. I told Ms. Parrish I would get to the bottom of what happened, and I do not break my word. Of course, y'all know we are going to have to be tightlipped, Bill."

"Don't worry about me, Sheriff. I have learned my lesson." Mildred was on the speakerphone again, "Sheriff, the administrative assistant to Senator Jackson has him holding on the line for you. He's on line one." Everyone's eyebrows raised one inch. Roland said, "Let's let him wait a minute, Mildred. Tell him I am getting the results from the DNA. That should make him sweat a little. Guys, this is the person who has been behind the suits, interfering with everything we have been trying to do." Cobb spoke up, "You want we should leave the room?"

"Hell, no. Grab a seat." After a couple of minutes, Roland picked up the phone. "Hello?"

"Do you know who this is? And what took you so long to get to the phone, Mr. Smith? I'm Senator Jackson, and I am not used to waiting." Roland had the phone on speaker so his deputies could hear. "Sorry, Senator, I was taking a shit. It was a longer than usual one. I ate Mexican last night, and boy, I'll tell you, it gave me a workout."

"Roland, that was not necessary. Anyway, my reason for the call is I would like to meet with you here in DC to go over the dual investigations that were occurring when our paths collided. This is in the spirit of cooperation. Your secretary said you got a DNA match?"

"Administrative assistant, Senator."

"What the hell, your AA then. What have you got?"

"Senator, I'm sure you realize that my investigation of these rapes is out of your purview, and it would be unethical for me to discuss the case unless you were read in."

"What kind of game are you pulling here? I'm offering an olive branch by having you come up here to DC to mend fences and share resources so you can catch the culprit. Are we on the same page?"

"Ok, but the county cannot afford the flight. Have you any suggestions?"

"That is such a little problem. I'm sending an FBI Lear jet to Andalusia to pick you up. One of my agents will escort you to my office."

"May I ask the agent's name?"

"Sure, James Woollcott. Been with me for ten years. Good man. The jet will arrive on Tuesday at 1 pm, and you will return on the same day around 8 pm. Will that work for you?"

"Consider it done, Senator." When Roland was off the phone, all the deputies broke out laughing. "Taking a shit." Another one said, "Mexican food." Everybody left the office except Cobb. He turned to Roland and said, "You know it's a trap. He has already tried to kill you once. This time, he will make sure. I'm going with you."

Roland felt deeply honored. "Cobb, I need you here. You are the best I've got. I have someone in mind to accompany me, and believe me, I'll be safe."

"You'd better be, or I'll kill the senator myself."

"Speaking of the senator, do you know where his family plantation is?"

"Yes, sir. I think everyone has some idea where it is."

"I need you out of uniform to go over there and snoop around, especially around the courtyard. North of the gazebo and south of it."

"What am I looking for?"

"Graves." With that comment, Cobb left the office. Roland pulled out the burner phone Joey had given him. He dialed up the preprogrammed number, and Joey answered, "How'd you like that willy?"

"Like a true professional."

"OK, what's up?"

"Senator Jackson is sending an FBI plane for me Tuesday to take me to DC for a peace meeting. Should I be worried?"

"Is he sending you an escort?"

"Why yes, how did you know?"

"He only sends an escort when it's a hit."

"Did he give you a name of your escort?"

"Yes, James Woolworth."

"I'm coming with you. He's a CIA hit man. His specialty is to make it look like an accident. Probably, in your case, a heart attack. We will need to pad you up a bit. Though you already have quite a bit of padding."

"Thanks."

"No problem, truth hurts." Joey began to laugh.

"Are you sure it should be you to come with me?"

"I'm your best hope, and I'm the last one they would expect to be traveling with you. The only problem is the CIA is now involved. I'm going to have to wear my full prosthetics. You will not even recognize me. This is also the best time to swipe a DNA sample from the senator. Let's just hope he plans to kill you after the meeting. Either way, I will have to kill James on the plane. Ok, I'll be back in touch in two days. We have three days to prepare. And please get me an XX large uniform with a badge. Bye." With that, Joey hung up. Roland had put a lot of faith on Joey, but he believed in him. He had a gut instinct that Joey was stronger because of all the scars life had dealt him. He felt his next move would be to notify Trent at the FBI. He had Mildred get Trent on the phone, and he went over to the switch to turn off any scrambling. Mildred came over the phone, "Trent on line two."

Roland picked up line two. "Hey, Trent, I'll bet you'll never guess who called me and wants to set up a meeting?" There was a small pause, and Trent said, "Senator Jackson."

"How did you know?"

"It's his style. He likes to look his enemies in the face before he destroys them. Not saying he is going to destroy you. Besides, I saw the request for one of the jets to go to Andalusia Tuesday. Wonder why he doesn't want to see me?"

"You know, that's a good question. You have been on this case for years. Maybe you should meet us, at my request, at his office at 3pm."

"I'll be there."

"I can't stress, with all the leaks, how important it is to keep this between us."

"Good point, Roland. My lips are sealed. See ya Tuesday." In Roland's mind, the stage was being set. The only problem was who would kill him? Was it James, like Joey said, or someone else? Either way, Roland felt he needed to be prepared. He called Mildred into his office. Once she entered, he asked her, "That cousin of yours, the one who invented the puncture-proof jumpsuit?"

"Yes."

"Does he still have the prototype? The reason I'm asking is I'm going to need it before Tuesday. Let's say it's a matter of life or death."

"What's going on, Roland?"

"Mildred, I cannot say. Is it possible?"

"I'll have it here this afternoon. Of course, it will have to be let out for your girth."

"Well, that wasn't necessary." They both laughed, but it was short-lived. Roland was a brave man, and he had come up with an idea that could solve everything. He went over to the scrambling switch and turned it on again. He called Joey back. "You again, what's up?"

"How good are you with this makeup thing? I mean, can you look like someone else?"

"Are you going where I think you're going?"

"Yes, I probably am."

"Then you need to come home. I need to make a mold of your face. And yes, I have fooled many people with my "makeup" as you say. It's prosthetics."

"Why do I need to come home?"

"Because, that's where I'm staying, of course. Is there a problem?"

"You are full of surprises. Be there in a while."

"I suggest you tell your staff you are going to be gone three days, one of which will be spent in DC."

"Good idea."

Roland went back to the switch and turned it off. He told Mildred he would be gone for three days, and Cobb would be out for two days. Mildred looked at him with those suspecting eyes, and Roland just said, "Understand, Mildred."

"What about that suit?"

"Oh, have him drop it by my house." Mildred, having known Roland a long time, had learned not to ask questions. The answer always became clear later.

"Ok."

Roland left the office to drive to Cobb's house, a short distance away. He lived on five acres outside of the city limits. His place was right off a path road, unlike Roland's, and had a chain-linked fence surrounding the property to keep in his two dogs, both beautiful black Labs. One adopted by Cobb, used to be a service dog for the military. Its job was to sniff out dead bodies. This was the dog Roland had thought about. As Roland pulled up, Cobb walked out the front door to calm the dogs' barking upon Roland's arrival. Cobb invited him into his double-wide where his girlfriend had been getting ready for work. She was an RN at a local nursing home. She had looked cute in her white scrubs, and Cobb caught Roland looking. He gave him the evil eye. Roland just winked back at him, and he smiled. Her name was Ruth Smith, no relation.

Ruth, heading for the front door, turned and said, "I know when I'm not wanted, so I'm leaving."

Cobb turned to her, "You know that's not the case, honey."

"When was the last time Roland was here?" Then Roland spoke up, "Well, it looks like I should come around more often. Ruth, I never knew you cared so much?"

"That's not what I meant, and you know it, Roland Smith. You better watch your step, buddy." She cracked a smile and left. Cobb looked at Roland rather curiously and asked, "Why are you here?"

"Cobb, you, me, and your dog are going to that plantation for a sneak-and-peek. And when we find out what we need, we are going to Judge Spurlin and get a warrant for a full inspection of that property."

"Thought you had to go to DC?"

"Get the dog, you are coming with me." Cobb had an old white Chevy Silverado, which his dog loved to ride in the back of. They both pulled off to Roland's house.

They arrived at Roland's house at the same time. Cobb let his dog loose from the back of the truck, and it ran into the barn. The Lab loved horses for some odd reason. Roland motioned Cobb to come in the house. When Cobb entered, he saw Joey right off the bat. He quickly pulled his gun and said, "Don't move or I'll shoot." Roland raised his arms and said, "Cool your jets, Cobb. Joey is helping us."

"He killed Ronnie!"

"He was under orders. There is a lot you don't know. Now, please put the gun away." Cobb reluctantly holstered his gun. Joey spoke up, "I don't blame you, Cobb. Ronnie didn't deserve to die."

"Then why in the fuck did you kill him?" Roland jumped in again, "Cobb, it will all become clear very soon. Let's keep our emotions in check for now. Ok Joey, I'm here. What are you going to do to me?"

"Well, I got all my stuff. You just need to take a seat in the dining room chair. I need a mold of your face." Cobb kept quiet. Roland sat down, and Joey began. He had already mixed the plaster to put on Roland's face. For breathing purposes, he put two straws in Roland's nose, and one in his mouth. Then he patted the plaster all over Roland's face until they could only see the straws. Cobb sat across from the table, extremely interested. Joey said, "Now, this has to stay on for 30 to 40 minutes. Do not talk, Roland, and keep completely still. While the plaster dried, Joey mixed a latex solution in another container. Cobb watched everything with a boyish curiosity. Finally, Cobb spoke, "Not to be a spoiler, but what the hell are you doing?"

"I'm becoming Roland."

"What the fuck? No way. Nobody is going to believe this. You are about his size, but no way you can talk or look like him. What about that scar on his face?"

"Just watch, and you may learn something."

An hour later, the plaster mold was off Roland's face, much to his relief, and the latex had been poured into the mold. Joey worked like a surgeon who had done this procedure many times. He also worked on a wig to match Roland's hair. One more hour passed, and Joey asked Cobb to feed the livestock.

"Now, look here, I will only go so far with this charade." Then Roland asked him to please just help for a moment. Cobb reluctantly left the house. Joey asked Roland to help him put on the mask and change into Roland's sheriff uniform. Roland had also been wearing his uniform. They put on the wig. It had taken some intricate gluing of the latex to match the wrinkles in Roland's face. When they had finished, both had looked in the mirror and said, "By God, this might work." As they viewed themselves in the mirror, Cobb came through the front door. When they turned around, he was flabbergasted. He stood there for a moment, speechless. And that was hard for Cobb. Finally, words formed, "I can tell who the fake is right away. Told you so. It's not going to work. One of the Rolands spoke, "All right dumbass, which one of us is fake?"

"It's obviously the one on the right, because the one who spoke is a dead giveaway. It's Roland. Nobody can talk like Roland." As soon as Cobb had spoken, he had to eat his words. The one who spoke had been Joey, who removed the mask. "Well, I'll be a horse's ass." Roland looked at Cobb with sympathy in his eyes and said, "I certainly hope not. Well, now you see what he can do. Do you think it will work for eight hours?"

"You've got a good question there. Joey, how long will the mask last with perspiration and all? I know that will have an effect."

"You're right, Cobb. We will be pushing the time limit. The longest has been six hours. Hopefully, I'll be out of the senator's office and back to the plane to be killed by James before time expires. And I'll have some of the senator's DNA. All in a day's work."

"Senator? James by kill? Have I passed out and awakened in a new reality?"

Joey jumped in and looked at Roland, "Should I tell him or you?"

"Why, you, of course."

"Ok, well you see, Cobb, since my defection, I'm number 1 on a hit list. Also, there's my association, which was revealed by my Harley's presence at your office..."

"Wait, that was you on the Harley?"

"Yes."

"Damn good willy, from what I hear."

"Thanks."

Roland looked peeved. "Joey, if you don't mind."

"Oh yes, of course. Well, that brought in the CIA. You see, Cobb, I have worked for the CIA, NSA, black ops for the SEALS, and am currently retired from black ops with the Homeland Security domestic division. Basically, homegrown terrorism. I'm afraid a hit has been put out on Roland. As you well know, they tried in Homerville."

"That was you who shot that guy?"

"Yes. Now we are walking a delicate path. While I'm being Roland going to DC, y'all will be inspecting Jackson's plantation for where I'm sure he has the bodies buried."

"That's why you wanted me to bring my dog." Roland looked at Cobb with a very serious look. "You are the only one I trust, besides Mildred." Right then, then there was a knock at the door. Joey ducked into a closet while Roland went to the door. He signaled Cobb to clean up the stuff in the kitchen. He opened the door. It was Mildred's cousin with a jumpsuit that looked more like a scuba suit. Roland spoke up, "Damn, Alphonse, when are you going to cut that afro?"

"As soon as you quit being a redneck."

"Oh hell, that's not fair."

"If the shoe fits." They laughed. "Hey, Cobb, saw your dog out there. You going to breed her? I would love to have one of her pups."

"If I do, I promise you one for free."

"Cool, gotta go. You owe me for the suit."

"How much?"

"$250.00 is fair."

"Highway robbery."

"Just give it to Mildred. See ya later." Alphonse went out the front door to pet the Lab a bit, then took off in his truck. Joey exited the closet and looked at the jumpsuit, rather puzzled. Roland explained, "Mildred said it was puncture proof. Something a needle couldn't penetrate. Thought I would need it." "It won't be needed, but I will sure as hell take it. Good thinking."

Cobb's head had been spinning from all this information. His feelings toward Joey had changed. He was not sure what he would have done. And now Joey was a wanted man and marked for death. What he had been doing for Roland and the case was admirable. There had to be something he and Roland could do to help him. He had a thought. "Roland, Joey, or whoever you are, let's get drunk, and I mean drunk and now. Roland, you got anything?" Roland took everyone to the barn. There was a deck off to one side with picnic tables and a regulation horseshoe pit. Close to the barn were two refrigerators and a freezer. "Open the fridge, Cobb." When he opened it, he was in awe. It was full of three brands of beer. "Joey, open the second fridge." Same results. "Ok, guys, let's pop some tops." The next few days would be the make-or-break of Roland's case. There still had been no match to the DNA. He had decided it was a time for a well-deserved break. Cobb and Joey seemed to agree. They sat in the patio chairs. After three beers, Roland began to contemplate what was ahead of them. He had been most worried for Joey. He hoped the disguise would work, especially with him going in front of his old boss, the senator. Then there was the sneak-and-peek warrant he had to get from Judge Spurlin. He and Cobb would take his Labrador to check out the old plantation. He hoped the dog would still be able to detect cadavers or remains of humans. The dog had been military-trained, so Roland had faith in the dog's abilities. All had to go well. And everything would have to be done the same day as Joey's flight to DC. He could not let his face be seen at all that fateful day. It would be on that day that he and Cobb would execute a search warrant on the plantation, and it had to be covert. So many things could go wrong. Roland dismissed the negative thinking, and asserted faith and justice were on their side. They could not fail.

Chapter 33

T ime flew and it was go time. Joey, Roland's lookalike, had
been in Roland's jeep on the way to the airport. He thought
about his time at Roland's farm. It had been so peaceful. It had
been the first time in a while he could completely relax. It was
there where Cobb came up with the ingenious idea of making
everybody around Joey miserable. He and Roland both came up
with the recipe. They had decided the night before the flight Joey
would drink plenty of beer and eat boiled peanuts, pickled eggs,
and boiled cabbage with Vidalia onions. They all knew this would
result in some gasses that would be devastating to the nose. They
all had laughed at the idea, but did not hesitate to put it into action.
Roland 2 had pulled into the airport, where he had seen the plane
on the tarmac ready to go. He parked the jeep and headed to
the plane.

The real Roland, warrant in hand, and Cobb with the trusty
black Lab, were almost at the plantation. As they scouted the
property, they had decided not to go in by way of the front road.
It would be obvious if they broke in that way. Instead, they had
circled the property to find the best entry point. The property had
been enclosed with an eight-foot chain-link fence, with razor wire
at the top. Roland and Cobb knew they would have to cut the
fence at a pole and squeeze through. Finally, toward the side of
the plantation, on a dirt road, they found their spot. There was
heavy undergrowth and tall pine trees. They concealed the truck,

grabbed the dog, bolt cutters, and their guns. They were not in uniform, but had their badges in plain sight. They had wanted no confusion in case they encountered any resistance. Once at the fence, Cobb used the bolt cutters to work on the fence. He cut a perfect tear in the fence where Roland, Cobb, and the dog could pass through. They kept the dog on a leash until it would be safe to let him roam. Once through the fence, they began their track toward the plantation house. It was a magnificent site from afar. It took one back to the Old South era, with lazy days spent on the porch, sipping mint juleps or sweet iced tea.

Roland 2 walked up to the steps to the plane and was greeted by the pilots. "You Roland Smith?"

"Yes, sir, and ready to roll."

"Climb aboard. We are on a tight schedule. We plan to get you back around 7 pm. Sound ok to you?"

"Perfect." At that moment, he had seen James at the head of the stairs who looked at him. He entered the plane with the pilots who went to their cockpit to begin the pre-flight checklist. James closed the flight door and proceeded to where Roland 2 had been sitting. "I was going to sit at the back, if you don't mind."

"Well, you see, that's going to be a problem. This here door is the bathroom, right?"

"Yes, it is."

"You see it's like this. I had me some Mexican food last night and my tummy is rumbling like a volcano. I believe it is in both our self-interest if I stay back here. I do hope you understand?"

James looked disappointed and had preferred to sit behind his target. He realized he would have to act on the flight back. "Well, if you must."

"Oh, I must."

Roland 2's stomach rumbled as the plane took off. Once the plane leveled off at cruising altitude, he could not hold back a massive gaseous release. And this release had not been silent in the least. It reverberated through the seat, and had made a rumbling sound in the beginning, and a squeaking sound toward the end. Roland 2 just sat there and felt a sense of relief, while James looked back at the commotion. It did not take long for the tainted

219

air to reach James' nostrils. He looked back at Roland 2 again. "Good God, man. What the hell did you eat? Was it spoiled?" His eyes had watered, and Roland 2 had enjoyed every moment. "Told ya." James opened the pilots' door, letting the noxious air drift in. James asked, "Can you do something with the air back here?"

The pilots, exceptionally upset, said, "Shut the damn door and deal with it. Did something die back there?"

"No, our guest ate Mexican."

"Close the door, asshole." James returned to his seat and covered his nose with his hand. Meanwhile, the pilots had put on their oxygen masks and locked the cockpit door. Roland 2 savored the moment and built up to the second release. He thought how amazing Cobb and Roland had been to come up with this idea. In the cockpit, the pilots commented, "Let's kick up the air speed. This is going to be a rough one." Both nodded in agreement.

Roland and Cobb made it to the front door of the massive house. There was a locked chain through what was once brass door handles. Not wanting to breach the house, they both had looked through the side windows. They could see a once elegant foyer and back doors, which led to a courtyard. Roland could see the gazebo Joey had mentioned. The house had been built like a horseshoe surrounding the courtyard. Roland looked at Cobb and said, "Well, looks like we are going to have to walk around." They both noted the dog's alert features. Ears had been perked up, tail had not wagged, and nostrils had been sniffing incessantly. They had begun their track around the house while the Lab had pulled increasingly at the leash. Cobb asked, "Should I let him go?"

"No, let's wait till we are in the courtyard." In a few minutes, they rounded the bend of the house. The courtyard was completely visible. There used to be a fountain next to the gazebo, and flowerbeds were now totally overgrown. The Lab choked itself to get free from the leash. Roland instructed, "Let him go." The Lab took off at a run, scoured the entire courtyard with his nose to the ground. He stopped at a spot and had started digging. Cobb caught up with the dog, and tried to remember the commands for a cadaver. Finally, he remembered, and Cobb patted the dog and said, "Good Blacky, more, more?" The dog took off again, stopped two feet away, and had started digging again. This went on for thirty minutes, and the dog had tried to dig up twenty-five spots. Roland looked at Cobb. "Let's get some pictures of the dog digging up at least 10 areas. This will prove beyond a shadow of a doubt that there are remains here." They proceeded with their documentation, uninterrupted because Roland had been on a plane to DC, or everyone thought he had been. Once the documentation had been done, they made a hasty retreat to the truck. On the outside of the fence, Cobb asked, "Should we repair the fence?"

"No, hell no." They got into the truck and headed to Roland's farm, realizing this was only part one. Now it was mandatory Roland not be seen by anyone. The imposter Roland had his phone and all his IDs. He in no way wanted to jeopardize part two. The two took all back roads and dirt roads to Roland's farm. They even came into the farm from the back way no one knew about. Once they had parked, Roland ran to the house to find that it had been ransacked. Someone had been waiting for him to leave his house, not expecting him to come back. As Cobb entered with the dog, his face was in complete shock. "Who did this, Roland?"

"The people who work for the senator. Let's just hope they are through and not coming back. Better pull the shades and secure the doors and windows. We have eight more hours of waiting."

Thirty minutes prior to landing, Roland 2 unleashed round two of the toxic gaseous mixture. His rear had been feeling the heat. This time, James was about to cry. He looked around at Roland 2 and said, "You better go to the bathroom and see if you didn't shit yourself. You're killing me!"

"Good idea, James. That last one felt a little wet." He entered the bathroom and checked all his prosthetics to make sure they had adhered perfectly. He had to do a few touchups because of his incessant grinning. Everything looked good. He was ready for the big test, the senator. He had with him two Cuban cigars in two separate cases. Roland had confiscated these and had figured they would be a good way to capture the senator's DNA. He knew how the senator loved Cuban cigars with his scotch. Everything had been in place and holding well; he exited the bathroom to see

James with an oxygen mask on. He looked at him, "All's good. Not wet." He then sat down.

"So damn glad to hear it. Man, you really need to watch your diet." The pilot came over the intercom to say they would be landing and to buckle up. The landing had been quick, for they landed at a private airport used by the Justice Department. The plane pulled up by a hanger, where a car had been waiting. Once the plane stopped, James opened the door and ran down the steps. The pilots remained in the cockpit. Roland 2 gathered himself and departed the plane. He carried only a small leather case. As he hit the tarmac, a car pulled up to take him to the congressman's office. Roland 2 yelled at James, who had been giving instructions to a flight crew to fumigate the plane. "Hey James, are you riding back with me?"

"Unfortunately, yes."

"See ya soon." He got in the car. As James saw him drive off, he had never felt so relieved. He decided not to call Senator Alex about the ride. He would let the senator discover on his own the perils of dealing with Roland. The pilots had finally exited the plane, having used every profanity known to man. "I pray he's empty on the way back. Either way, we need to be prepared."

Roland 2 was escorted in the back way to the senator's office, a way he had been many times before. He was finally seated in the senator's office. He only had to wait briefly before the senator had entered. "Hope you had a pleasant flight."

"Yes I did, but nothing to drink."

"You like scotch?"

"Love it. As a matter of fact, prefer it with a good Cuban."

"You got good taste. Sorry, no Cubans here." He pulled out two glasses with his bottle of scotch and poured two healthy portions. Roland 2 looked over at him and said, as he had reached into his pocket, "Just so happens, I have two Cubans here." He handed one to the senator.

The senator quickly produced an ashtray. "I'll be damned. You know these are still illegal? But such a minor infraction. I say we both enjoy. Let me turn on this smoke eater. We are not supposed to smoke cigarettes in the building. Said nothing about cigars." He laughed. He licked the cigar all over, seeming to enjoy it, then lit it up as Roland 2 lit his. Roland 2 thought, *Mission accomplished. Now, just get that cigar.* Then he thought a couple of farts would do the trick. Alex started the conversation. "Roland, I hope you realize you have stirred up quite a hornet's nest. That Adams boy got the criminal released from Atmore. Now I thought for sure he was guilty. What the hell is going on down there?"

Roland 2 sipped the scotch and took a puff off his cigar and watched as Alex did the same. "Well, Senator, we have discovered a serial killer has been living among us. The man at Atmore was innocent. He was just a drunk, stumbling in the wrong place at the wrong time. And we have this guy, Joey something, who killed our witness in jail. Then we found out the guards were paid off. So, we have a little problem."

"It seems you have been quite busy. What's the FBI got to do with it?"

"They were the ones to discover it was a serial killer. It has spanned decades. Trent seems to think there are 21 bodies unaccounted for."

Alex had leaned back in his chair. Roland 2 had seen this as the perfect time to let one go, and he did. It was a squeaker, ear-piercing. "Oh, I'm so sorry, Senator, I had Mexican before I left, and it has played havoc with my stomach." The senator looked at him for a moment, until the noxious smell hit his nose. "Oh, my God, son. That's horrible. Excuse me, I have some refresher in the other room. Lord have mercy!"

As he had turned, Roland 2 quickly switched out the cigars. They were evenly matched. He put the cigar in its case to choke it out and save the DNA. When Alex returned, he sprayed Febreze all over the room. "There, please warn me before another attack."

"Sure. Well, what do you want me to do? We are currently looking for this Joey guy. We feel we could get some leads from him, and the FBI is helping with the body search. Only problem is we have no useable DNA. So, that makes our case a needle in the haystack." Alex had been waiting for this statement about DNA. He felt a bit of relief. He picked up his cigar, puffing on, while thinking. He noticed Roland's cigar was gone. "Where is your cigar?"

"I think it was upsetting my stomach, so I stubbed it to save for later."

He showed the case to Alex. Alex didn't want to argue and said, "Yes, I agree we should let your stomach rest. Well, I don't want this meeting to prolong itself. What can I do to help you?"

"It's this Joey guy. It's like he has military training. I was wondering if you could get his military records. That should help a lot. I feel he has been around me and I have had no idea. Could you do that?"

"I'll do it right away." Then, so Roland 2 could get out of there, he had let another one loose. This had been silent, but deadly. It hit Alex's nose with a vengeance. He almost got sick. Choking out the words as he pushed a button, he said, "Will do. Now if that's all, this man will get you back to the airport."

"Why, thank you." Roland 2 immediately turned to go with the man. He couldn't help but notice the man had been holding his nose. Alex left the room to avoid the nauseating smell. He called to James. "He's on his way back to you. Do us a favor. Make sure he has a heart attack and no longer pollutes the air. My God, you could have warned me."

"Not sure what to say, boss. You should have been on the plane. It was hell."

"Just get it done."

Roland 2 was back at the airport in no time. This time, the pilots had not been there to greet him. They had already gone into the cockpit to start pre-flight. James had waited at the head of the stairs. Roland 2 could see he had been cupping his right hand. So, they would do it here and now. He had been ready. As he climbed the steps, he saw James move back to let him pass to the backseat. Roland 2 said, "Don't worry. It's over. You can have your seat. I'll follow you."

James had felt relieved. He would get him mid-flight. So, with James having expected nothing as he turned, Joey immediately karate-chopped him on the neck. When he went down, Joey put him in a sleeper hold. James was out like a light in two minutes.

He placed him in a seat, buckled him up, and closed the door to the plane. Having heard the commotion, one of the pilots opened the flight door and asked, "Everything ok?"

"Sure, you might want to keep your door closed." "No argument here." The pilot went back in and locked the door with a click. Joey picked up the syringe to use on James. He removed James' shoe and sock, and emptied the syringe between his toes. He put the sock and shoe back on James' foot. The plane took off. He sat behind James and checked the pulse on James' neck. It had been rapid at first, then slowed until there was nothing. Joey sat back to enjoy the ride home. He thought there might be backup at the airport, so he had better check out the jeep before driving off.

Once the plane had leveled off, Joey went to the bathroom to remove his disguise. While in the bathroom, he put on a wig so that he would not be immediately recognized when he departed the plane. His purpose had been to confuse everyone as much as possible. He also did not want anyone to investigate Roland for James' death. He figured he had better call Roland as to his status.

He dialed Roland's phone. "Hello."

"Roland, all has gone as planned. The person who was to assassinate you is no more."

"My God, Joey, the bodies are starting to mount up. Are you sure that was wise?"

"Roland, I was left no choice. Anyway, I need you to go to your office and conduct business as usual. Make sure plenty of people see you, even the chief of police. This is imperative. They will try to pin this death on you."

"Well, you need to know we found evidence of twenty-five graves on Jackson's plantation. We are sure these are all the missing people that have been reported."

"Awesome, I have the senator's DNA. I will drive your jeep to your office. Get my motorcycle, and I can leave from there."

"Where in the hell is your motor bike?"

"In your barn in the third stall hidden behind some hay bales."

"Will do. By the way, while I was gone, somebody trashed my house looking for something."

"Don't worry. That was just a ploy to scare you and get something of yours to plant for a frame job. Now get to your office and be seen."

"On my way."

Joey picked up a phone for the cockpit, "How long till landing?"

The pilot responded, "We are now on our approach."

"You might want to phone ahead for an ambulance, I think James had a heart attack."

The pilot was shocked and responded, "What? Is there anything you can do?"

"He apparently passed out while I was sleeping."

"I'm sending back the co-pilot to help." Within seconds the co-pilot emerged from the cockpit and observed James lying lifeless in his chair, he checked for a pulse at his neck. There had been none. He looked up at Joey and had seen someone who appeared to be a completely different person. "What the hell? Who are you?"

Joey produced an NSA badge and had explained that the senator and some of his associates were under investigation. The pilot, dumbfounded, recognized the badge. He sat down as if exhausted. "Look, we are just the pilots. We have no knowledge of anything except our destinations."

"I know that. I have flown with y'all several times."

"I thought you looked familiar. So, what happens now?"

"Well, when we land, I want you to give me some time to get to my car. Delay talking to the entourage that will be attacking this plane since an ambulance will be waiting. Do not allow anybody on board except the paramedics. That should give me enough time. And when turning the plane, open the door to let me slip out, then taxi to the terminal. Can you do that?"

"Sure. NSA, wow."

"I can't explain how important this is. It's a matter of national security."

"We are here to serve." With that, he entered the cockpit and left the door open. Then the captain spoke up, "Was that you farting? Because if it was, son, my God, that odor was lethal."

"Sorry, Captain. It was a Southern recipe."

Landing the plane in Andalusia, the pilots took a long path and circled by the hangar where Roland's jeep had been parked. As the plane turned toward the terminal, Joey snuck out and made a run for the jeep, unseen. There had been an ambulance waiting at the terminal with three other people in suits. As Joey arrived at the jeep, he immediately checked it out for an improvised explosive device. He raised the hood and nothing. He crawled under the jeep near the gas tank, and there it had been. He had been familiar with this device, for he had used one before. It was a magnetic device controlled by a cell phone signal. He removed it very carefully and placed it on a government car used by the "others." He did another sweep of the jeep and found nothing else. His search completed, he took off in his jeep at a high rate of speed. This caught the attention of the men in suits, who ran to their government vehicle, none the wiser about the switch. The paramedics removed the body from the plane and treated the whole situation as a heart attack. There had been no cooperation from the pilots since they had been in the cockpit the whole time.

Roland and Cobb arrived at their office ten minutes after they had received the call from Joey. Cobb rode the motorcycle, while Roland drove Cobb's truck. As they had walked into the office, Mildred was shocked. "I thought you were in DC?"

"That's what we wanted everyone to think."

"Why, you sneaky bastard. There have been at least four people in suits looking for you. I told them you were out of state. Then they just left. Strange, they had the personality of a dead skunk."

"Mildred, come to my office. Cobb, the guy we have on ice, release him. I feel they really don't care about him anymore."

"But, boss, he accepted a bribe that resulted in death. We just can't let that slide."

"Think about it, Cobb. We can put him back into place and use him to rat out the administrator and anyone else who has been a part of this conspiracy."

"I guess that is why you get paid the big bucks. Ok, but I do not like it."

"Mildred, we are on the brink of bringing down a US senator. So, anything, and I mean anything, needs to be looked at again.

And most importantly, I want you to call the chief of OPD and tell him I would like to talk to him, as well as the mayor. Also, call my buddy, Johnny, at the radio station and tell him I got a scoop he will need to put on the wire. Oh, and tell him there is a dead body at the airport, and to send one of his mentors there. Also, get Judge Spurlin on the phone."

Mildred took all this in and replied sarcastically, "Ok, will that be all, my lordship?"

"Work with me. We have solved over twenty murders."

When Mildred heard that, she replied "Sorry, so sorry. Love you, Roland, I knew you were the man. On it now." Mildred ran out of the room to perform her tasks.

One of the suits had seen Roland's jeep tearing out of the airport parking lot and pointed it out to the suit in charge. The lead man called for the other suit in the airplane. He asked him, "What's up in the plane?"

"James is dead."

"All right, guys, no time to waste. Let's follow the jeep and blow that bitch up."

"Another suit asked, "Shouldn't we call Alex?"

"Yes, get on it now." The other suit called Senator Jackson's encrypted phone to report the findings. Within a moment, Alex had answered, "Tell me good news."

"Well, sir, James is dead. We are in pursuit of the person who ran to Roland's jeep and took off from the airport."

"You mean that's not Roland in the jeep?"

"No, sir. Apparently, it was someone made to look like Roland."

"Damn it, man. Didn't you put a bomb on that jeep?"

"Yes, sir."

"Then blow it now. I mean blow it now."

The person with the phone detonator dialed the number. Before pushing the enter button, he had said, "Die, you motherfucker." Little did they know they would blow themselves up in spectacular fashion. There was a massive explosion with no survivors. Alex, still on the other line, had heard the explosion. He realized his assets had blown up. He slammed down the phone and cursed profusely. He called his mole at the police station. "Hello."

"Yes, Alex."

"Has there been any activity at the sheriff's office?"

"Well, Roland and Cobb rolled in about an hour ago."

"That's impossible, Roland was on a plane. Are you positive?"

"Yes, sir. There's no mistaking Roland with that gun on his side, and Mildred greeted him. Oh, it's him all right."

"Keep up the surveillance. Well, boys, we all have been played. That guy on the plane was a dead ringer for Roland. Now we have three more dead agents in a car explosion." With that, Alex hung up. Who the hell was in his office? What had they been planning? Why the rouse? He had to get to the bottom of this and quickly. Was James ok? He'd better call the airport. "Hello, this is Senator Jackson. I NEED TO TALK TO ONE OF MY PILOTS. Please patch me through."

"Yes, sir, Senator," responded the air traffic controller. Once connected, the senator said tersely, "Captain, this is Senator Jackson. I need you to tell me exactly what happened on that plane and spare no detail."

"Well, sir, when we departed DC, we kind of kept ourselves in the cockpit because of the foul gasses this passenger was emitting."

"Yes. I'm aware they were quite noxious. What I want to know is, who died?"

"The other passenger stated he took a nap, and when he awoke, James was not breathing or moving. It was like he had a heart attack. And I have to say, it was not Roland on the flight back. He must have been wearing makeup. He looked like a totally different person. He flashed an NSA badge and mentioned this was a matter of national security. We let him escape the plane secretly."

"You did what? Didn't this look at all suspicious to you?"

"Yes, sir. But, he said you were under investigation. We took a wide birth and let him go by the hangar where his jeep was parked. We had no choice."

"Do you think James had a heart attack?"

"Yes, sir. We had an ambulance here when we landed, and they believe it was a heart attack. They have taken the body to the hospital to verify."

"Good job, guys. Thanks for the information." Alex hung up. He thought to himself he had been duped. What did they have now? No witnesses. Only hearsay. No evidence. No, wait, they had DNA. But they did not have his DNA, or did they? He ran into the office to check where he had laid his cigar. It had been in the ashtray. He picked it up and looked at the teeth marks. It had been in his sight at all times, or had it? Then he dismissed his worries. No way anyone could have changed out the cigar. What had they been planning? His execution had always been flawless. Maybe it was time to take a trip down to L.A. just to rally his base. Yes, that was it. He would go see the real Roland Smith and put the fear of God in him.

Chapter 34

J oey had heard the explosion behind him and thought that could
have been him. He thanked God for all the training he had
received throughout the years. He was in a hurry to switch vehicles and get the DNA evidence to his friend, the pathologist. It
wasn't long before he had arrived at Roland's office, and dashed
through the front door to meet Mildred. Mildred stood up, "Ok,
boy, cool your jets. What's the hurry? No one is pregnant here."

"Roland is expecting me, and this is life or death."

"Isn't everything? He's got the mayor and chief of police back
there. You will just have to wait your turn."

"Mildred, right?

Buzz me in now or someone will die. You see those suits
across the street? They don't care who they kill, even you."

"Since you put it that way." Mildred buzzed Roland, and he
responded, "Mildred, I told you no interruptions!"

"Sorry, sir, but I have a gent stating it's life or death, and there
are men in suits across the street." There was no response. Roland
ran out of his office and left the mayor and chief in there. "Joey,
thank God you made it. I heard there was an explosion near the
airport, and I feared the worse. Who are the guys across the street?"

"Not sure, but I do believe they want to finish the job."

"Hurry, in my office. Warning, there are hostiles in there." As
Joey entered the office, the only one who had recognized him was

the chief, who responded, "What's he doing here? He's a murderer and assassin. Roland, arrest him immediately."

Roland, composed as usual, said, "Him or you, Chief. It appears you have a bank account in the Cayman Islands with 1.5 million dollars in it. And Joey here just happens to work for the NSA. Show them your badge. "Joey produced his badge (which was fake but no one knew any better). The chief shut up. The mayor looked nervous. Roland took the floor once again. He looked at the mayor and asked, "What's your relationship with Senator Alex Jackson?" The mayor was taken aback, not sure how to answer. "Well, we are both Republicans, and I helped get him re-elected."

"You mean, you didn't look away when he was brutalizing young women under your nose or operating two fully operational meth labs. Don't worry, Chief, the same question goes to you, too." Both individuals had denied involvement. Finally, Joey chimed in, gun in hand. "I'm so tired of lies. There are three men in suits across the street. Roland, just say they cooperated and release them. At the door, make sure you thank them for their help. Now, if there is a back way, I've got to go, and quick. We need these results ASAP. I'M SURE OUR FAVORITE SENATOR IS UP TO SPEED NOW!"

"Of course, how stupid of me. I suppose you are taking Cobb's truck? It's got a full tank."

"Why would I take anything else?" They had intentionally misled so the suits would follow the wrong vehicle. Joey would take the bike and Cobb the truck.

"I'll have Cobb bring the keys to you." Roland called for Cobb, and he and Joey embraced as if they had not seen each other in years. Roland broke up the "bromance." "Cobb, Joey's taking your truck, and you can use his bike."

Cobb followed Joey out the back door. Once outside, Joey said, "Give me my bike keys." Cobb complied. "Now drive like a bat out of hell. I want them to follow you. Head toward Montgomery and cut off on some dirt roads and double back."

"Hell, yea. I love mudding. They don't know what they are in for."

"Have fun."

"You bet ya." Cobb headed off at a rapid speed from the front of the sheriff's office. All suits piled into a car and followed. Joey got on his bike and proceeded in the opposite direction. Back in Roland's office, the mayor and chief felt it had been time to depart. Roland left them with a final thought. "You know my grandmother used to say, 'Oh, what a tangled web you weave when you first practice to deceive.' Makes a lot of sense to me." With that comment, both had stomped out of his office.

Joey drove at a high rate of speed to Selma. He had already called ahead to his CSI friend, the same one who had performed the autopsy on the girl. It took only forty-five minutes to arrive at his destination. He hopped off his bike and ran to the morgue, where his friend had eagerly awaited him. Joey pulled the cigar case from his pocket. His friend said, "I didn't realize this was a cigar-smoking occasion."

"It's not. This cigar has the senator's saliva all over it, and teeth marks on the end."

"Well, I must say that is overkill. We should get an excellent DNA profile. Let's put it through the extracting process and analysis, and we will have your profile. It will take three hours. Care to wait?"

"I'm not going anywhere."

"Whose DNA am I extracting exactly?"

"The serial killer's."

"Cool, this is exciting."

"Trust me, after this, you will become famous."

"Please leave me out of it. I do not care for fame, just the integrity of my work."

"Thanks, let's get started."

"I apologize. It's because of your work I come to you." Joey had tried to settle down, but his anxiety had the best of him. He paced relentlessly. He was like a dog in heat. Finally, he had walked across the street to a diner to grab a bite to eat. After consuming some greasy dumplings, he had walked back over to the morgue. He sat down in a chair, which was as comfortable as sitting on a porcupine. Time would not move fast enough for him.

Joey had noticed Dr. Wilkins walking down the hall. Not saying anything, but bridled with anticipation, he anxiously waited for him to speak. Dr. Wilkins took a deep breath and said, "Robert, Joey, or whoever, this DNA is a positive match to both victims brought to me. The Parrish girl and the one bagged up. There is no doubt the DNA strands were a positive match. This is the DNA of your killer. And, I might add, a sick son of a bitch, considering the manner of their deaths."

"Doctor, I need these results in triplicate."

"Ahead of you. Here is a USB drive with the results. It has also been recorded in the database of the coroner's report, backed up by another external drive, and another USB backup put in the file. If I may ask, who is this mysterious serial killer? You owe it to me."

"Can you keep your mouth shut?"

"You should know by now, I can."

"Senator Alex Bodacious Jackson."

"Holy shit! Boy, is this going to be a shitstorm. When is the news going to break?"

"There are a few loose ends to tie up. However, we will be slapping cuffs on him today." Joey pocketed the USB drive and called Roland on their secured phone. "Roland."

"Oh, please tell me good news. I have the local media here, ready to go."

"You might want to go national."

"He's our man. Call Trent to get a warrant for his arrest from the FBI first. We need to get over there now and arrest him. Then get the warrant to excavate the land at the plantation."

"Joey, or whoever you are, I already got the warrant, and Judge Spurlin wants to be present at the dig. He stuck his neck out several times. Got a backhoe in route along with our friends with the state trooper's office. They all should be there in twenty minutes. What about you, Joey? Where are you going to be? You saved my bacon more than once."

"Sorry, Roland, I want to stay in the background. Don't fool yourself. Alex wasn't the lone ranger on the meth production. He was, though, the lone ranger on the killings. If it wasn't for you sticking your nose where it didn't belong, this would never have come out. Thanks, and good job." Joey hung up. Roland dialed Trent "Hey, Trent."

"Yes?"

"I have a warrant for the arrest of Senator Jackson. Think you could execute it for me since you're up there?"

"You damn straight. It's solid, isn't it?"

"It's a complete DNA match."

"My pleasure. This has been my lifelong dream. I'll call you when I have him in custody."

"Looking forward to that call." Roland sat down at his desk with a feeling of accomplishment. All those tormented souls would now rest, knowing their killer had been caught. He redirected his thoughts to all the ones on the payroll of deceit. The money trail would be a challenge.

Chapter 35

S enator Jackson had been sitting in his office when he had gotten the call from his lead agent.

"Senator, I do believe it has all blown up. Joey, or Robert, got away from us through a vehicle decoy. Roland has an escort of state troopers going to your old plantation with a backhoe in tow. It appears they have a warrant to dig up the courtyard of your family home. Roland also has been interviewing the mayor and chief of police of Hope. Judge Spurlin is accompanying the caravan to your home. They say he wants to see what all the fuss is about. Senator, I hate to say this, but FBI Agent Trent is on the way to your office with an arrest warrant for you. What do you want us to do?"

The senator slumped down in his chair and realized the gig was up. He opened the drawer to his desk and pulled out his scotch. He poured himself a healthy shot and downed it in one gulp. On the phone, he heard, "Alex, Senator, hello? What do we do?"

"Stand down. Report to the Homeland Security Division and deny anything I asked you to do. Save your ass. My game is over." The senator buzzed his assistant, "Susan I'm leaving early today. Cancel all my appointments."

"Ok, Senator. Is everything ok?"

"Couldn't be better." He took the back route out of his office and went to the parking garage, got in his car, and went to his DC apartment. Once through the door, he scavenged around for a rope, but had found only a frayed extension cord. His thoughts had raced in his head. He knew he could not face anyone publicly. The shame alone would be overwhelming; the humiliation of what he had done to those women. He threw the frayed cord around a rafter in the living room and got on a chair. He tied a secure knot around his neck with exposed wires, and kicked the chair away. He dangled there and kicked madly for about one minute, when the frayed wires severed his jugular artery resulting in an arterial spray of blood all over the apartment. It had been a ghastly sight of human blood dispersed in every direction. Horror movies couldn't reproduce this scene.

Back at the senator's office, Trent came to arrest the senator. "Susan, where was he?" She said he took the day off. Trent broadcasted on his radio, "This is Agent Trent, and I'm issuing an APB on Senator Alex Jackson. Start with his apartment. I'm heading there now. From her desk, Susan asked, "What did he do?"

Trent responded, "Consider yourself lucky, very lucky." Then Trent left the office. His destination would be the senator's apartment. There were already two squad cars there when he had arrived. The officers stood outside the door, and one had puked on the sidewalk. "Well?"

The officers responded, "Go look for yourself." As Trent entered, he saw a horrible site. The frayed extension cord wire had cut the jugular vein and had sprayed blood all over the room. It had been a ghastly mess. Trent thought, *Karma*. He instructed them that only the authorized were to enter. He ordered them to cordon off a block radius.

Trent felt it would be his duty to call Roland. "Roland, Alex will not be going to trial."

Roland had been exceptionally upset. "And why the hell not?"

"He nearly decapitated himself in a hanging suicide."

"Why, that chicken-shit bastard. You'll never believe how many bodies we got already. Ten, and still digging. All had smashed-in skulls. I have invited all the media, CNN, FOX, MSNBC, NBC, CBS, BBC, and some I cannot pronounce. I am getting them to film all of it. That son of a bitch will pay in his afterlife. Besides, I endowed myself with all publishing and film rights through Ms.

Parrish. We got a lawyer, and I'm making things right for her. She said I could have a cut. I swear I'm going to marry that woman."

All in total, there had been 25 victims killed in the same manner. Many communities were in mourning for weeks. As for Roland, he had been affected deeply by witnessing the depravity of one man and the ones who had helped him.

Chapter 36

CONCLUSION

I t had been just another typical day at Fred's Pub and Package. All the regulars were in their respective spots. Sparky, on his second drink, talked with Johnny from the radio station. Good ole Molly tried to get lucky. As usual, you could cut the smoke in there with a knife. Vicky had been bartending when Doc rolled in through the front doors. The whole crowd wooed him. Doc had been motioned to sit by Sparky, who whispered, "You know why you are getting wooed, don't ya?"

"No."

"Why, you dumb ass. Didn't you realize your time at the boarding house was on the underground wire, meaning gossip central? Why, it was told you "did" everybody in the house, and they wanted more. Hell, it was even said they didn't charge you. You must be one stud muffin. Molly's even looking at you."

"My God, Sparky, protect me."

"I'll be your body guard." Johnny jumped in, "Good God, we have our own Casanova here in Hope Alabama."

"All right, guys." Vicky handed Doc beer and said, "It's on the house, Romeo." Everybody had fun with Doc, then Roland rolled in through the doors. Everybody had become silent. Roland bellied up to the bar and yelled, "Where's that gigolo Doc? I have to buy that expensive ass a beer." Everybody laughed. It would now be a time to put a most tragic time behind them.

Lightning Source UK Ltd.
Milton Keynes UK
UKHW020818151220
375245UK00003B/615